DRENCHED SUNFLOWERS

THE WATER STREET CHRONICLES

TAMMERA COOPER

AUTHORS NOTE

This story and all the characters in it are purely fictional.

The city of Washington, North Carolina is a real and fantastic place. Many of the places my fictional characters visit in my book are real and open for your business. I hope you feel the need to visit our charming Southern town.

Abram and Selah are fictional characters based on the heroes of the Washington Underground Railroad. Hundreds were secretly smuggled through the Port of Washington to freedom in the North during the period before and during the Civil War. Without the conductors risking their lives every day, the dreams of freedom would not come true.

Locals will be tempted to guess who my contemporary characters are inspired by. Please know that every person in this book lives only in my imagination.

ACKNOWLEDGMENTS

I would like to thank the people who have made this book possible. There are many behind the scenes.

Thank you

~to Patrick, who wears a tool belt every day so I can follow my dreams

~to Sabrina, who corrects my splices

~to Jeni, who makes my thoughts shine

~to Joan and Shannon for reading it chapter by chapter and pushing me to finish so they would know the ending

~to Leesa, who did the research to uncover Washington's hidden past

~to the Campbell family for giving me Washington to love

Finally, thank you Little Washington for being my home

DEMOLITION

*W*HEN I PROMISED MY FAMILY, I WOULD WORK FOREVER TO FREE THEM, I DIDN'T KNOW IT WOULD BE TRUE. WHEN I PROMISED YOU THAT I WOULD WAIT FOREVER FOR YOUR RETURN, I DIDN'T KNOW IT WOULD BE AN ETERNITY. A PERSON'S EXISTENCE IS SUPPOSED TO CEASE WHEN THEY DIE. MINE, WELL, LET'S JUST SAY, IT DIDN'T.

SELAH BROWN (1839-1861), WASHINGTON, NORTH CAROLINA.

~~~

Water Street, Washington, NC, September 9, 2014

Plaster crumbled down onto Selah's head as she struggled to wake. Brushing the large pieces off her face, her fingers felt butter bean size welts on her cheeks and forehead.

"What is going on upstairs?" She rolled over on her bedroll. "It has been peaceful for years and…" A bang echoed in the space of her safe haven. She bolted upright and looked around. Beams of light shone through the dark room. "Maybe it's Abram trying to break

1

me free? Perhaps he has returned?" A tear escaped as the reality of how long she waited for him came to mind. She promised him so many years ago, she would be ready no matter how long. Too much time had passed. She knew it.

Another impact shook the floor above her. *Someone is trying to come this way for sure.* She scrambled to her feet and pulled her bed linens back. The pop of her quilt sent dust and plaster flying breaking the silence again. Selah grabbed her sewing tools, packed them in a handy pouch and hid it behind the tool crates on the large shelves on the wall. The footsteps above her head became louder as she hurried to hide all the evidence of her squatting.

"Where will I go? I have to stay in case Abram comes." She looked around making sure she didn't miss anything as another cloud of plaster rained down, turning her into a ghostly gray figure. "I will never get this out of my braids," she ran her fingers over her hair trying to pick the small bits out of her coarse hair without success. She strained to listen to the voices upstairs, but the hammering muffled the words that would give her a clue to the happenings.

The whole building started to shake, dust grew thicker in the air, and she cowered in the corner. She was convinced the ceiling was going to fall on her and kill her dead, maybe permanently this time. She saw a bar slide between the timbers, straining against the floorboards. More light appeared on the floor beside her. Selah tried to avoid it and pressed closer to the wall, daring the light to touch her she pulled her skirt tight around her legs. Her hands began to shake. Wood splintered allowing more light to invade the space. She watched the bright spot grow. *What will I do, if he comes and I am not here?* Suddenly, Selah disappeared.

* * *

BETH AWOKE coughing to a loud banging noise. Her chest hurt from labored breathing, and her eyes tried to focus. Then she heard her name.

"Miss Beth, wake up! Wake up! You need to see this!" Jose was knocking on the car window.

She blinked her eyes, nodded her head, and held up her finger to acknowledge him. She turned off the car and stepped out. *Oh God, how long had she been out?* She checked her watch. *Two hours. No way, that medicine must have hit me hard.* What did Jose need? He was usually pretty self-reliant. Hopefully, the men were more productive while she was asleep. She couldn't read his face, and her imagination went crazy inventing the worse. Had there been an accident? Maybe someone had razed something they weren't supposed to. "Oh, Jose I am so sorry. I didn't mean to sleep that long."

"It's okay. You didn't feel well. I wouldn't have woken you, but you need to see what we found."

"Okay. Show me what it is."

Jose took her hand and led her through the rubble of the day. *Wow, they had made a mess today.* There were plaster and wood all over the lawn. They were going to have to get this straight before they finished for the day. "It looks like a bomb went off. You better get this cleaned up."

"We got this," Jose reassured her.

"Okay, but you are better than what I have seen today. Letting the guys run things; that's not like you."

"You weren't yourself today either. Watch your step," Jose warned. He took her hand again as she slipped on some wood when she jumped a hole in the pitted yard.

3

"Thanks." She knew he didn't approve of her being here and only put up with it because Sam said it was okay, even though she was the one paying them.

The two-story Federal-style house Beth bought last month was exactly what she needed to make the changes she promised herself when she lost her husband. Brad would have loved it, and it was all hers. The history of the building piqued her interest, and she could imagine a thriving art gallery here. Every day she worked with her contractor, Sam, her vision grew closer to reality. He made sure she stuck to the original aesthetics of the house. When she hired him, she didn't know what a pain his Tuesdays off would be, or the paperwork swamp a historical project produced. She made a mental note to visit with him about it later.

Jose led her through the front door into what used to be the foyer. The only thing still standing was the staircase leading to the second floor. All the plaster and slats were removed exposing the wires and plumbing weaving in and out of the studs. A group of men stared at the floor. *Why are they always just standing around?* She glanced over at Jose with frustration. He pulled her toward the group. The smell of sweaty construction workers was not what she wanted after her morning migraine. The men looked up when they heard her footsteps echo through the empty building. She realized they were waiting on her and picked up her pace only to stop and stare down into an open hole in her floor.

"Look, Miss Beth. We took up the floor and there it was."

What in the world? "Hand me a flashlight." One of the guys placed one in her outstretched hand. She stepped onto old cobblestone stairs leading her down into a newly discovered cellar. She was thankful she wasn't tall. Ducking her head, she stepped onto a dirt floor and back in time; the cold, damp air raised goosebumps on her skin. Shelves containing stoneware, wooden crates, old tools, and other household items lined the walls. The spider webs hung thickly between the timbers supporting the floorboards above. It was a good thing she didn't startle easily. She brushed them off her face so she could see more clearly. Scanning the room, she decided they needed to be careful with this section of the house. It didn't require a historian to tell these items were antiques. There was no knowing how long this cellar had remained sealed. *I need to call Sam. Wonder if he will pick up his phone today?* Carefully, she headed back up the stairs to the kitchen area before turning to Jose. "Tell the men to stop work inside for the day. We need to finish the roof and clean up the yard. I know Sam will not be happy when he gets here. Get them going."

Jose looked at her with anxious eyes. "Shit, the boss is coming. Gotta get cleaned up fast. He didn't say he was stopping by when I talked to him earlier."

"No, Jose. The boss is here," she reminded with a glare. "Sam is *also* coming." She added in frustration.

"Sorry." He quickly turned and started barking orders to the crew. The men reacted right away as if a fire blazed under their feet.

She pulled her cell phone out of her pocket and dialed Sam's number. "Please pick up, please pick up. Damn it." She disconnected when it went to voicemail and instead typed a text.

Beth: Found something of significance under subfloor. Call me ASAP.

PEELING BACK THE SHEATHING

*S*am's iPhone vibrated against the wood grain of his office desk under layers of papers waiting to be graded. He didn't take phone calls during his office hours here at the local community college, but the name on the screen distracted him, instantly pulling him from his work. Beth was at the project house today, and the men were not happy about it. Jose called him earlier to vent about her giving directions. The weather was clearing this week getting them back on schedule by Saturday. But no, she had to push without him there.

His crew didn't like a woman supervising them, and it didn't help that she was so attractive. He looked at the pic on the screen as the cell continued to shake. A brunette in her mid-thirties, she'd had a rough life and wasn't afraid of hard work. The day he took the photo she shot him that stubborn look, her green eyes bright with determination during an argument about a detail on the house. End the end she listened to his long-winded explanations and made the right decision. Her commitment to this project was even sexier than her curves. *Damn it. Not right now.* He was busy. She would just have to wait until he had a free moment.

He slammed the phone in the desk drawer, closed it, and went back to work. The paperwork on his desk required his full attention, and he promised himself that he would not check his phone until he was available.

At one o'clock he left his office for the rest of the afternoon, stepping into a lecture hall full of half-interested college students.

It wasn't until late evening when he made it back to his desk to recover his phone. The evening sunset painted with swirls of orange and purple pulled him to the window looking out into the parking lot. Man, he loved the sky here. He glanced at the notifications on the phone. While she had called three times, the messages didn't interest him. It was the single text that made him anxious. What had they uncovered? *Shit.* Now he wanted to kick himself for ignoring the first call.

Gathering his papers from the desk, he wished he didn't have to take work home with him tonight and stuffed them into his briefcase. He made it out to the truck in record time and the heat of the day flushed his face when it escaped from the open driver's side door. He tossed his briefcase on the floorboard and pulled out his phone to call her back while it aired out.

The phone rang, and Beth picked up. "Hi. I've been waiting for you to call back. Can you come by the site, please? I have something fantastic to show you."

"Okay, fine. I need to change first, but I will be over in about thirty minutes." Adjusting the rearview mirror, he ran his fingers through his hair.

"Better hurry, it's getting dark fast, and the guys have totally stripped the house. We will only have flashlights."

"Get Jose to see if he can put some lights up for you. Should I bring something to eat?"

"Nah. I'm not hungry. Besides, I'm not sure Jose will do anything for me. He's been pretty stubborn today."

"Really? I'll talk to him. See you in a while."

He started the old truck and took off out of the lot. As he pulled onto Highway 264 and headed east, he noticed a traffic jam ahead. He laughed to himself. *Well, a traffic jam by Beaufort County standards was twenty cars lined up both ways.* Sam sighed, *how his perspective had changed over the years.* It appeared to only be a license check, but what a pain. Slowly, the cars pulled up to the sheriff's car. As he pulled through the checkpoint, he recognized the officer. "How are you doing tonight, Bill?"

"Okay. It's been pretty quiet here lately, and everyone's behaving themselves as well as can be expected. License and registration, please. How are things up at the college, Professor Howard?"

"Pretty good. That beard is looking pretty healthy," he said, handing the Deputy his paperwork and laughing at his formal tone. Bill and he had known each other since they were in junior high.

"Yeah, I'm growing it for the next play down at the theater. I'll have some tickets to sell in a couple of weeks. Can I put you down for a couple?"

"Sure"

He handed back the paperwork with a smile. "Thanks. Have a good night."

"See you later."

"I hope not," Bill replied with a big toothy grin that mimicked Grizzly Adams.

Sam waved as he drove through to turn off the main road to his house. As he pulled up to the house, he threw the truck in park and jogged into the house. He changed into blue jeans and a white button-up shirt. He traded his dress shoes for work boots and headed back out to the truck. *Hopefully, I don't need anything special. What in the world did they find today?* Now he wished he had asked her some more questions. But he had been frustrated and didn't want to chat at the time. It wasn't her fault. She didn't know about his real job; that teaching was his priority. He started his truck and headed up the road back into town. He really wasn't planning on this tonight. He had things to do. This side job had turned out to be more than he had bargained for. This was not a simple remodel. After seeing the house, he fell in love with it. He knew it was going to be a big job, but he didn't care. The privilege was all his.

A blaring horn brought him back to the now green stoplight. *Damn it, you're driving* he reminded himself. He waved to the driver behind him, hoping he didn't piss someone off. He turned down the street and pulled into Beth's drive. The dumpster overflowed, but the new roof looked good in the twilight. *Wow, the guys got a lot done today.* Maybe it wasn't a bad thing for them to work without him. He would inspect it more thoroughly in the morning. He could see spotlights blazing through the windows. Jose must have hooked her up so Beth could stay after dark. The days were getting shorter now, and they would need the lights anyway to get a good day's work in. He knocked loudly on the door and yelled, "Beth!"

"Down here!" He heard from the kitchen floor. She poked her head up through a new opening. She was absolutely filthy.

"Hahaha. You should see yourself." She was beaming with excitement. *God, she looked good right now. No woman has the right to look that good covered with cobwebs and dirt.* Sam reminded himself that he was mad at her but realized no one could stay mad at her long.

"Shut up! Stop laughing at me. Will you get down here?!" It was a demand, not a request. "Wait till you see. I can't believe it." She disappeared back down into the hole.

Sam looked at the construction of the opening. The nails in the molding were eighteenth century. He stepped down the worn stone stairs into the cellar. He could see from the coloration they were local stone. The ceiling was low, but there was enough room for Beth to walk around. He had to bend down to move around in the space. She had placed the lights, so the space was well lit. As he started a mental inventory of the items throughout the room, he understood her excitement. *Oh man, this is fantastic.*

"Have you moved anything?" He asked.

"No. I was waiting for you. It was hard to be patient, but you said we should document things as we went through the process. I took pictures before it got too dark, but I think the lights help a lot. I'm going to take another set."

"Good thinking. Looks like most everything is from the nineteenth century or older. We will want to be careful. This is awesome. I'm glad you called."

"You took your sweet time getting back to me. What was so important today anyway?" She jabbed at him, wrinkling her nose.

"I was busy. This is supposed to be just a side gig. Of course, this one has required more work than usual, which I don't mind. You must give me my Tuesdays. Okay?" He looked at her.

* * *

SHE SHRUGGED. "You still should have called me back. I had a lot of trouble with the guys today. Jose said you took his call." She went back to snapping pictures. Her mind was too occupied to care at the moment. She forgot the anger she had felt toward him earlier in the day for not being there. For a moment, the camera's focus centered on Sam. He looked different today. His short brown hair peppered with cobwebs and bits of dust. He studied a crock and its contents like he had found the crown jewels. *Look at that amazing sexy grin.* The lines around his mouth gave him a rugged outdoorsy look. He glanced up from his treasure in her direction.

Their eyes met, and heat ran through her body. She quickly turned and pulled a crate from the shelf. Hoping he didn't notice her staring, she sat it on the floor next to a light. Gently she pulled out a set of awls, setting them off to the left. Then a set of hand planers, an old hammer, and a hand drill. In the bottom were newspapers the original owner had used to line the crate.

Dated October 24, 1862

Yellow Fever Outbreak Kills Hundreds

Beth felt Sam reading over her shoulder. As she looked up at him, he said, "It devastated Wilmington. The cemeteries are full of graves from that period."

She glanced over the brittle yellowing paper, carefully turning the pages. There were so many ads for runaway slaves. "Why would they advertise here for a slave from Alabama?"

"Because of the port, Washington was a main stop on the Underground Railroad."

Sweat started to bead on Beth's forehead. The lights were heating up the room at a rapid pace.

Sam wiped his face with the back of his hand. "We should turn off the lights. The heat might damage some of our finds. Did you get all the pictures you needed?"

"I think I documented everything. What time is it?"

"Nine o'clock."

"Holy shit. I've been down here for five hours." She smiled. "I love this house. I better head to the apartment. Thanks for letting me be at the site today."

Sam started turning off the lights one by one. "You're welcome. Looks like you got a lot done today. Jose isn't going to want you back. You must have pushed them hard. Did you yell at them?" He offered her a hand as they went upstairs to the kitchen.

"No, I just reminded them that you were coming and wouldn't like the mess they left. Well, maybe I yelled a few times. Why do they push back so much? I can tell they are dedicated to you."

"You have to give them a little slack. They work really hard at getting it right. Sometimes that takes a little longer. You'll get a feel for the way they work eventually."

"Hopefully before the project is over." She laughed.

He joined in, their laughter echoed through the empty building as they walked toward the front door "Hope so. I'll see you later in the week."

"Thanks, Sam. See ya later."

As Beth emerged from the house, the cool breeze hit her damp shirt sending a chill over her body. She had been down in the cellar for hours and sweat had soaked her through. Sam gave a quick wave as he pulled out of the driveway. She walked across the street to the waterfront to relax. The excitement of the day still had her adrenaline flowing. She needed to get some rest, but it would be impossible right now. Her hands ran along the railing as she walked listening to the waves lap at the retaining wall.

There were so many people downtown tonight. On a Tuesday? How weird. The wind lifted her hair off the nape of her neck cooling her skin. Her head quieted. Focusing on the sound of her shoes on the brick walkway, she headed toward her Main Street loft. She had lucked out when she found this place only two blocks away offering month-to-month rent. Lord knows how long the house was going to take. Maybe she should have signed a lease. Of course, she hadn't been expecting to gut the place, but it became necessary to pass code for both her home and a retail shop. She couldn't wait to open. Now she had the historical cellar, what was she going to do with all the antiques? Perhaps a local museum would be interested in them. She made a mental note to check this week.

She climbed the stairs and unlocked the door. Crossing the room, she laid her phone on the bedside table. As she straightened, her reflection caught her attention in the mirror hanging on the wall. The figure staring at her startled her. She laughed to herself. Layer upon layer of dirt caked every surface of her skin. First impressions notwithstanding, she felt a sense of accomplishment. She stripped and jumped in the shower. A trail of dirty water ran down the middle of the tub adding to her satisfaction. She toweled off and headed straight to bed.

BETH PEERED INTO THE DARKNESS, blinking to focus while confusion took hold. An unfamiliar shed with a dirt floor? Water came into the building from an unseen source. It flowed with force, holding her feet fast to the ground. She couldn't move. Panic overtook her senses. She willed her feet to move, but they were as stuck as if they were in hardened concrete. The water became deeper. She heard a noise from the corner of the room.

A young black woman holding a bundle close to her, her eyes huge with fear, huddled in the shadows. Beth's eyes started to adjust to the darkness. The girl was dressed in a long cotton gown. Her hair wrapped with a scarf. She tried to speak, but her mouth wouldn't form the words. *We have to get out of here.* The shed boards creaked against the strain of the water. It was going to collapse. *We have to get out.* The young girl waded toward the door. She pushed on the latch, but it was locked on the outside. She began to scream. She banged on the door, but it only made the building sway. The water sloshed at Beth's waist now. The beams supporting the roof gave way. Beth tried to dodge the pieces as they fell, but her body refused to respond. A beam broke free. Everything went black.

Beth sat up in bed. *Shit, what was that?* She tried to catch her breath. "It was only a dream. It was only a dream," she repeated to the darkness.

PERMITS AND PAPERWORK

September 12, 2014

"You sure are punishing that bread." Hellen heard her husband's voice coming up the hall into their small kitchen.

She turned and glared at Jose, slapped more peanut butter on the bread, before shoving it into a baggy. The peanut butter pressed against the plastic blocking the view of its contents. She rolled her eyes and let out a breath of frustration.

"I just don't understand why you are working late *again* today." She brushed her hair out of her eyes and wiped the perspiration from her forehead. *Why do you have to make this so hard? A little help, that's all. Can't you help just a little?*

"We have an important inspection today and are way behind. It's been raining so much the project isn't going as quickly as Sam wants it to."

She pulled out another slice. "But the boys want to go fishing after school, and you haven't been home on time since you've been working on Water Street. Don't you think it's a little weird she has all that money to spend? I heard she killed her husband."

Jose looked directly at her. "Who told you that?"

"Just something I heard. But what if it's true? I don't think you should be working for someone like that. I'm worried about you."

"You know how it works. I don't pick our clients, and you shouldn't believe everything you hear down at the store."

"I wouldn't have to worry if you had your own company. When are you going to talk to Sam?"

"I will, I will. Now is not the time. If you wanted to be married to the boss, you should have married him."

Hellen turned around and faced him. "I picked the one I wanted." She winked at him and spun back around.

Jose crossed the kitchen to wrap his arms around his wife. He nuzzled her ear and whispered. "How about a little night fishing later?"

Temptation and want filled her. She had to stay on track. Hellen whipped around to face him. "Jose," she intoned, emphasizing the last syllable, "I have to get everybody's lunch packed and take the boys to school. I have a meeting so I will have to drop you off at the site. Better get your stuff together."

"What if I need to run to the lumber yard?"

Hellen poked him in the ribs, "You should have thought about that before you took the car apart last week. Now, get everyone in the truck." She kissed him on the cheek and slapped his behind to get him to move out of her way so she could finish the lunches.

"Boys, get in the truck and don't forget your backpacks." He yelled down the hall.

Hellen jumped. "You don't have to yell. Inside voice, please."

"But yelling gets them going. We'll be in the truck." He strutted across the kitchen floor as two brown haired boys raced past him and out the screen door. He turned around and winked at her, mouthing the words "Later" with a huge grin on his face.

Minutes later, she heard the truck engine fire up. Sprinting to the back door, she cracked the screen door and shook her finger at him. If he knew what was good for him, he wouldn't take off with those boys. She had stuff to do today. His brilliant smile through the windshield melted her anger. God, he was sexy.

"Wait a minute," she yelled across the yard. Grabbing the lunches and her purse, she locked the door behind her and dashed to the truck.

* * *

SAM WOKE WITH THE SUN. He had always been an early riser since construction was no fun in the Southern heat and humidity. Beth's house was coming along nicely, but now he needed a few inspections on the site. The cellar needed to be declared to the city on paper, so there was a record of it in the historic registry. It was a lot of additional work, but the house was going to be fantastic when finished. Bob, the county building inspector, was coming to look at the framing. He would just tack on the new Certificate of Appropriateness during the visit. He also needed to schedule the appointment for the electrical and plumbing inspections. The cellar would make the plumbing a little more complicated, but he had dealt with that sort of thing before.

He sent Beth a text. He learned when the project first started that she was also always up early. In the beginning, her text messages full of questions about this and that had been annoying. Now, her enthusiasm struck a chord. She was invested in this project as much as he was, if not more. They haven't had much time to get to know each other. The rush on the house had pushed their respective schedules to the extreme. He might have to remedy that. Maybe, after the house was complete, she would accept an invitation for dinner one night. He had struggled with whether he should ask her out or not. Although she was his boss, he was attracted to her, and he believed she felt the same way. He laughed at the thought. He never had a problem asking someone out before. What was the worst that could happen?

Perhaps a celebration dinner. He stepped into the shower. He would ask her after the inspection. He knew it would go well. Bob's a good guy, and there wasn't anything unusual about the project. He made a mental note to ask about the plumbing. Maybe he would have some ideas.

Finishing his shower, he toweled off and absentmindedly ran his fingers through his short hair. He pulled on his blue jeans and white button-up. His steel toe boots sat beside the bedroom chair. He sighed. How long had it been since he had taken a day off? Too long.

Maybe he'd take a weekend soon. He shoved his feet into the boots and laced them up, grabbed his phone, keys, and wallet, and headed out the door.

* * *

"MAN, I FEEL LIKE CRAP." Beth stretched, trying to wake up from her sleepiness. She didn't sleep much again last night. The intense nightmares had felt so real. After three nights in a row, she needed a good night sleep. Hopefully, like before, they would disappear and not return.

Her cell phone chimed with a text message.

Sam: Need to have an additional inspection this afternoon. The historical COA must be amended because of the cellar. 2pm apt if you want to be there.

Beth: I'll be there.

She had a teleconference at eleven with Martin about the art coming from Paris. Other than that, she planned to spend her time in the cellar. Sam had said it would get complicated now that historical content needed to be documented. They had to be careful. He was definitely living up to his professional reputation. The way he sorted through all the antiques they had found was very methodical like he had done it many times before. The Washington Underground Railroad Museum was thrilled with the artifacts being donated. They would make a fantastic exhibit.

She had to get up and get going. There was way too much to do today. She picked out a t-shirt and khaki shorts. She would change before the inspection. A button-up blouse and khaki pants should be fine for the building inspector. She laid those aside and headed to the shower. Catching a glimpse in the mirror, she jumped. Dark circles under her eyes made her look ten years older. She would have to take a nap later if she was going to prevent a migraine.

She stripped down and stepped in the shower. The hot water relaxed the tension in her shoulders. She tried to recall what had the nightmare been about. An unfocused figure left her head as soon as it appeared. She wished she had written the details down when she woke during the night. It bothered her that something so simple had thrown off her schedule.

She stepped from the shower, toweled off and quickly ran a comb through her hair before twisting it up. It was the only style that would do working in the heat of Indian summer. Quick and easy, the way she liked it. She dressed and headed off to Rachel's for some breakfast. It was a quick walk to the old city hall, now a heavenly bakery. She had to watch herself; the croissants were incredible. Better schedule a run for this afternoon.

She glanced up at the old building. Rachel had done a great job with her remodel. The raw masonry of the bakery's walls gave the place a fantastic atmosphere. Beth opened the door and was met with the line of customers waiting for their choice of the delicious pastries and freshly brewed coffee. Washingtonians were early risers, trying to beat the heat no doubt. She waited patiently smelling the heavenly scents from the kitchen and people watching.

There were the natives, usually dressed in their summer casual. You saw a lot of preppy outfits. The tattered cut-offs were only worn in the garden at home. There was the old money who didn't care what they wore or what others thought and new money whose appearance screamed, 'notice and approve of me' to the latter. You could always tell from their carefully thought-out ensembles. No doubt with some help from the boutiques down on Main Street. Then there were the people who had moved here to find a new way of life. She smiled to herself, thinking how fast she adjusted to the relaxed downtown style here on the waterfront. She had been nervous at first, and now she wondered why. The relaxed atmosphere suited her. She was so glad she moved to Washington.

The young man behind the counter dazzled her with a bright smile as he handed over her usual. "Good morning, Beth. Here you go. You are running a little behind today? I didn't see you on your morning jog when I came into work."

"Morning, Rick." She laughed as she reached for her purchase. "Thanks. Am I so predictable?"

Rick laughed. "I'll see you tomorrow." He handed her the change with a wink.

"I guess I am. See ya." She stepped over to the counter with creamer and turned her tea to a milky mocha color.

A deep male voice came from behind her. "Would you like some honey with that?"

"Yes, thank you." She took the honey dipper from a strong hand reaching over her shoulder. She turned and looked into the deep blue eyes of a tall sheriff's deputy.

"Anytime." He touched his fingers to his hat brim, turned, and left through the back door.

Beth paused and watched him go. Such manners. She took some time to perfect her morning wake-up drink before heading toward the waterfront.

The breeze coming off the river felt wonderful. A bench called her name as seagulls inched closer, eyeballing her breakfast. She gave them a glare wishing them away knowing they were not going anywhere until all the food was gone. The buttery croissant went perfectly with her iced citrus mint tea. The caffeine hit her system, and her brain went into hyperdrive as she thought about the art she was selecting with Martin this afternoon. He was doing such a great job finding the bright colored masterpieces for the gallery. He said there were a few surprises for her in this afternoons batch. She couldn't wait.

MONEY AND THE PASS

*I*t was a shame to return to the apartment on a beautiful day like this. Beth turned on her laptop to prepare for her meeting. She couldn't wait to see what he had found. Martin had been purchasing art from Paris for six months now. He promised that he found some 'superb' items. It made her laugh every time he said it. Martin was one of Brad's most trusted friends, and the only one she trusted with the huge purchases she was making. He sent her a list of pieces last week, and from it, she made her wish list. He promised to have a slide presentation of the actual pieces ready for today. Goosebumps rose on her skin thinking of the pieces she had chosen. Was she overshooting the quality of the pieces she wanted to purchase? She shook her head. No, there was a customer base for this kind of quality in North Carolina. Plus, her application to sell online was in its final stages.

Martin joined her on the WebEx meeting. He was an older Frenchman on the edge of fashion. The scarf tied around his neck gave him that extra flair, while his glasses created a studious appearance. A paradox. "Bonjour, Madame Beth. Comment ça va?"

"Ça va bien, Martin. How are you?"

"Bien. I will not keep you long. I wanted you to see the pieces I have available for you today. I'm afraid we missed the Miró I included in the presentation. Someone purchased it last night."

Shoot. "Please, keep looking for one. I really want a piece by Miró."

"Okay. Let's go through the list. Here is the Gateaux. I think the style and subject matter will suit the beach. You said you were looking for water scenes. I have included several Hillary Hassells. She paints exactly what you described. "

Clicking through the pastel beach scenes, she agreed they were perfect. The vigorous brushstrokes gave it exactly the right sense of movement. "Oh, I love these."

Martin continued, "I know this is more modern and abstract, but I thought a Dufy with the strong blue pallet might also suit your customers."

He continued through about thirty slides of pieces, describing their high points. The dates ranged from the 1850s to the 1950s, and the prices were in the fine art category. All of them within her nautical theme requirement. Beth jotted down notes as he spoke. She made a list of pieces she would buy today and a wish list for later after the gallery opened. All the sudden, little blond heads bobbed into the screen.

"Hi, Beth!" Martin's kids giggled.

"Sophie! Come and get the children please," Martin yelled. Their mother came rushing into the room. "Sortez de la chambre, enfants! Votre père travaille." She turned to the screen. "Salut Beth. Ça va?"

"Ça va bien. How are you? I miss you." Beth had become close to

Sophie in the months following her husband's death. She never failed to pick up the phone or answer a late-night text.

"I miss you too. You must come and visit soon." Sophie waved, grabbed the kids, and headed out of the room.

"Sorry, Beth. Shall we get back to business?" They turned back to the slides again to review the pieces.

The price of the initial start-up was going to be painful. "I will take the Dufy, all the Hassell's." She liked the fact they were by a woman artist during the turn of the century. "Send the first two Gateaux's, the Boudin, and the Thomson. Keep looking for a Miró, please."

"Absolutely."

"Thanks for all your hard work." Her cell phone announced a text.

"You are welcome. I am happy to help a fellow art lover and friend. Call me if you have any other requests. We were thinking about bringing the children to the opening. Will that be okay? Are you still on schedule?"

"Of course, they are welcome. I have missed Sophie and the kids. It will be chaos of course, but Sophie's company will calm me. The kids will love the river. Construction is taking longer than expected, but the opening should be on schedule. I will contact you when I am ready for you to start shipping."

"Okay. I look forward to hearing from you. Bonne chance. Au revoir."

"Au revoir." Beth disconnected and grabbed her phone. It was from Sam.

Sam: Inspector will be prompt at 2pm. See you

. . .

WHAT TIME WAS IT? *Shit.* It was already one. The meeting took way longer than she expected. It was good to see Sophie and the kids, though. She needed to get ready for the inspection. Thank goodness, Sam texted. Beth threw on the khakis she picked out earlier in the day. She considered taking something to change into after the inspection while she pulled her hair down and brushed it out. Who was she kidding? There was nowhere to change on the property except the porta john in the front yard. Just thinking about it turned her stomach. There was no way she was going to hang out at the site in her good clothes after the inspector left. She shoved a pair of jeans and a t-shirt into her bag and headed out the door.

The walk to the house was refreshing. The breeze off the water cooled her skin from the heat of the day. She turned down Main taking in the old buildings. The storefronts hadn't changed since the fifties. *God, I love this place.* She waved at a blond in one window fixing the display of the latest Southern fashion. The new generation had taken over where the last left off. Yes, it was a small town, but you couldn't tell by their retail tradition. This is why her gallery would fit in with the rest. There were several in town with fine reputations, but her online shop for the business would make hers stand out. Her love of art had been her passion for years. Her husband spoiled her, taking her to museums all over the world. She networked with all the gallery owners and museum curators, and it was finally paying off. The stores were busy this afternoon. It was a great sign.

Beth rounded the corner to her house. It was so beautiful. There was an extra vehicle in the drive. Maybe the inspector's. He was early. *Shoot.* She jogged up the drive. The site looked oddly empty without all the guys working.

As she walked in the front door, she found Sam standing with an older gentleman in the foyer. He appeared to be in his mid-50's, short, bald, and as wide as he was tall. He smiled politely putting out his hand.

"Good afternoon, Ms. Pearse. I'm Bob. Nice to meet you. Sam was just talking to me about your discovery. I'm afraid that it does add some extra paperwork. But it shouldn't delay your project too much. Sam has assured us that it will stay intact, and he has done excellent work in the past." He nodded in Sam's direction with an air of confidence. "I would like to take a look at the cellar. We need to make sure that the footings are in good shape, especially considering the age of the building. Sam has also mentioned the new plumbing."

Sam smiled behind him. Beth caught his eye. She hoped Sam knew what he was doing because she had no idea what needed to be done.

Dropping her duffle bag by the front door, she took Bob's hand and smiled. "Thank you for helping us with the plans." She turned toward the kitchen.

Sam slid the plywood cover for the cellar away from the opening and headed down the stairs. Beth followed him, steadying herself against the wall. Sam switched on the lamps around the room giving the group light to see by. Much to Beth's surprise, Bob pulled out his flashlight and walked over to the corner of the room. He shined the light up into the corners. He walked the edges occasionally only letting out a "Hmmm."

Beth couldn't keep still. Her nerves were getting the best of her. Why couldn't he say something that meant something? She shifted her weight. Suddenly, the room grew fuzzy, and her legs started to give way. Sam stepped over, placing his hand on her shoulder to steady her. All she could think of was how great his hands felt. His long fingers brushed her collarbone. The touch set her skin on fire through the cotton of her blouse. Suddenly he stepped away, and she realized they were being spoken to.

"Ms. Pearse, everything looks good here. Sam, you might want to reinforce the floor joists since this is going to be a busy business." He winked at Beth.

"From your mouth to God's ears." Beth smiled.

"I would recommend removing the shelving in here. I would worry about their stability for storage. Just a recommendation, though. Take it if you like. Then they can be used elsewhere."

"Thank you so much."

"Let's go upstairs, and I'll look at the framing."

Bob led the way upstairs and stepped into the kitchen. He toured both floors with her and Sam in tow. There were no walls, only two by four framing boxing out the rooms. The sound of their footsteps changed as they moved from the original wood flooring in some places to the subfloor made of thick plywood in others. Their conversation filled the building echoing in the empty space. From what she could understand, Bob inspected the wiring and the plumbing while Sam took notes to ensure they complied for the next inspection.

The empty space began to close in around her, getting smaller with every suggestion Bob made. Her pulse jumped, and her breathing became shallow. Excusing herself, Beth stepped out into the yard for some fresh air.

Away from Sam, everything normalized. Could be that anxious over the inspection? It seemed to be going well. Or was the more likely answer her reaction to Sam's touch? At the mere thought, butterflies in her belly nearly made her float away. She plopped down on a lawn chair under the shade of the big oak tree. She shook her head and laughed out loud. It had only been a hand.

Sam and Bob came out of the front door. They talked and laughed. The contrast between the two men only emphasized Sam's tall, athletic form. The jeans suited him. She wondered how he might look all dressed up. Shaking the slowly derailing train in her brain, she focused on their body language and determined it must have been a successful inspection. The men shook hands before Bob got into his truck. Beth's nerves resurfaced as she watched him drive away. Sam walked to where Beth was sitting, his long strides covering the yard quickly, a heart-melting grin was plastered across his face.

* * *

"Congratulations, we did great." He winked. Now was his chance. "You want to get a bite to celebrate?"

Her head jerked up, and he looked deep into her eyes. There was something there. What was it? Why was she hesitating?

"Of course. Where should we go?"

"What are you in the mood for? Italian? Southern? Steak or Seafood? Maybe you want a Bill's hot dog?"

She laughed. God, he loved her laugh. It eased the worry on her forehead he saw so often. "Let's do Southern. You have an idea of where you want to go?"

"Grub Brothers, definitely." Plus, they could get a table upstairs for a little privacy, so he could really get to know her. "Do you mind if I change first though? You look great, and I don't want to embarrass you." Beth blushed and confirmed his suspected feelings. "Would you like me to come back and pick you up or are you up for a drive?"

"I'll come with you."

"Hop in the truck. I need to turn everything off and lock up." He ran inside trying to hurry. First, he hit the lights downstairs, thought about grabbing her bag sitting by the door but thought better of it, before he locked the door behind himself. He almost fell off the front stoop, he turned so fast, rushing to the truck.

"Come on; I'm starving." She was laughing at him from the cab of the truck.

He jumped in, fumbling with the keys in the ignition. He was never nervous about dates, but this one felt different. He promised himself not to spend too much time at the house. Just a quick change. He had to at least get out of the dirty jeans and shirt. He had been at her house all morning, trying to clean up. He rolled down the windows in the truck and glanced at her as he backed down the drive. Her eyes lit with excitement.

Maybe the risk was worth it.

ELECTRICITY

*B*eth's hair blew around like crazy in the cab. The knots she would deal with later. She should've left her hair up this afternoon. The fresh air felt good though, and she didn't dare ask him to roll up the windows. The air was thick and sticky signaling the rain that would soon come. She could smell it in the air. The dark, lush landscape turned an emerald green with the darkening sky. She loved the color pallet here. It was one of the reasons she had chosen this part of the country, it spoke to her. She glanced at Sam. "Do you mind if I turn on the radio?"

"Help yourself. It's on a country station, but you can change it if you like."

She flipped on the newer-looking radio. It reminded her of Brad; he had also been the kind of man to have a stereo newer than his truck. Music filled the truck, and she turned up the volume. As they headed down Hwy 264, she sang along with the music.

"You're in a good mood," Sam yelled over the music and the wind, glancing at her.

"Today went well. It's a big relief." Beth leaned back in the seat.

"It did. Bob gave me a lot of notes so we will be good in a couple of weeks for his follow-up inspection."

She nodded in acknowledgment and sang out another note. Sam smiled as he turned the truck up a driveway. Her voice trailed off as she caught his house in her view. This didn't fit the farmhouse style she expected. She closed her mouth consciously. The gray two-story house looked like it had been transported from California with its modern style and huge front windows. A large overhang with slender supports at each corner protected the truck as they pulled up. "Wow, it's beautiful."

"Thanks. You can come in if you want, while I change." Sam smiled, "I'll just be about ten minutes." He put it in park and stepped from the truck. Beth opened her door slowly taking in the view. It was an impressive place. The longer she looked at it, the less it reminded her of its owner.

She followed Sam through the front door into a vast living room. The floor was a beautiful light oak that reflected the light from the lighted ceiling fan hanging high above them. The décor was as impressive as the style on the outside. The open floor plan suited the modern look. Drawn to the massive built-in desk on the far side of the room, she moved in that direction.

"Make yourself at home. I'll be ready in a bit." Sam called over his shoulder as he disappeared down the hall.

Beth strode over to the desk. Artifacts were placed carefully on top. There were small tools on a cotton cloth laid in a row. She recognized some old bullets and shards of pottery. There were some other questionable things she couldn't identify. She glanced to the other side of the room. Above the fireplace hung a Miró painting. *Oh, my God. Amazing.* The lines were so fluid, with bright red, yellow, and blue colors. The painting called to her. She moved across the floor to take in the piece. A woman stood on a beach, alone. Waiting. What was she waiting for?

Beth contemplated the multitude of possibilities as she stared at the canvas until she felt eyes on her. His eyes. She turned around and found him standing behind her. Close. His eyes twinkled.

"How do you have a Miró? I have been trying to locate one of these for the gallery for months."

"It was a graduation present from my parents. It inspired my house when I built it. I love the clean lines but still captures so much chaotic emotion. There is a story in there, but it seems the story is different for everyone who views it. You're buying pieces like this for our small town?" He asked, disbelief laced in his voice.

"My gallery will be primarily online. But there is a market for fine art here in North Carolina. A few years ago, I visited a gallery in Charlotte, and it had some amazing pieces. I knew this would be a perfect place to set up shop."

"Washington is a long way from Charlotte, Beth."

"I know. But Charlotte doesn't have the water. I have to be close to the water. It's part of who I am." Her mind flashed back to the nightmares she'd been having over the last week. Water had been a huge part of them. Hmm. She had never feared the water even after her husband's accident. She didn't dare consider why this was surfacing now. A knot formed in her throat.

Sam studied her and quickly added, "I'm not saying that it won't work. I was just wondering why you chose Washington? The online business is brilliant by the way."

Beth's mind swung back to Sam. She needed to enjoy this evening. "Oh, I know. That will be the primary selling point. The physical gallery will be a showplace to entertain clients and attract new ones. The art world has been changing for several years now. It is expensive to set up a large space in a big city. You must realize most people have an interest in collecting fine art. The internet has opened up the art world. Someone in Milwaukee can purchase a piece from someone in Los Angeles or London. There are no travel costs, just shipping. A truly global marketplace."

"I had no idea. It sounds awesome." He winked at her motioning to the front door. "Okay, let's get you fed. You can explain some more to me over food."

Beth's cheeks flamed. She'd forgotten how hungry she was while distracted by both the Miró and the man leading the way toward the front door. She took in the house one last time. What a surprise. She thought she read people well, but Sam was an exception. She followed him out to the truck. Slipping into the passenger seat, she smiled. This was shaping up to be a surprising turn for her evening.

HISTORICAL ACCURACY

*S*am's heart skipped a beat when she blushed. She looked so beautiful talking about her passion. He didn't want to stop her, but his stomach was starting to sound off in protest. He would make sure to bring it up again while they were eating even if only for a few moments to see the spark speaking about art spurred in her green eyes. He started the truck, and the radio blared. He absentmindedly turned it down. "Sorry about that."

He steered out onto the highway and headed back toward town. The windows still down allowed a cool breeze to blow through the cab. Beth's hair whipped around like crazy. He clicked on the AC and put up the windows. "Might save you some time later," he offered in explanation.

She smiled at him. "Thanks. Looks like there is a storm brewing. Those clouds look nasty."

The clouds hung huge and dark over the town. His foot pressed the accelerator in hopes they'd beat the storm. The radio kept them entertained until they arrived at the restaurant, so the silence in the truck didn't feed his nervousness.

As Sam parked the truck on the street in front, big drops of rain began hitting the windshield.

"Better hurry," she said and jumped out, heading to the front door.

He locked the truck and followed her. Sam asked the hostess for a table upstairs. With a conspiratorial nod, she led the way and seated them in a booth in the corner.

They both ordered tea and settled in to continue their earlier conversation. "Okay, you know why I'm here. Now, I want to know why you moved here," Beth asked Sam.

"I grew up here. I moved away to go to college, but the city didn't agree with me. The politics I had to deal with weren't worth it. I love what I do, and it just wasn't working there."

"You can't tell me there are no politics in Washington."

They both laughed.

"There are politics, but at least you can see them coming a mile away. You can take people at face value here. Yes, there is pettiness and gossips, but for the most part, everyone knows everyone, so you know who the storytellers are. I like that. Besides, having grown up here makes it easier to navigate the small-town politics. Of course, occasionally, you get new blood that stirs the pot, and the stories start up again." He winked at her.

"So, I've stirred the pot, have I? Tell me more." Beth batted her eyelashes, teasing.

"Well, there is a certain mystery to you. A single, young woman comes to town, buys an old, can I say that again? *Old* house *and* applies for a business license. These things combined raised a few eyebrows. You have to remember, we are fairly traditional around here. Wait till they see your art. They will really be curious."

The waitress stopped by, dropped off their tea, and took their orders. Sam chose the Southern Fried Smiles to start and then a Black and Blue burger for dinner. "Homemade chips with that?

"Of course."

"I'm going to have the shrimp and grits and a salad. Thank you." She handed her menu back to the waitress and turned back to Sam. "Don't tell me you are wondering what's up." The amusement reflected in Beth's voice.

"How can I not? You're a very unique client. I have been wondering about your decision to move here. You answered that. So, tell me how you came to love art. I can tell it's a passion."

"I also grew up in a small town. My father loved art, and he shared that love with me every chance he got. We studied his books every Friday; looking at masterpieces all over the world. When I went to college, it was excited to discover I could study art history and share my love of art with other people. You know, to kind of pass on my father's legacy. College was where I met my late husband. He shared my love of art. He came from a good family, and he had been to all the museums and galleries that I only experienced in my dreams. After college, we were married, and he took me with him when he traveled on business.

"We would visit museums and galleries. I made friends with a lot of the gallery owners. Sophie is my best friend in Paris. Her husband helps me with my European purchases." A smile spread across Beth's face, and her expression softened.

"Whatcha thinking about?"

Beth laughed. "Sophie with her little ones running around her legs, trying to clean the house while they created more and more clutter. Their two little boys are a handful."

"I can imagine. So how did you find Washington?"

"One of our trips was to Washington. I forget why Brad had to be here. While he was in meetings, I walked the streets of downtown. I loved the galleries and antique shops. Of course, that was six years ago, downtown has changed a bit." She took a long swig of iced tea. Her eyes brimmed with unshed tears. "Brad died in an accident five years ago. Since then, I have been sorting out life, trying to find a direction. The online gallery idea combined Brad's company and my love of art, so that's what I went with."

"Sorry about your husband," Sam said uncomfortably. He had no idea her wounds ran so deep.

"It's okay. I miss him. He was my best friend for so long. Our adventures were amazing. The happy memories have helped me heal. I'm ready for my next adventure." She smiled.

* * *

THE SAMPLER SAM ordered was dropped off at the table, breaking the awkward silence. Beth dipped an okra fritter in the remoulade sauce and tried a bite while Sam chose a fried green tomato. Sauce dripped down her chin.

"Sorry." She smiled at Sam. "Good choice. It lives up to its name," she said with a laugh.

"It's your turn. Tell me about you. Tell me what made you choose Washington. You are very talented. I'm sure you would make a fortune in a place like Savannah or even Richmond." She continued to snack while he talked.

"Like I said, I grew up here. I like it here. My dad was one of the few architects in Beaufort County. So, I have been on building sites since I could walk. My parents wanted me to be an architect and sent me to NC State for my degree. I discovered that I loved history more than design. Learning why something was made a certain way, centuries ago, fascinates me. I get pulled in looking at blueprints of old churches and houses and try to get into the brain of the original builder."

Beth watched him as he talked about history and teaching. His hands moved with his words. Those hands, so strong and creative, with their rough calluses. She smiled as he continued the narrative of his life as a struggling young professor.

"I decided that I wanted to stay here, but I had to come up with a way to pay the bills. As you know, teachers don't make much. So, I started my renovation business. The growth in the historical district here has helped a lot. The families who buy in the district must follow specific rules, as you already know. I work really hard to be as historically accurate as possible. Sometimes it requires research. I take a few jobs out of state if they interest me, but usually, only during a school break when I don't have to be in the classroom on Tuesday."

"The mysterious Tuesday. You could have told me." Beth teased.

"Not everyone would trust a history professor to rip their house apart and put it back together in a livable state. I try to keep the two separate."

TRIPPING THE BREAKER

*W*hen the main course arrived, and they both were so hungry, that their eating interrupted the conversation. Sam smiled at Beth enjoying her salad. Her face became unreadable when she tasted her grits.

"How are the grits?"

"Very creamy and... Salty? I've never eaten savory grits before. I've only had them prepared sweet. They are delicious though and compliment the wasabi cucumber dressing."

With a crack of thunder outside, they both glanced up at the ceiling and then back at each other. The rain sounded as if it would come through the roof. They burst into laughter. They had beaten the storm, and it was a doozy. Another huge boom made the lights flicker. "We better eat before we lose our lights." He smiled. "I'm going to go ahead and pay the bill just in case they lose the power."

"Let me give you some cash for my half." Beth reached into her pocket.

"Thanks, but this is my treat. You can get the tip if you want after we see how our service is," he tossed over his shoulder as he headed downstairs. He quickly reappeared with a candle. "Just in case."

"Why Sam, I thought you were getting romantic on me," she teased in a cute pretend southern drawl and giggled.

"Ma'am, you have no idea," Sam teased back, enjoying Beth's blush. The rain continued to fall on the roof.

"So, tell me about your house. It seems like a total contradiction to the rest of your style. It is so sleek and modern. Don't get me wrong, it's beautiful, just different."

"It was an experiment. My first set of plans I did after school. Mom and dad gave me the Miró, and I decided that I would design and build a house worthy of the painting."

"So, you built a house for a painting? You are a strange man." She smiled. "Why did you put your bid in on my job?"

"I like the idea of a gallery to showcase fine art for the public. Of course, I had no idea the quality you were planning. Your presentation showed your dedication to public access. It did require some extra planning for security and other things, but I like the idea of having museum quality in our town. Young people will not have to go to Raleigh anymore. It will be fantastic."

"Always the teacher." Beth laughed.

They finished up their food and Beth reached in her pocket for the tip. Sam gave her a look and dropped a tip on the table. They walked down the stairs. "Careful, the stairs are a little steep." He grabbed Beth's hand. It fit perfectly in his palm. So comfortable. They made their way to the front door, just to face the torrential downpour. It was raining hard, and they had no umbrellas.

The young hostess poked her head into the foyer glancing at Sam and Beth. "Professor Howard, here, borrow my umbrella. You can get it back to me later." She gave Beth a quick sideways look.

"Thanks, Liz. I'll get it right back to you. We're just going down a couple of doors. Don't get too wet later. Maybe the storm will stop soon." He smiled and waved as they headed out the door. Beth stood close to Sam trying to stay dry under the umbrella. The wind blew the rain sideways, and they soon realized the umbrella wasn't going to be much use.

They sprinted down Main to Beth's building; the rain drenching them. When they finally made it to the entrance of the lofts, they were both soaked through. Beth's white shirt clung to her skin leaving little to the imagination. Sam stood behind her at the door trying to be a gentleman but could not ignore the heat between their bodies. He could see a path of goosebumps his hot breath left on the back of her neck as she tried to unlock the door. Droplets of rain fell from her dark hair. The umbrella was a total failure at that point, and a sudden clap of thunder made them jump. Beth squealed in triumph as the lock released and the door finally opened. He could see the invitation in her eyes as he leaned down touching his lips to hers. Her lips softly parted, and he deepened the kiss gently. He slipped his arm around her waist pulling her close, their bodies melting together. He was losing himself in her. Another crack of thunder broke the spell as Beth jumped at the noise.

"I better go. We have a lot to get done in the morning. I had a great time. Maybe we can do it again on a much dryer night," Sam said hurriedly trying not to lose his determination. He was not going to ruin this by rushing her. He saw the disappointment in her eyes. "Are you busy next weekend, maybe next Saturday night?"

"Nope, what do you want to do?"

"We will figure something out. I'll plan something special." He reached down and touched her cheek. "See you in the morning," he said as he kissed her again before he turned toward his truck and ran through the rain. He ducked into the restaurant, knocked on the window of the inside door and pointed to the umbrella as he leaned it in the corner of the foyer. He smiled and waved, mouthing "Thank you." With a wave, he was back out in the rain and sprinting to the truck. He slid in and started the engine. He couldn't believe how good he felt.

UNEXPECTED CURRENT

*B*eth stepped into the hallway, watching him go. Her heart was going a mile a minute. She didn't expect this when the evening started. It happened so easily, so naturally. She had been so careful not to get involved with anyone since Brad's death. It was nothing serious. At least it didn't have to be. She would have fun while it lasted. She watched him return the umbrella before jumping into his truck and her breath caught in her throat as heat filled her whole body. She knew she was lying to herself.

She headed up the stairs to her loft and stripped off her wet clothes, going over the night in her head. He was very impressive with all his accomplishments. Her eyes closed as she remembered his kiss. *Wow.* It had been incredible. She stepped into the shower, the hot water warming her chilled skin. The water massaged her, chasing away the cold. The steam filled the bathroom fogging the mirror and the air. The lights blinked and then went out.

Oh man. She stood in the dark shower. She reached down and cut off the water. She remembered some candles under the sink. Stepping out of the bathtub, goosebumps rose on her skin as a chill ran over her. The room felt ice cold despite the steam hanging in the air. She reached for the hook on the back of the door grabbing her robe to shield her from the cold air. Under the sink, she fumbled through the bottles of various cleaners and beauty products looking for a candle while wishing she was more organized and prepared for a situation like this. Where was it?

She finally found one in the very back with a lighter sitting on top. She sat it on the vanity top and flashed the lighter. Out of the corner of her eye, she thought she saw a figure. She caught her breath. She tried the lighter again, and the flame flickered in the damp air. In the reflection of the mirror, she saw a young black woman.

She turned around quickly, the lighter going out with the breeze. She lit it again, holding her breath, her hands shaking. *How did she get in? Did she follow me in?* She wasn't paying attention when she came into the building. "Anyone there?" The light of the flame ignited, and the room was empty. Beth looked around, her fingers aching form keeping the flame alive. She lit the candle to have a brighter light. The candle illuminated the room with a warm glow, once again revealing she was alone.

She opened the bathroom door quickly and searched the bedroom with the candle. A loud clap of thunder proceeded a flash of lightning that lit the room with light. A shadow cast on the wall in front of her. Someone was standing beside her.

She whipped around the light disappearing with the lightning. There was no one there. Beth called out hoping for no answer. "Who's there? I saw you. What do you want?"

A female voice came out of the darkness. "A friend of a friend sent me. Are you the conductor?"

There was another flash of lightning, and the room stayed empty. The lights flickered on, and the bedroom lamps beside her bed came back to life. She stood in the room by herself. *Where did she hide?* She glanced under the bed, in the closet. Shaking, she went to the front door and confirmed the deadbolt was thrown. She was alone. She pulled on some shorts and a t-shirt and climbed into bed.

She needed to sleep. Beth scanned the room as her heart raced in her chest, then she got up again to recheck the front door and windows. She needed to calm down. She made herself a cup of tea and curled up under the covers with a book. She knew sleep would not come easy. Her hands, still unsteady, caused the spoon to clank against the teacup as she stirred.

RUNNING WATER

*B*eth ran to the back of the house. Her chest hurt as she gasped for her next breath. Screams came from the small outbuilding at the corner of the yard. Rain poured down in sheets as the lightning flashed around her. Sunflowers waved in the wind, bending, almost touching the lawn. The trees joined in the harsh dance forced to follow the rhythm of the storm. It had gotten worse. Someone was stuck, and they couldn't get out of the shed. She kept running, but it seemed the shed was getting farther away. The yard was starting to flood.

"I'm coming," she yelled, but no words came out of her mouth. The screaming got louder. She finally reached to the door. The lightning flashed with a loud clap of thunder. Beth jumped because it was so loud. She reached for the doorknob, but the handle was gone.

"Help! The water is coming in. I can't get out."

It was a woman on the other side of the door. The banging was so loud. Beth tried to get some leverage on the door, but there was nothing to grab. The rough water was getting deep, up to Beth's waist. It wouldn't stop coming. It must be coming over the river bank.

She looked around the yard for something to pry the door open as the structure started to sway. She had to get her out of there. She ran back to the shed just as it collapsed. A horrible scream split the night air. The roof fell, and the walls ripped apart in the surf as they disappeared into the darkness. Maybe she could still save the woman. Maybe she wasn't badly hurt. Beth grabbed at the debris tossing it out of her way like a mad woman. Under a broad beam, she found a young black woman strangely dressed. The beam held her pinned under the water. Yard tools and other rubble floated in the waves that churned around her. A basket floated by Beth as she bent to move the massive beam. She looked down at the person struggling under the water. It was the woman she had seen in the bathroom mirror, her eyes pleading for help. She tried to grab Beth as air bubbles escaped her mouth.

"Oh, my God, it won't move." Beth looked down at her, the hope draining from her spirit. The beam wouldn't move. She tried again, but the water was too deep now. With a quick glance back toward the house, she spied an older woman standing in the window. Beth waved her arms, hoping for some bit of salvation, but the woman turned away as if she couldn't see Beth at all. Beth turned back to the woman and reached out to lay a reassuring hand on her arm only to find, there was no life left to be saved.

* * *

BETH SAT UP IN BED, tears running down her face. "I'm sorry. I'm so sorry. I tried." Her sobbing was loud, but there was no one to hear her. She was alone. She started to shake. It had been a long time since she'd cried so hard. Not since Brad's accident. She leaned over for the pen and paper she had parked by the bed earlier in the week. Through the tears, she wrote down the details of the dream. It was so real. No wonder she wasn't sleeping. Especially since her subconscious was breaking through, placing the woman in her bathroom earlier. Teardrops fell on her paper making it hard to write. She experienced nightmares like this after Brad's accident, but they faded away with the memory of what had happened.

Beth tried hard to remember that day on the lake. It started out fantastic. Martin and Sophie were in from Paris, and they had breakfast. The guys left the cabin laughing and joking, and then decided to go for a swim. It had been a beautiful summer day, and the water perfect. She loved it when they had company at their mountain home. Everyone was having a great time and then all the sudden, Brad was gone.

She shook her head trying to clear the memory. She hated feeling helpless. It was the same feeling she relived tonight. Standing there, trying to figure out what to do and not being able to do a thing. She walked into the kitchen and prepared another cup of tea. Standing at the counter, she cleared her mind, willing herself not to think about that day or the nightmare. She would look at what she had written in the light of day. She hoped the walls weren't too thin. She didn't want to wake everyone else up.

She turned on the TV and flipped it on the local news. She was curious how long this rain could last. The thunder and lightning had stopped, but the rain continued to beat on the roof. She could hear it flowing through the gutters on the front of the building. So, soothing when she concentrated on it. The weatherman on the TV said the tropical depression would be around for a couple of days, which meant rain. Hopefully, the guys would be able to work inside the house. She was tired of delays. She couldn't wait until she would be able to sleep under her own roof.

The loft was supposed to be a temporary situation, and she had not moved in a lot of her personal items because of it. They were still in storage in Colorado. She was ready to be able to snuggle on her own couch and watch her own TV under her own quilts. All the memories of her life with Brad. It was weird how she had become so attached to her home when they used to travel so much. It made the feeling of being home that much more precious. Beth turned off the TV and headed back to bed. She glanced at the notebook on the side table. Hopefully writing down the dream would keep it away for tonight so she could get some sleep. She turned on her iPod and climbed under the covers.

A CASE OF METAL FATIGUE

*S*eptember 13, 2014

The alarm rang way too early, and Sam swung his feet to the floor. The sun was not up yet; he shouldn't have to be. He tried to wake himself as he put on his running shoes. He headed out under the overhang at the front of the house. The rain poured as he stretched out his muscles warming them up and convincing himself the run was more important than the weather before he took off out into the downpour. He turned on his iPod, listening to his latest country rock mix. It kept him going. He thought of her face. Her smile as she looked across the table at him. She had listened intently as he talked about his boring work. She seemed genuinely interested. Was that even possible? He jogged along the highway.

There was no traffic this time of the morning. It gave him time to think. The rain beat his face as he trekked on down the road. He wondered if she would stop by the house today. She had been spending a lot of time inside these days. She had other things to worry about besides the house. That's why she hired him. He laughed. He knew his name was at the top of the list for renovation contractors, but he felt lucky she called him. He saw the college up ahead, his turn around point. He headed back to the house. The rain and wind pelted his back now. He was already soaked through, and he was only at the halfway point.

His feet pounded the pavement, and his mind drifted back to last night. Hopefully, she wasn't disappointed that he didn't come up to her place. He thought the kiss had been great. And he liked the way she fit perfectly in his arms. His body warmed with the memory of her lips on his. He turned up the driveway toward the house, the gravel crunching beneath his feet. He headed into the house to get ready for work.

As he came down the hall, he heard his ringer. Work was calling. This couldn't be good. He sprinted to the phone and hit the button. "Sam here. What? Slow down. Okay, hook up the generator then place the sump pump. I'll be there in twenty minutes. You're in charge until I get there. Make sure everyone gets busy as they arrive." Sam threw down his phone. "Damn it. We can't catch a break." He jumped in the shower, then got ready. As soon as he was in the truck, he dialed Beth. It went to voicemail. "Good morning. Hope you slept well. The property is flooded. I'm heading over to see how bad it is. Jose is there if you want to head over now. I will call in a little while with an update." He started the truck and headed out spinning the tires in the wet gravel of his lane.

When he pulled into the yard of the Water Street house, it was alive with activity. Jose must've gotten the pump to work because water poured out onto the street from a basement window. He parked the truck and headed in. There was at least a foot of water standing in the yard. He didn't want to see how much was in the cellar. It was a good thing they had removed the artifacts. His feet slushed, creating waves as he walked through what used to be a lawn. He stepped up on the stoop of the front steps and tapped his boots on the side of the step. As he stepped inside, his hopes for a dry cellar disappeared. The hose was stiff with the flow of water, and he could hear the pump straining. Wow, it was deep. Thank goodness, she had not brought anything into the store. "Jose, how is the pumping going?"

"It should be dry in a few hours. We don't have anything seeping in. It all flowed in last night through the windows into the cellar. I would recommend a permanent sump pump. I called the hardware store already. They said to stop by and take a look at what they have."

"I agree. I will include it in the plan for the cellar. Let's continue pumping until it's completely dry. Have you seen Ms. Pearse this morning?"

"No, not yet."

Sam was relieved at the answer. Her heart would be devastated if she saw how bad it was. He grabbed his phone from his hip and dialed Beth. Again, it went to voicemail. He started to worry. Maybe something went wrong last night, and she was avoiding him. He pushed his concern to the back of his mind and dealt with the task at hand. "The flooding is primarily in the yard and the cellar. We have started pumping, and it should be dry in a few hours. Give me a call when you get this message." He took another look inside the cellar. Baskets and papers floated in the water. They must have missed some items when they cleared the cellar. Another hour or two and he should be able to clear the remainder.

* * *

SELAH ROCKED in the corner sewing a quilt patch she was working on. It had been quite a few days since she was evicted from her waterfront home, but she didn't mind. Having another person moving around in her space made her comfortable. She hadn't been among the living for a very long time, centuries in fact. But she had a feeling that her roommate did not feel the same way about her. The look of panic on the woman's face a few nights before when she confronted her was horrendous. She looked over at the woman sleeping in the bed, tossing and turning throughout the night. Selah watched her every night yelling in her sleep. Distracted by her thoughts, she pricked her finger with her sewing needle. She let out a small gasp, but no blood appeared. Shaking her finger, she peeked at the woman across the room. There was no movement in the bed.

It was the perfect day for sewing and staying inside. The raindrops created a rhythm that matched the sway of the rocker. The small box on the bedside table started to play music and move against the wood top. Selah wondered what it could be. She had watched the woman talk to it sometimes, but it didn't make sense to her.

The small music box chimed, and the woman turned over in the bed, reaching out to grab it. She picked it up and dropped it back to the table. She mumbled something and then stared right at Selah. This made her stop in mid-rock. Selah reminded herself that the woman couldn't see her without permission. So, she started to rock again.

The woman shook her head and said, "Must be dreaming," before she rolled over and pulled the quilt up around her.

Selah laughed to herself. "Yep, you're dreaming, girl. Get some rest." She pulled out another square of fabric and worked on attaching the next section of her freedom quilt.

* * *

SAM CALLED up from the cellar, "Hey, Jose give me a hand."

Jose peered down the stairs into the dark room.

"I want to clear it out down here so that we can treat it for mold. Let's take everything and place it in the kitchen. Be careful of any paper. It will tear easily if it's wet." They started with the shelves that surrounded the room. The water was still knee-high, and they had to be careful of the stairs. The smell of the brackish water already started to permeate the house. A couple more guys joined them as they struggled to get the unit up the stairs. The thick damp wood weighed a ton. "Set it over there," Sam said trying to catch his breath.

He went down with a crowbar to separate the next piece off the salt-encrusted wall. The salt would start to eat the brick if he didn't get it done soon. As he forced the bar between the wood and wall, he noticed a hole in the red brick. He pushed against the wood, pulling on it. He could see a bundle. His adrenaline pumping, he pulled the wood away and grabbed the cotton bundle out of the hole. He threw it up into the kitchen. "Come on guys, we have to get this done." The pump was still sucking the water up and out of the cellar, shooting it down the drive. He wanted to get it as dry as possible before Beth showed up. He pulled another unit away from the wall. The guys heaved it up into the kitchen. One more and then he could start clearing the debris. He grabbed the crowbar and wedged it against the brick wall. The shelves became unbalanced and began to lean toward Sam. He didn't notice the huge bookcase until it was too late, and it fell on top of him. The weight of the wet oak knocked the breath out of him. He heard the guys coming down the stairs and wading through the water.

"Hold on boss."

Sam heard Jose's voice. He felt the wood lift off his chest and his lungs filled with air. *God, it felt good to be able to breathe, again.* He gasped for the oxygen he had lacked for a few seconds, but what seemed like an eternity. He stood up and regained his footing. Then the pain started to shoot up his arm. His arm hung at an awkward angle, and the pain worsened.

He looked at Jose, and Jose just shook his head. "Boss, you gotta go to the hospital. I can't put a Band-Aid on that."

He hated doctors and hospitals. Half the time, he would get Jose to stitch him up on the job site. Usually, it was something small: a misplaced hammer or box-knife. This, his foreman could not fix. Sam tried to move his arm and winced with pain.

"Come on I'll drive you," Jose insisted.

"Don't anyone touch anything!" he ordered already feeling grumpy, dreading the wait at the hospital. "Just get the water out of the cellar. I will be back as soon as I can."

He typed left-handed a quick text before jumping in Jose's truck.

Sam: Had small accident, on the way to hospital, call me for update.

WRAPPING THE THREAD

*B*eth rolled over in bed looking at the sun finally peeking through the lace curtains. She wondered how long she had slept. She stretched lazily to reach her phone and looked at the time. Two PM. *Holy cow.* Five missed calls and a couple of texts. *Shit, an accident.* She dialed Sam right away. "Sam, pick up, pick up, pick up." It went to voicemail. He must still be at the hospital. Would it presumptuous to go to the hospital to check on what was going on? Oh God, what if it was him? Her stomach turned.

She dressed and grabbed her car keys. She glanced in the mirror. She should at least run a brush through her hair. And maybe apply some lip gloss. He had taken her out for dinner last night, and she shouldn't show up looking like she'd slept on a bench in the storm. She ran back to the bathroom and made a little more effort. She made another dash for the door and locked it behind her. She flew down the stairs trying not to trip over her feet. Now she was freaking herself out. Luckily, it was a short drive, and she would have her answers soon. She grabbed her phone.

Beth: On my way to the hospital. What happened?

The response came back immediately.

Sam: No need to worry or come. Gotta get x-rays, then they will make decision.

Beth: Do you mind if I come? Worried.

Sam: No problem. I'm in ER. I'll send Jose to waiting room

Beth: Ok omw...

Beth parked by the ER and hurried to the waiting area. There was Jose, soaked and wet. He smelled like river water, but he smiled at Beth when he saw her.

"Thank God you are here. You can take over. I'm out of here. That man is making me crazy. I'll take you back, and then you are responsible for him." They walked and talked weaving through the hospital corridors.

"What happened?"

"He was rushing, trying to get everything out of the cellar before it got ruined by the water. It's probably too late if you want my opinion. He was being pig-headed like always, and one of the storage units fell, pinning him."

"What water?" She stopped in her tracks.

"It's flooded. The cellar was flooded last night when the surf came over the banks in the storm."

"I didn't know. I should have…" Her voice trailed off. She glanced at her phone and saw the voice messages from Sam. Just like in her dream.

"Anyway, it knocked the breath out of him, and his arm is pretty banged up. He will probably need a cast. He does not like doctors, just an FYI, and I am relinquishing my babysitting duties to you." He turned down another hallway and motioned with his hand to give her the right-away. She could hear Sam giving the nurse a hard time.

"But I don't want to take off my pants. There is nothing wrong with my legs. It's my arm. Damn it, where is the doctor? I don't need this hassle."

Jose winked at Beth. "Here you go, Madame. Bye." He turned on his heels and retraced his steps as quickly as he could. Sam was yelling as soon as he heard Jose.

"Jose, go get me some clean, dry clothes out of the truck. This lady wants me to get naked." His surprise was evident when it wasn't Jose but Beth that came through the door. Sam blushed, and Beth laughed. She had never seen him blush before.

"Sorry, I didn't know you were there. Where is Jose?"

"He wanted to go and check on the guys. I'm his replacement." Sam was sitting on hospital bed, no doubt he was refusing to lie down. He was naked waist up, and there was a hospital gown sitting beside him. Beth felt heat flood her body as her eyes took in the perfect specimen of a man in front of her, his chest muscles taut with tension and washboard abs to die for. She looked at the bewildered nurse standing next to him. "Are you giving her a hard time?"

"No, I just don't see why they need me to put this thing on," Sam said, slinging the gown around with his good arm.

"Professor Howard, we need to check you for any other injuries. Apparently, you were underwater a while, and the bookcase could have landed on something else. I know the pain in your arm is extreme. But it may be masking pain in another area," the nurse explained, looking at Beth with a pleading expression.

"Sam, you better do as she says. I can't have you passing out later because you have a concussion or something. I'll step outside into the hallway so you can change."

The nurse pulled the drapes around his bed and stepped out into the hallway with Beth. "He is a hand full. I need your help. He should get checked out. He is not listening to the Doctor or me."

"And you think he will listen to me?"

"Jose seems to think so, or he wouldn't have left you here."

"No, I think he just wanted to leave. Has he been that bad?" Just then Sam started yelling from the room. The nurse smiled at Beth. "Apparently." Beth laughed.

"I'm ready to be tortured," Sam yelled.

The ladies walked back in the room and peeked around the curtain. Sam was sitting on the bed in his hospital gown squirming. It was evident he was uncomfortable. "I don't understand why I have to stay here. I am fine. Just put the cast on and let me go back to the house."

"Sam, they said that you might have hit your head. They need to do some tests. Now, will you just be patient? You are being a royal pain, and they are going to kick you out if you don't stop."

"Really? Good. I've been here way too long anyway." He started to stand up but began to sway and tried to catch himself with his broken arm without thinking. He winced in pain. "Shit."

"Not so fast. Sit down before you fall down. See, this is why you need to have the tests. Quit being such a baby. I'm not in the mood today."

"Wow, okay. You don't have to be mean about it." He sat down and gave her a pout.

She looked at him and rolled her eyes. "Seriously, Sam, the faster you cooperate, the faster you will be out of here."

The nurse checked Sam's vitals and helped him get into the wheelchair. "Miss, if you want to wait here, we should be back soon. They were ready for him twenty minutes ago." Catching Beth's attention, she mouthed *Thank You.*

"See you in a little while." She kissed Sam on the head. Sam smiled and leaned back in the chair wincing.

Beth watched the two of them head down the hall then pulled out her cell and started checking messages. There was one from Martin. He had finalized the purchase of all the paintings that she had selected. He was bringing the family to the gallery opening. That's fantastic. She couldn't wait to see Sophia and the kids. It had been ages since she had seen them. They looked so big over the Skype screen. She couldn't believe how fast they were growing.

The next message was from City Hall. There would be a review of her amended COA. Hopefully, that would be painless. Sam submitted a couple of plans on how to deal with a cover for the cellar. It would keep the historical integrity of the construction but functionality in the kitchen. Fingers crossed it would be approved quickly.

Deputy Felton wanted to ask her some questions about something. Hopefully, it wasn't about her certificate approval.

Sam called about the house. The cellar was full of water. They were pumping it out. He didn't know how much damage there was at that point.

She remembered her notes about the nightmare she had in her shorts pocket. She pulled them out and read over them. The storm was horrible. There was so much water coming into the yard. The young woman. She didn't recognize her face as someone she knew. She thought it was the figure she saw in the bathroom, but it seemed unlikely. Maybe she was someone in a movie. She wracked her brain trying to place her with no luck. Maybe Sam could help her talk through the dream and figure out what was going on. She had felt a connection last night during dinner. She sensed he had felt it too.

She heard Sam's laugh coming down the hall. Well, that was a good thing. The nurse was laughing as well. Maybe he wasn't being a pain anymore. They joined her in the room, and the nurse helped Sam lay down on the bed. "How's everything looking?" she asked Sam.

"Well, the Doctor said I'm okay besides my arm. Cast for a month, and that should be good. Nothing permanent. And I'm just as cranky and crazy as ever." He laughed and winked at the nurse.

The nurse smiled at Beth. He must have behaved himself. He was his usual charming self. "That's good. How long before they can put the cast on?"

"The tech will come in a little while to do that. You guys should be out of here within a couple of hours." The nurse turned and left them alone.

Beth turned to Sam. "How are you really feeling?"

"Like shit. My arm hurts like hell and the painkillers they gave me are taking their sweet time kicking in." He shined an exaggerated smile at her, the pain visible on his face.

"Just relax and let the meds take effect. I have something I need to talk to you about." She saw Sam tense, almost like he was preparing for the worst. "It's nothing awful. It's just I've been having nightmares, and I wanted to see if you could help me with it. Maybe while we are waiting, we can talk through some of the details. I haven't slept well this week, and I need some rest."

"Okay. What'cha got?" He laid back holding his arm next to his body awkwardly and groaning. Beth pulled out her notes, and he laughed. "You have notes?"

"Yes. I had been having these dreams, but I couldn't remember anything in the morning. I just knew that I hadn't slept well. So, last night I stopped and wrote everything down so I could figure it out. I haven't had nightmares like this in a long time."

"Okay. Let's hear it."

"I'm at the house, and it is storming. The water is rising, and a young woman is screaming for help. When I get to the shed, I can't open the door to let her out. A woman is peeking out of the window of the house. She is an elegant lady with her hair pulled back in a black dress, and the curtains are lace.

"Then all the sudden I am inside the shed. I still can't open the door. The lady screaming is African American in an ole timey dress. She keeps beating on the door, and the water is rising. The shed starts to shake and shift, then collapses. One of the roofs supports falls on the young woman. I try to move it, but I can't. She is flailing, and air is escaping from her mouth because she is stuck under the weight of the wood. I keep trying, but she is gone. Then I wake up. "

"Describe her clothes to me."

"It's a long dress, full, made of cotton, a brown check pattern I think."

"Okay, so that would place it around the civil war. The black girl is probably a slave or a fugitive slave. We did look at the advertise-ments in the old newspapers. As far as the lady in the window, I will check and see which family owned the house during that period. Don't worry, we will figure it out. Is that why you didn't pick up this morning?"

"Yeah. I was just drifting off to sleep, so I let it go to voicemail. I'm sorry. I was just so tired."

He looked relieved. "I was worried you were upset with me or disappointed about last night. I had a good time, and I thought…"

"No, no. I had a great time last night. The dreams just have me so freaked out. I can't sleep, and then I can't concentrate during the day." She looked at him, moisture pooling her eyes. "I can't save her. I try and try but I can't."

He put out his good hand, and she grabbed it. "I understand."

"No, I don't think you do. You see, my late husband drowned. We were on vacation. He went swimming with a friend, and he got a muscle cramp. One minute they were having a good time and the next he was gone. I wasn't there to save him. The nightmares kept happening for years. I tried every night to undo what had happened. I have come to terms with it, but now it seems to be happening all over again." The grief in her voice made it quiver.

He pulled her to him, and she laid her head on his chest. He ran his fingers through her hair in a slow rhythmic motion. She relaxed and shut her eyes. He shifted to one side of the bed and whispered in her ear. "Come up here so you can relax." He shifted in the small hospital bed. "Let me give you some more room. I don't want you to fall out of bed. I think we both can squeeze in here. I see it in the movies all the time."

She looked up, trying to guess his intentions. She didn't see anything but honesty and sympathy in his eyes. She climbed up on the hospital bed and laid beside him. He was not a small man and they just barely fit in the hospital bed. It was a good thing that the railing was up on the other side. He continued to stroke her in the gentle way that let her release of all the tension from the week.

She raised up quickly. "The nurse will be here soon to do your cast."

* * *

HE PUSHED her back down into a reclining position. "Shh, I will adjust when they get here. You relax. Now it's my turn to be bossy." He laughed. He placed his hurt arm on top of his lap out of the way. She laid back down and shut her eyes again. "My mother used to do this to me when I had trouble sleeping. I would lay back, and she would run her fingers through my hair. She would tell me stories of the boats on the river and fishing with her father. The way the boat rocked with the tide. Her voice was so quiet I would let everything go. And soon I would be …" He glanced down, and she was asleep. He smiled to himself. This felt so right, so perfect.

There was a knock at the door, and the Doctor came in. "Can we make this work to put the cast on? She hasn't slept for a couple of days," he whispered to not wake Beth.

"You are going to have to turn toward me, but we will make it work. As we discussed before, you have a break right below your elbow, so I'm going to have to stabilize the whole arm. We will leave it on for four weeks and then reevaluate. We may be able to cut you down to a half-cast at that point." The Doctor lowered the rail and rolled the table over to the bedside. He had a bowl of water and a roll of cast bandage. He held up the roll. "Blue, okay?"

"What are my options?"

"I have some pink with butterflies in the office." The doctor laughed. Sam crinkled his nose. "I'll take that as a no on the pink. Sorry, you had to wait so long. We had some call-ins on the staff. My tech didn't show up, so you're stuck with me this afternoon." The doc rolled a stool over to get comfortable.

"No problem. We needed some time to talk." He gestured toward Beth. "I completely understand filling in as the boss. Nothing wrong with the expert taking care of things." He smiled a huge smile. His demeanor had completely changed with Beth here. He didn't mind the extra wait. He did need to get back to the site, but it could wait. The doctor set the arm and then wrapped cotton and damp plaster up to his bicep. It was going to be a little inconvenient, but he'd make due. What about fishing? "Doc what about keeping it dry? I was going fishing this weekend."

"Go to the feed store and get you some of the large animal gloves. They work perfect to keep it dry. You do have to wear your sling, though."

"Great." No canceled plans there. Beth shifted in her sleep. He glanced over. Good, she was still asleep. She must be exhausted to sleep through this. The doctor was very conversational. He wanted to know where Sam was going to fish, what he was using as bait, and what he was planning on catching. Sam filled him in and even told him that he would take him one Sunday if he would like to join him. It's the polite way of the South.

"All done. I'll send a nurse in with your release paperwork, but you are going to have to wake her up. I assume she's your ride."

"Yep. I'll wake her up when I need my good arm back." Sam smiled at the doc.

"Your prescription will be ready as well. Take them as you need them but not more than four a day. Here's my card. Let me know if you need anything else, especially a fishing partner." He dropped the card on the table and waved to Sam since both of his hands were occupied as he walked out the door.

Moments later there was another knock at the door. Regret haunted him as he turned to Beth to wake her up. She was sleeping so well. He stroked her cheek with his fingers and brushed her hair off her face. He whispered in her ear, "Beth, time to wake up. They are kicking us out." She started to giggle his breath tickling her ear. She sat up on the side of the bed and Sam rubbed his arm to regain his circulation.

There were just a few things to sign and then they were ready to go. Sam grabbed his paperwork and the Doctor's card and tucked it in his sling. The prescription bottle fit in the corner of the sling too. "I could get used to having this thing on, it's kind of handy." He smiled at Beth as he grabbed her hand with his good one. "Hopefully we don't get lost trying to leave."

Beth laughed. He knew she had no sense of direction at all, so he hoped she knew where they were headed. They weaved through the corridors and finally ended up at the ER entrance where Beth had parked. Sam squeezed into her little hatchback. She laughed as he tried to fold his legs into his side. She hit the button, and the seat flew back with the resistance of his legs trying to fit into the little compartment. They both busted out laughing.

"Phew, I thought I was going to be permanently folded in half." He winked at her.

Beth smiled. She felt so much better now that she had grabbed a nap. "I'll drive you back over to the house. When you left the message this morning, you said it was a mess. How bad was it?"

"It filled the cellar. The pump was working well though. It should be dry by now, but there was a lot of stuff that got wet. Some things floating that we didn't even know was down there. I told the guys not to touch anything that I would handle it. The water might have ruined everything, but we will see. We will have to be careful handling anything. It will be muddy, and the salt was soaking into the brick. I don't want to think the worst. Sorry about my arm. This probably set us back quite a bit of time. But Jose and the guys are professionals. They probably haven't touched a thing except for the pump all afternoon."

DRIPPING EAVES

*B*eth laughed as she turned out of the hospital parking lot and cut across town. It didn't take long to get back to the house. They pulled up into the drive behind Sam's truck. Sure enough, the guys were sitting out front. There was no water draining out of the hoses from the house, and they were all laughing and talking. Jose met Sam halfway across the yard.

"Hi, Beth. Boss, the cellar is dry. There is a lot of debris, so I didn't want to have the guys clean up the mud. You said there was a lot of the paper items that were floating. I left the one bag in the kitchen but moved it to the corner so it wouldn't get damaged. We put the shelving units in the living room area so they would be out of the way. These guys don't have anything to do until you clear the cellar. Let me send them home."

"Okay, I'll let them know." Sam walked over to the guys. Beth waved to them as she walked into the house. She laughed as she heard the groans. She walked into the living room. Shelving units filled the room. The wood was soaked through. Maybe they would dry by morning. The smell in the house was almost overwhelming. It smelled like brackish water that had been standing.

Musty salt water muck was not the most inviting smell. She hoped she could get rid of it. Sam walked into the kitchen. "What was that all about?"

He started to laugh. "They were not thrilled about their five am start in the morning. I told them they better go get some rest. "

"Please, tell me you have some magic spell to get rid of the smell."

"Of course, I have a specialist for this sort of thing. He will take care of the smell and the mud. But we have a bigger job this afternoon. Let's head down and see what we can save." She followed him down the stairs. Mud covered everything, and salt was leaching up the brick walls. Sam disappeared upstairs and returned with a dishpan of clean water. Beth watched him pick up what looked like piles of mud and put it in the pan. The mud melted away, and there appeared a newspaper page or a piece of cloth. It was incredible the things that were appearing like magic. It reminded her of the magic eggs that she played with as a child that would melt away, and a dinosaur or bug would appear. He filled another dishpan and sent Beth to lay their finds on the kitchen countertop. She couldn't believe that a newspaper would survive years, much less all the water and mud. Her fingers brushed the items: a small quilt, a handmade doll, quilt squares, a few newspaper clippings, and advertisements for runaway slaves. Sam brought up the other pan full of stuff. They laid the rest of the stuff out together flat on paper towels.

Sam peeked over her shoulder, "I can't believe how lucky we are. Looks like we won't lose much. The Formica countertop should be a good slick surface for the items not to stick to. Oh, I almost forgot." He turned and snatched up the bundle of cotton in the corner of the room. "I'll give you the honors." He handed it to Beth.

Beth took the bundle and gently untied the corners. It was made of blue plaid cotton. She laid the fabric out flat. There was a book with papers sticking out of it. A small bundle of lavender. Some buttons tied together with a string. A wooden spool of thread with a needle. She picked up the book and very slowly opened it. The pages were handwritten. Inside the cover was a sketch of a sunflower with an inscription. *To my daughter on her 15th year, may she always remember from where she came and always have the courage to follow her name. 4th of May 1854.* Tucked a few pages back was a tintype photo. It was an African American girl with a baby. The picture was cloudy with the dampness inside the cover. She tried to focus on the face.

"Oh, my God," she whispered. She began to tremble. Sam looked at her. She felt the color drain from her face. She caught her breath.

Sam grabbed her arm "What is it? I need you to breathe."

"It's her. It's the girl, the woman, the lady from the shed."

"What do you mean? You have to breathe. You are going to pass out."

"It's the girl that drowned." She froze with fear.

INEVITABLE DELAYS

*B*eth sat down on the floor leaning against the cabinet and held her head in her hands. Her head started to hurt. She tried to jog her memory. Where had she seen her before? Sam sat down beside her. "You're not running for the hills, are you? We've only been on one date. I would completely understand if you didn't want to go out again. I must seem totally insane to you."

"Was that a date? I thought it was just a celebratory dinner." He looked at her with a serious face. Her mouth fell open with shock. He broke into a laugh, the tension dispersed. "I'm teasing. I had a great time, and I think you're great. We will figure this out. You had to have seen her somewhere. Now, we know that she existed. There is photographic proof. The diary is a fantastic find, and maybe it will tell us something about her. I think you should be the one to read it first. It's your find." He smiled at her. "Don't get too frustrated reading the old handwriting. A lot of times you should skip a word to keep from getting bogged down in the details. You will get the rhythm of the writer, and then it will come easier."

"Thanks for the pointers. You already know me so well." She laughed. "Did we get everything out of the cellar? I don't want to miss anything. You guys are going to start cleaning early in the morning, right?"

Beth watched him struggle to get up trying to use his broken arm for support. "I'll go check it out so that we can be sure."

"I'll go with you."

"They are going to get started at five AM. I can't believe I broke my arm. This is so ridiculous." He looked down at his cast, and she could see the frustration on his face. He offered her his good hand and slowly lead the way down the slippery stairs. She knew there wasn't much left in the cellar, lots of mud and salt. *What a mess!* The guys did do a good job getting all the water out. Now, all that was left was to bring in the water damage specialist to fix the rest. Sam double checked all the piles of mud to make sure there wasn't anything left that needed to be rescued then turned and headed up the stairs, careful not to bump his head as he poked it up into the kitchen.

Beth followed him up. The stuff was organized on the countertop. She walked over to a stack of fabric and subconsciously brushed it with her fingers. It was a soft, vibrant blue cotton.

Sam started to gather his lunch box and other items he left earlier in the day. "What'cha got there?"

"It looks like a baby quilt. The stitches are so tiny. I can't imagine sewing such a small detailed project."

"Someone was quite the seamstress." The small quilt had black birds flying across a patchwork of flying geese patches. They were so tiny. "We will leave everything here. I will bring some stuff tomorrow to package everything for transport. You can take the diary if you want. Make sure you fan the pages every once in a while, to keep them from sticking. The book is probably ruined, but at least you will get a chance to read it."

Beth grabbed the diary and walked through the house. "Wow, what a day, huh?" She looked at Sam.

"Yep, we better go home before anything else happens." His laugh echoed through the empty building. "Think about what you want to do with the shelves and let me know tomorrow."

"Okay. Sam, what did you want to do Saturday night?"

"It's a surprise. And you are not getting it out of me before then." He winked at her. She thought she saw a bit of mischief in his eyes.

"Okay, what should I wear? Do I need to go shopping?" she said, smiling at him and hoping it would trick him.

"Just wear something light and comfortable, tennis shoes will be good. Maybe a jacket. You can go shopping if you like, but that's up to you." He paused and wagged a finger on his good hand. "I know what you're doing." His finger poked her in the side. "Do you want me to take you home?

"Company would be good. Do you want to walk or drive?"

"I think a walk would do me good. I feel like I've been inside all day. I hate that."

"Okay, a walk it is. Let's go." Beth grabbed her stuff from the car, and they headed down the waterfront. The harbor lights illuminated the walkway along the waterside. "Looks like another busy night." She watched the people enjoying the summer night on the decks of the boats moored along the dock. Families rode by on their bikes. Someone had 'Sweet Home Alabama' playing on their stereo.

* * *

"I THINK THEY'RE LOST," Sam said breaking the silence. Beth laughed. They slowly walked, taking in the lazy night and relaxing from the stress of the day. As they neared the music, a man jumped off the boat and started waving.

"Sam, Beth, hey. Come and meet the wife." It was Jose. He looked at his boss with a big grin. A petite blonde popped up out of the galley with her hands full of a platter of food. "This is Hellen, doing what she does best." He turned to his wife. "Be nice."

She shook her head and set down her tray. "Beth, hi. Ignore him, I don't know what he's talking about. Come aboard and give me a hand." Hellen grabbed Beth's hand as she stepped aboard. "How are you liking Washington? I know you've had a crazy day. Sorry, my husband is such a coward, leaving you at the hospital with this big grump. Don't worry, I gave him a hard time already." She stuck her tongue out at Jose like a toddler.

"Hey. I wasn't that bad today."

All three adults turned to Sam and said "Really?" in unison.

"Oh man. I *was* that bad." He laughed. "Sorry."

The ladies disappeared into the galley, and Jose turned to Sam. "What's up boss? What's going on here?" He jabbed Sam in the side.

"I'll never tell." He poked Jose back with his cast. "Don't give me a hard time dude. There is too much going on with the house, and I just don't know. We are trying to de-stress."

"Well relax and enjoy yourself tonight. We have a shrimp boil coming from the galley. There are Coronas in the cooler, and you need to let work go for a while."

"As long as we aren't up too late. It's an early start in the morning, remember."

"I got ya, boss. Will you relax? Sit down and enjoy the music. Here, have a beer." He pushed Sam down into the chair. Jimmy Buffett came over the speakers.

"Okay, okay, but we have to leave after dinner."

"No problem." He handed Sam the bottle opener.

Sam popped the top off the bottle and took a long sip. "Thanks. I'm starting to stress about the paperwork for the house. I should have heard something by now."

"We've never had an issue before. We'll be fine. The plans maintain the historical value of the house. We are working clean, and the neighbors haven't complained once. I don't think there is any reason for a delay. The commissioners are on vacation and haven't had a meeting in a month. I heard down at the Piggly Wiggly that Frank Monroe has been in Florida for the last three weeks. You know they can't have a meeting without Commissioner Monroe."

"You're right. I'm just worrying. We can't do the kitchen area until we get the floor squared away. I'm ready to get that cellar closed and move on."

"So, what did you decide on the covering?"

"I was talking to Robert down at the hardware store about our options. We decided on using thick fiberglass so it can be seen by visitors, but it will be safe. He went ahead and placed it on order. "

"Who the heck is Robert?" Jose leaned forward in his chair.

"Some new guy Mike hired. He's been super helpful. You haven't met him yet?"

"Nope. Will it be removable? "

"I'm still working on that. Maybe some hinges or something of the sort. Robert's come up with some pretty cool stuff." Sam sat down on the lid of the cooler.

"About time Mike hired somebody who knows what they're doing. Where is he from?"

"He doesn't say much. Not from around here. You'll know who I mean when you see him. He's kind of scruffy looking, but he definitely knows what he's talking about."

"Well, at least something's going on while we wait for the go-ahead from the city. The storage is going to be incredible for the gallery. It would be a shame to waste the space. I know you're worried about flooding, but Beth will just have to be careful what she stores." Jose took a swig of his beer. "I'm going to go see how the ladies are doing with the shrimp."

"Okay." Sam leaned back in his chair and closed his eyes.

* * *

BETH AND HELLEN both jumped when Jose's voice came down the stairs into the galley.

"What is going on here?" His head appeared in the doorway, and Hellen had no idea how long her husband had been standing there.

"What?" Hellen gave him a frown and spotted the pot beside him was boiling on the stove. "Oh, crap. Sorry, it will be ten minutes." She stepped over to the stove top and popped the corn in, covering it quickly. "Really. Sorry. We got distracted."

"It's okay, babe. I'm just starving. What are you guys looking at?"

"A diary that Beth and Sam found. Did Sam tell you about it? It's cool."

"Nope. Call me when it's ready. I'll help you bring up the food. You shouldn't have that around all the mess." Jose winked as he turned and headed back up to the deck.

"Eek, I don't want to mess it up." Hellen looked at Beth.

"I'll put it away soon as we get ready to eat. Look, the girl is talking about how she learned how to write and why she should keep it a secret. Such beautiful handwriting. Her mother taught her in secret to carry on the tradition. Says here that her mother learned to help her mistress with invitations and correspondences. Apparently, the Browns were major entertainers, and handwritten invitations were expected to all their events. Such a terrible thing to keep such a talent hidden. Her form is perfect."

Hellen threw the rest of the food in the steamer pot and joined Beth at the table for a minute. "I wonder if it was really against the law or if they just told them that to keep them afraid of telling anyone. Their owner probably just didn't want anyone to know she wasn't doing all the work herself. I bet Sam would know. He is smart about this sort of thing. He goes to Raleigh for conferences giving speeches on history at the universities."

"Really? I thought he would be too busy for that sort of thing."

"Oh yeah. Here lately, Sam's teaching has been his priority. It helps us out though because he puts Jose in charge while he's gone. Jose loves it." She walked over to the stove and lifted the heavy pot over to the sink. "Jose, it's ready; come and help me!" Jose and Sam appeared in the galley. Hellen grabbed the lid as Jose took the pot from her and tipped it to drain through a colander. Steam filled the air, swirling around the men at the sink and smells of Old Bay and sage filled the air.

"Nothing like a nightly facial to keep those baby faces fresh." Hellen's huge laugh joined Beth's as she headed up to the cooler. "You want something, Beth?"

"Yeah, I'll take a beer."

Hellen smiled as she watched Sam give Beth directions on how to cover the table. "Got it." She reached into the small fridge and retrieved a couple of beers.

Beth smoothed out the newspaper tablecloth. Soon it was covered with a massive pile of shrimp, sausage, corn, and onions. Sam put a couple of bowls on the table and handed Beth a kitchen towel. "Trust me, you are going to need one of these. Might want to let it cool for a while. Don't want to burn your fingers."

Sam and Jose grabbed some shrimp and tried to peel them quickly, blowing on the steaming food. "Ouch, ouch, ouch. Hot, hot." Beth burst out laughing.

"What happened to waiting?"

"I'm starving. Sometimes you have to bear the pain." Jose said in a manly voice.

Hellen grabbed some butter for her corn and started to enjoy the food. She tried not to choke as the men continued to ignore the heat of the steaming shrimp. "Sam, you might want to cover your cast. Or you will smell really rank tomorrow with all that shrimp juice dripping down your arm."

"That's okay, I'll just go get a new cast put on."

Beth shot Hellen a look.

Hellen winked at her, reached across the table, and smacked Sam's good hand. "You will be lucky if they let you back in the hospital after your behavior today. What a whiney baby. I have never seen a grown man make such a fuss."

"What? I don't like doctors."

"Or hospitals, nurses, sitting still, being inside," Hellen poked fun at him.

"Cut a guy a break, will you. I was injured today." He grabbed his cast and gave Hellen the most pitiful look she had ever seen.

"Give me a break." Hellen turned to Beth. "Thanks for staying. It's nice to have an adult around. Especially with these two. I never did hear how you like it here. Tell me how you're adjusting."

"I love it. It's awesome walking on the waterfront after a busy day. I'm a little frustrated with how things move at their own pace. But I know I will get used to it. I'm just anxious to get the gallery open. Right now, everything is in Europe waiting for a wall to hang on. My partner picked some great work to sell and master-pieces to ground the collection. The house is amazing, and Sam is doing a good job with the renovation. We are only waiting for approval of the plans for the flooring on the first story to finish the gallery. The flooding sucked."

"Jose was telling me about that. I've never known that property to flood, but then again, we have had a ton of rain lately. It's been flooding in some unusual places around town. Hopefully, the waterproofing will help in the future. Now tell me about Colorado. Sam told me that's where you moved from. What's it like in the Rockies? I've only seen it on TV. It looks beautiful."

Beth described the hiking trails and outdoor life so Hellen could picture the blue skies and all the sunshine. Fly fishing in the mountain streams and sunbathing on huge boulders by the river-side. The grizzly bears and elk showing up in the yard on a lazy afternoon. Then there were the water restrictions from no rain and fire season. Hellen shuddered along with the story of Beth standing in a store parking lot, a forest fire consuming the side of a mountain. "All that was left were black stumps when the flames retreated over the summit. It was a sad day."

"It sounds incredible. Despite the fires. Why did you ever leave?"

"There was nothing left for me there. My life there was with Brad, and when he died, it ruined it all for me. I mean it was still all the great stuff, but there were too many memories. Every corner there was a story of Brad and me doing this or that. I couldn't keep breaking my heart every day. Not anymore. It was time to move on." Tears started to roll down Beth's face. Hellen reached across the table and brushed her hand, motioning to go above deck.

"Guys, we're going up for some fresh air." Hellen grabbed a roll of paper towels, a hand full of lemons and Beth's hand. "Don't touch your face. We need to get the spice off your hands first."

Beth blindly followed the Hellen, the tears flowing freely now. She stumbled up the stairs. "I'm sorry to ruin the fun. I don't know what's wrong with me."

Hellen tightened her grip on Beth's hand. "You are okay. It's terrible to lose someone you love. Here, let's rinse your hands in the river quick. Then take some of the lemons to get rid of the fishy smell."

Beth leaned over the side of the boat and rinsed her hands in the brackish water. "You sure this will work?" Beth's voice quivered as she leaned down to reach into the water. Hellen rinsed hers as well and then started to squeeze the lemon wedges over Beth's hands.

"Tell me about Brad. I'm so sorry that I pushed you for information. I heard you lost your husband, I shouldn't have pushed."

Drying her hands, Beth turned to Hellen and gave her a hug. "It's okay," she squeaked sounding like she was reassuring herself more than Hellen. "I really don't know why I'm so emotional. It was a while ago. I have worked through what happened. I guess sometimes it just hits me. I've been so busy with everything. I haven't really had time to think about it since moving here. Brad was my husband, amazing and smart. My college sweetheart." Her tears slowed.

"I can't imagine losing Jose. It must have been horrible."

"We were on vacation with our friends, Martin and Sophie. The guys went out for a quick swim. I stayed behind to help Sophie with something." Beth gazed toward the river as if she forgot Hellen was there. "I was busy when the phone rang. I didn't pick it up because I was on vacation. It rang again, and I glanced down to see who was being so persistent. I remember being so angry that someone would call me while I was on holiday. It was Martin. I knew something was wrong because they were just a short walk away from the cabin. I picked up, and he was screaming. 'Brad is missing. He went under, and I can't find him, Beth. I can't find him. Search and Rescue is on their way.' Oh, my God, the panic I felt. Why didn't I go with them?"

Hellen lightly touched Beth's arm bringing her back to the present. She handed her a clean paper towel for her face. "Here. So, he didn't come back from the lake."

Beth shook her head.

"But that's not your fault. It was an accident. No one can be blamed for that." Hellen reassured her. "Did they find him?"

"No, they never did. The investigation just wrapped up last year. They finally declared him assumed dead. I didn't even get to bury him. To say goodbye." The tears returned full force.

The other woman wrapped her arms around Beth. "Oh my, I am so sorry. I'm torturing you. All to satisfy my own curiosity. Some of the rumors flying are unbelievable. I'm so glad you guys stopped by tonight, but I feel terrible for bringing all this up."

Beth's head jerked as she faced Hellen. "Rumors? What could they have to talk about? They don't even know me. Sam told me there were questions, but I had no idea they were making shit up."

"You don't need to worry about it tonight. Let's get you presentable for the guys and get you some dinner. We can talk about the busybodies later." She wiped off Beth's face and grabbed her hand. "Come on, we have left the guys alone long enough. No telling what they're talking about."

The two ladies headed back down to see the guys still stuffing their faces. The pile of food had almost disappeared. "Everything okay?" Sam asked to which Beth only nodded. "Better get you some food. Jose is eating it all."

Jose grinned, his smile covered in spice and butter. "I can't help it. It's good."

Beth and Hellen sat down, and the tension of Beth's outburst was soon only in the back of her company's minds. Hellen was glad the men monopolized the conversation. Fishing and the tidal schedule. It was nice to just listen to their chatting. Soon dinner was completely gone, and they ran out of subjects. The men pushed back from the table both rubbing their stomachs.

"It was delicious. Thanks, Hellen for feeding us." Sam stood up and signaled to Beth it was time to go.

Beth turned and gave Hellen a long hug. "Thank you so much for listening," she whispered. "It was so good to meet you. We'll have to have lunch one day."

Hellen smiled, "You'll have to put up with the kids. Date night and a babysitter only come once a month."

"You can bring them along. Maybe we could have a picnic at the park. "

"That would be a great idea."

* * *

Sam grabbed Beth's hand and helped her step off the boat. Her footing was unsure as she tried to gain her land legs back. They both turned and waved to the couple. "Good night guys, thanks again."

Sam grabbed Beth's hand and pulled her across the wet lawn. "You are going to get my shoes soaked. I may as well have jumped in back at the boat."

"That can be arranged. Come on, let's get you home. I have to get some sleep."

"But can't we take our time? Ah, look at this." Beth held up her left foot showing the wet canvas shoes she was wearing.

"We're almost to the sidewalk." Sam leaned down in one swoop and lifted Beth off her feet. She squealed and then snuggled in with her arms around Sam's neck. "Don't get too comfortable Ma'am. I'm not going to carry you far with this cast on my arm."

"Yes, sir," Beth whispered into his ear, the warmth of her breath heating more than just his cheek.

"You sure are a wimp. I'm beginning to doubt if you can handle what I had planned for Saturday," he teased.

"What? No way. I can handle anything you throw at me. I just don't want my sneakers to be soaked."

"Okay." He planted her feet on the sidewalk. She stood, leaning into him to regain her balance.

"You sure you don't want to carry me a little further? What kind of Southern gentleman are you?" She leaned into the crook of Sam's arm.

"Hey, miss, those big eyes won't change the answer. I really can't carry you. Don't make me feel guilty." She leaned in, even more, stretching up on her tiptoes, and touched her lips to his. "No guilt necessary."

His good arm slid around her waist molding his body against her, lifting her off her feet. The kiss deepened, and her lips parted. The flame he felt took over, and he forgot where they were. His hand slid under her t-shirt, and he only knew what he needed.

OFFICIAL WARNING

*B*weep bip Bweep. Red and blue lights reflected from the brick buildings across the street. Beth looked around dazed. She brushed her hair from her face and covered her mouth. Sam quickly pulled his hand from her shirt in a smooth motion. "Crap! You okay?" She nodded her head. Her hand raised blocking the light and hiding her embarrassment.

Deputy Whitaker slowly opened the patrol car door, stepping out and adjusting the spotlight in their faces. "Evening folks. Everything okay here?" He squinted into the darkness. "Sam, is that you? Christ, man, what are you doing out here making out like some...? Who are...? Ms. Pearse? I didn't expect to see you down here." Heads popped up from below the decks of all the boats along the waterfront. Why did she suddenly feel like the headliner in a Broadway play? And not a successful one. No doubt there will be plenty of reviews at the beauty salon tomorrow.

"Evening Deputy." She smoothed out her clothes again, fidgeting. Sam cued her to stand still by placing his hand on her shoulder.

"Tim, I was just walking Ms. Pearse home for the evening."

"I can see that, along with the rest of the world. You should really find a more private place to walk her home." He gave Sam a sideways smile.

Beth stepped in front of Sam into the light. "Deputy, I've had several calls from your office. Do you know why?"

"I sure don't. Let me check for you." He leaned down to his radio and pushed the button. "Mae, Deputy Whitaker here. Do you copy?"

"Go ahead Whitaker," blared from the speaker.

"Do you know why someone is calling Ms. Pearse, the new owner of the art gallery?"

"Let me check." There was a short silence. "Peter says that Bill was trying to schedule a time tomorrow to ask her some questions. "

She shrugged, turned and looked at Sam, "Okay. I have no idea why, but I'll be available at two. Tell him to give me a call before he comes over."

Tim nodded. "Two o'clock tomorrow Mae. Tell him to call in the morning."

"Copy that."

"Okay, now you two run along before someone pulls out a cell phone and starts filming." He reached in and turned off the flashing lights and spotlight.

Just as he closed the car door, a request came over his radio, "Deputy Whitaker, you are needed at the Walmart. They have a juvenile riding bikes through the store and being destructive."

"Copy that Mae. Let them know I will be there ASAP." He opened the door and jumped in, waved at the pair and sped away.

"What do you think that is about? Are you sure you're okay?"

Beth shrugged, "Just embarrassed. I can't believe we got caught by the cops." She smacked his good arm. "It's all your fault you know."

"All my fault? I don't think so. Let's go home before we star on YouTube." Holding hands, they strolled to her loft.

Beth savored the silence between them while letting the passion that had emerged earlier simmer as they walked down the street. The exchange of glances Sam was giving her made Beth blush. She knew what was on his mind and it was on her mind as well. She handed him the keys when they arrived at her building.

"Damn it, I can't get the key to work. Better grab some of that mail. Do you ever take in your mail?"

The letters and junk mail were overflowing from the box by the front door. "Yes! Here let me try. You have to caress it a bit." She smiled and laughed as the door instantly unlocked.

They rushed upstairs to the inner door. She saved time by unlocking it herself. He pulled her to him while she tried to concentrate on the lock. He raised her hair kissing the back of her neck. She turned around as the door opened and they stepped inside, closing the door behind them. The mail fell from her hand as she pushed the door shut, sliding across the hardwood floor.

Beth leaned in close and looked up at Sam. She needed him, and she didn't know how to show him. He leaned in to kiss her again, and she could feel his need as his long hard body pressed against hers. A vibration came from his front pocket. Sam stilled and released her from his arms. Beth caught her breath as she caught a chill as his warm left hers. Pulling out his phone to answer, he glanced at the screen and frowned.

"Hello, Sam here. Hi, Bill. What do you need?" The pause seemed to last forever. As Sam listened to the other end of the phone, he mouthed "Sorry" to Beth and stepped away from her. "Okay, can I meet you? Yes, I can be over there in a little while. I'll see you then. Thanks for calling."

Beth was getting a glass of water when Sam stepped behind her at the kitchen sink. The call was only a few minutes but the magic she felt moments before, was gone. She turned around and wrapped her arms around his waist.

"I have to go. Something is going on at the college, and the deputies would like me to meet them at the school."

Beth leaned her head against his chest. "Be careful."

Sam tipped her head up, kissed her forehead, and ran his finger down her cheek. "I'll be fine. Don't worry. I'll call you later. But I gotta go."

Beth turned him loose, and he crossed the flat. Turning as he opened the door, "Make sure you lock up after I leave. I'll call when I get home." With that, he closed the door behind him.

Beth watched Sam run down the street and turn the corner. She put on a pot of tea knowing she was not going to sleep easy tonight. She walked over to the door to throw the deadbolt and got the now familiar feeling of someone's presence in the room.

"Who's there?" Beth's skin covered with goosebumps. Frost left from Beth's mouth as she asked again. "Are you there?"

"Yes."

"What do you want?"

"Be mindful."

"Why? Why do I need to be careful?"

"He is watching."

And as fast as the ghostly presence had appeared, it disappeared, leaving Beth alone. Was it the girl in the picture? Did she mean to be careful with Sam? Her mind drifted back to the nap at the hospital. She felt so safe in his arms, listening to his memories of his childhood. She wondered what had pulled him away.

The kettle started to whistle bringing her back to fixing her cup of tea. She poured honey into the cup and started to stir, staring at the mail on the floor. Setting her cup on the table, she gathered up all the envelopes and sorted it on the table. "Bills, bills, bills, City of Washington." Tearing open the envelope it was an invitation to the hearing for her new permit on Wednesday. *Alright! Progress!* Now she could relax. She sipped her tea and drifted back to memories of the day.

* * *

THE RED AND blue lights of mayhem flashed in the darkness as Sam pulled up into the college parking lot. He wondered if they even had this many cops in Beaufort County? Two deputies taped off the building's entryway and Tim interviewed students next to the squad car.

Sam parked and sent Bill a text.

SAM: I'm here. Where do you need me?

Bill: Be right there.

IT DIDN'T TAKE LONG for Bill to appear at the caution tape. "Sam, I need you to stay calm."

"Okay, you said on the phone there was vandalism. Stuff like that happens all the time. Why do you need me?"

"This is a different situation. Let's go up to your office."

"My office? Really? Why?"

"You'll see."

Sam followed Deputy Felton down the winding hallway. Sam's first instinct was to rush in when he saw the broken window in the door. Glass covered the hallway floor. Bill shook his head. "We can't go in. They are still working the scene. I had to call some guys in from Greenville." Sam felt his body tense as anger started to build. He peered through the doorway at utter destruction. There were books thrown everywhere and shards of broken pottery. Sam could only look at the years of research destroyed. Flashes of light filled the air as a deputy took pictures. His first instinct was to try and save his work. Sam saw red.

Bill's firm voice and hand on Sam's bicep brought him back in line. "No Sam. Let them work."

Sam glanced over his shoulder. "I don't understand. Why someone would do something like this?"

"It looks personal. Sam, do you know anyone who would do this? We do have some bullet casings to send through ballistics. And Peter says he might have some fingerprints and a..."

"A Bullet? Really? Bill, are you telling me someone shot up my office?" His voice echoed down the hall.

"It appears that way. Is there anyone that is mad at you? A student? Maybe, a business rival?"

"Bill, I don't have any enemies. I teach basic History 101. Anyone who tries passes. I don't date. I don't have any real exes."

"What about the girl you were with tonight?"

"How do you know about that?"

"Tim told me about the call to the waterfront. Said you were awful friendly with her in public."

"Look, Beth is a great girl. You are not trying to say she is involved, are you? Besides, I was with her up until you called. She couldn't have anything to do with this."

"Just exploring the possibilities."

"You need to leave her out of this. Run your tests on the evidence and then I will talk to you about possibilities. You've got my number." Sam turned his back on Bill, feeling oddly protective over his new relationship, wondering where tonight could have led if Bill hadn't called. He stomped up the hallway, muttering under his breath.

He pushed his way through the few students standing in the parking lot. Their cell phones held out with lenses facing the building and cops. The whole student body must know now. Just great. Now he'd be fodder for the town gossips. This coming week is going to be impossible. Maybe he should cancel the date with Beth. He didn't want to put her in danger if there was a psycho. He'd anticipated it since their first meal though and believed it was exactly what he needed. He only had to survive the week, and then it would be Saturday again. Should he tell her what happened? He was supposed to call her when he finished here. What could he say without scaring her? Climbing into the truck, he sat in the driver's seat and laid his head against the steering wheel. His good hand tapped the dash. How did life get so complicated?

Not trusting his voice, Sam pulled out his phone and texted Beth. He told himself it was in case she was sleeping, but he knew it was a lie.

Sam: Just finished up. Headed home. See you Saturday. I had a great time tonight. Sweet dreams.

BUILDING ADDITIONS

*S*eptember 17, 2014

Beth sprinted across the street to the gazebo in Festival Park. Hellen waved and yelled something, but Beth couldn't hear because of the rain hitting the hood of her jacket.

"What did you say?" Beth asked as she lowered her hood.

"I said, I hope hot dogs are okay." She finished unloading the bag onto the table.

"Absolutely. I've acquired a taste for Bill's hot dogs in the last month." She slid onto the bench. "Thanks for the invite. I've been stuck in the loft working on the online business non-stop."

"Of course, gives me a chance to have some girl time. I'm extremely out-numbered at home. So how are things going? Are you almost ready?" She handed Beth two dogs and a can of soda.

"The gallery is coming along. It still looks like a mess to me, but Sam says they are making good progress." Beth unwrapped a dog and took a bite.

"And how are things with Sam? It looked like things were going really well on Saturday." The rain blew under the roof as the wind changed direction and drops hit the bag of chips Hellen was opening.

"Are you sure you want to eat out here?" Beth took another bite.

"If we wait for the good weather this year, it might be Christmas. The weather has been terrible." She grabbed a few chips. "Now about you and Sam."

"I'm not sure. There is definitely an attraction, but I don't know if I'm ready for dating. Nothing serious, anyway."

Hellen laughed, "If there is any hesitation, I'm sure it's not just you. Bless his heart, Sam can be a little distant." She unwrapped her hot dog and took a bite.

"Really? It doesn't seem that way to me."

"Sam has always put work first. Even in high school, when we were …" A gust of wind caught her bag of chips and blew it across the lawn to the waterfront railing. The contents scattered on the sidewalk and gulls swooped down to feast on the snack.

The ladies laughed and secured the rest of the food on the table. "They didn't waste time," Beth commented.

"They never do."

"What happened in high school? You didn't finish."

"Sam and I dated. I thought we were getting married, but he moved to Raleigh, swearing he was headed to California." She took a long sip from her can.

"He said the city wasn't for him." Beth thought about his comment about liking the slower pace.

"Is that what he told you?"

"Yes."

Hellen gave her a look of doubt. "Well, I would bet you he is headed to a big University the first offer that comes. He has invested too much time in his career to stay here. He sacrificed our future for it."

"But you have Jose and the boys. You seem very happy." Darker clouds threw shadows over the gazebo.

"Oh, I am very happy. Jose is a wonderful husband. I'm just saying, take care when it comes to Sam."

"Thanks for letting me know." Beth gave her a little smile.

"Sure, we girls have to stick together. Now, tell me about your online gallery."

EXPOSED CLAPBOARDS

*S*eptember 19, 2014

Steam rose from the large foam cup of coffee dispensing from the loud machine at Mom's Grill. Sam waited for his breakfast order at the small gas station. He didn't sleep a bit the night before, worrying about the situation at the office. He had no idea who would do something like that, and it was driving him crazy.

The older black lady on the other side of the grill yelled at him, "Samuel are you listening to me? You don't look like you're listening to me." She stirred the pot of chicken and pastry with a large spoon. "You shouldn't be working at that house. Evil things happen there. My momma told me stories of evil spirits in that house. She told me there is bad juju. I cannot believe you took that job. No good will come of it. Look what happened at the school."

"Ms. Martha, it's just a job. A job I happen to enjoy doing. Nothing is going to happen. I'm working to make it a good place."

"Nothing is going to happen; nothing is going to happen you say. But look at that cast on your arm. It's already got you once. You gonna push it to do something more harmful to you." She turned and flipped his eggs over on the griddle. Then, she fixed his plate and wrapped a cheese biscuit, passing it over the counter. "We both know that this is not 'just a job.' It is all over town how you are carrying on with that woman. You mark my word, you better be careful, Samuel. There is something not right at the house."

"Yes, Ms. Martha. I'm listening. I will be careful, promise. Thanks for breakfast." Grabbing his food, Sam paid the cashier and headed toward the hardware store. Robert promised to be there early so he could pick up what he needed, but he had some time to eat before he had to shop. Balancing his food plate on the dash, he parked his truck outside the store.

The lights in the small store came on, and Sam saw a shadow move through the building. Robert must be getting ready for the day. Sam finished up his biscuit, gathered up his notes, and locked up the truck. It was going to be an intense day. A day to make up time and get things done.

* * *

SELAH GLANCED at the wall clock as the doorbell rang, two-o'clock exactly. Beth had been pacing all morning, and Selah could tell the other woman was nervous. She didn't know why there was a lawman at the door. She had learned early that no good could come of questions from the law. She could tell Beth was cautious by how slowly she opened the door with her back straighter than a knitting needle. A middle-aged man stood before them looking down at Beth wearing a freshly pressed deputy's uniform. The creases and cuffs molded themselves to his very athletic body. Selah stepped back to her favorite corner to observe the exchange. Strange she did not request a chaperone. Beth should be more careful.

"Ms. Pearse, how are you today?" He asked with a charming southern drawl.

Beth invited the officer into the apartment. "I'm okay. A little taken back as to why there are still questions. Come on in. Would you like something to drink?"

"Maybe some coffee."

"Okay, let me put some on. We can sit in the kitchen."

"Wherever you are comfortable. I just have a few questions for you. I've been contacted by the sheriff's department in Colorado, and they requested we follow up with you."

"What in the world? What do they need to know? It's been five years. Nothing has changed from the first twenty times I was questioned."

Beth was being very forward with this man, Selah thought.

"I don't mean to upset you, Ms. Pearse. Please, let me do my job."

"What's your question?" Beth sat down at the table, a frown on her face.

The deputy pulled out his notes and a pen. "Ms. Pearse, were you aware that your husband was under the care of a doctor at the time of his accident?"

"I know that he went for his annual physical two weeks before we went on vacation. It was a good visit, and Brad didn't mention anything unusual. He was always physically fit. What do you mean?"

"Apparently, some prescription bottles with his name were found at your cabin recently. Any idea what they were for?"

"No, Brad didn't have any prescriptions. We did have guests in for a visit. Maybe they were theirs?"

"I will make sure that the sheriff knows. Are you sure Mr. Pearse didn't share anything that the doctor told him during his appointment?"

"He said that it was a routine visit. Nothing to worry about for another year."

"Can you tell me exactly what happened that morning?"

"Sure. We all had breakfast; Martin, Brad, Sophie and me. The guys wanted to go for a swim, but it was too chilly for me, so I stayed at the house. I was helping Sophie clean up from breakfast. The guys went down to the lake and the next thing I know I get a phone call from Martin panicking about Brad disappearing under the water." Beth looked down at her hands and squeezed her eyes shut. "I didn't believe that he was gone for a long time. They searched and searched for his body, but never found anything. The only thing left was his Gatorade bottle on shore and his towel."

"Who are Martin and Sophie? What is their last name?

"Pommier, P-O-M-M-I-E-R."

"Why were they staying with you?"

"They were our best friends from Paris. Brad met Martin on a business trip, and they hit it off. We would visit them when we traveled in Europe, and then they decided to come and visit us. I'm still in contact with them. In fact, Martin is helping me with my art purchases for the gallery." Beth rose and got the deputy his coffee. "Why so many questions? I thought the investigation was closed when they released the insurance money. It was a rough five years with no income. The insurance company took forever to decide whether it was an accident." She put the cup in front of the officer, and their fingers touched lightly. Beth jumped, and Selah knew she was uncomfortable now. "The coroner determined right away and issued a death certificate right away based on Martin's testimony." Beth walked around the table and slid back into her chair. "Was there anything else?"

"Can I get Mr. Pommier's contact information in case the sheriff would like to talk to him?"

"Of course, But he should already have that. Can I ask you about something? It's not related to this."

"What can I help you with?"

"I received a notice from city hall that there have been complaints about the construction from the neighbors. I have a hearing scheduled next week. Do you know of any complaints? No one has said anything in the neighborhood. If they had let us know we would have fixed whatever needs to be resolved."

"I have not received any complaints from anyone in the neighborhood. Your crew has worked relatively clean, and they start after the noise restrictions."

They are way too noisy for my tastes, Selah thought.

"I will check on it for you and get back with you but as far as I know nothing has come through my office. I would be glad to come to the hearing if you would like." He took a long sip of coffee and finished off his cup. "Is there anything else?" He walked over to the kitchen counter and sat the cup in the sink.

"No, that's all. If you hear anything else from the sheriff in Colorado will you let me know? I don't understand why there are still questions."

"I will let you know anything I hear. I'm sorry for your loss. Thank you for your time and the coffee. One last thing, who do you receive your checks from? Do they come directly from the insurance company?"

"No, they send it through my lawyer. He handles all the paper-work, so I don't have to worry about it."

"Thank you again." He held out his hand, and Beth reluctantly shook it.

Selah could see the lust in the deputy's eyes. He was up to no good, that's for sure, and Beth better be careful, she thought.

Beth closed the door behind the deputy and leaned against the door. Selah listened to his heavy footsteps headed down the stairs. She had seen that look before when the overseer found a girl to his liking. It was so frustrating. Things hadn't changed a bit.

Suddenly the deputy's coffee cup flew to the floor and landed in pieces on the kitchen floor. Beth jumped and ran to the kitchen.

"How did that happen?" Beth exclaimed as she grabbed a broom and cleaned up the shards.

Selah didn't mean for that to happen. Beth warmed some water and made herself a cup of tea. The other woman glanced at the mountain of mail and left it on the table. When the tea was ready, she grabbed Selah's diary and curled up on the couch to read some more of the book. Selah loved the way that Beth concen-trated when she was reading her diary. She could tell the woman was drawn into her life's story. Selah peeked over Beth's shoulder to see what part she was reading.

Ahh, a tragic day. The day her life changed.

COVERING THE FANLIGHT

*J*ohnson Farm, Just Outside of Wilmington, NC, October 21, 1859

There was movement by the well. Selah rubbed the back of her neck wiping the sweat between her braids and her collar. The bird trail had proven to be a challenge. Her mother taught her about the safe trail to Wilmington since she was little, but the hardship of the journey remained a mystery until now. Selah moved around the tree to get a better look at the person drawing water. It was not a slave but a plainly dressed white woman with her hair in a bun. The quilt hanging on the clothesline told Selah it was safe to approach the house, but she didn't want to have bad manners. The woman struggled to pull the rope that held the bucket for water.

This was her chance. "Can I help?"

"Well, hello. Yes, thank you."

Selah stepped to the side of the well and gave the rope a tug. The bucket was full of water, and she knew now why the woman was having a hard time. The other woman grabbed the rope along

Selah. The fact that she did not leave the proper space between them did not go unnoticed.

"Ma'am, I can do it for you. Let me…"

"Oh no, four hands are better than two. I will gladly help."

When the bucket finally arrived at the top, the woman gave Selah a hug. "Thank you so much for the help. How did you find yourself out this way?"

"A friend of a friend sent me. I'm looking for a safe place to stay."

The woman looked around with fear on her face. "Why are you traveling during the day, child? Let's go inside." She grabbed the bucket and began to run toward the house, the water splashing over the sides as she went.

"Ma'am, there is no hurry," Selah quickly said. "I have my Freeman papers."

The woman stopped and turned. "Then why would you follow the trail?"

"I need some assistance getting a message back to my family." She eyed the other woman. "And a safe place to stay while I wait for my man to arrive."

"I see. We have never had a person stay longer than a night. Perhaps you can stay at an inn in town, while you wait."

Selah shook her head, "They will not let a negro stay without an owner, so I have been sleeping along the trail in the hiding trees. Can you help me send a note?"

"Yes, we can do that. Now come inside and have a refreshing drink."

"No, ma'am. I will take some water and wait in the barn. I don't want to be any trouble."

"It's no trouble. You have already proven to be a help."

Selah turned toward the large red barn. "I will wait in the barn for you, ma'am." The other woman nodded and took the bucket, now only three-quarters full across the barnyard to the house. Selah wanted some time alone to write her note to William. She knew he would be able to safely make the journey and perhaps it wouldn't take him the two days it had taken her. He was such a big and strong man. The journey would be nothing to him. She found a nice corner in the hayloft.

MY DEAREST WILLIAM,

I have arrived at a friendly farm near Wilmington. The birds have shown me the way. I hope my news was not too hard for you. I am lonely without you.

I wait here to hear from you.

Your Love,

Selah

The note was a short one, but full of the code they were taught as children. She would have to convince the farmer to let her stay until William met her and then they would go north together.

Selah heard the barn door, and she peered over the edge. The woman had a man with her. He didn't look like a plantation owner. His dress was made of the same black fabric as the woman and was not very fancy.

"Hello, we've come to talk to you," he called out.

Selah made her way down the ladder to speak to them face to face. She brought her bag along with her. "Hello, Sir. I'm Selah, and I thank you very much for letting me rest in the barn."

"My wife says that you are a Freeman."

"Yes, sir. I have my papers with me and a pass from the plantation if you would like to see them."

"That won't be necessary. My wife said that you need lodging for a few days."

"That's correct."

"And what do you have to offer as payment for this lodging?" He looked at Selah's dirty clothes.

"I am a very good seamstress and quilter. I will be glad to do any mending you need done. My quilts sell for a very high price down south."

"Do they now?"

"Yes, sir. That is how I bought my freedom."

He turned to his wife. "I think you could use some help with the sewing, don't you?"

"Yes, that would be wonderful. Selah, do you have that note?"

Selah tore the back page of her book, folded it and handed it to the farmer's wife. "Thank you so much. He should be here two days after he gets the note and then we will leave you in peace."

"With God's grace, it will be sooner." She gave Selah a smile.

Thank goodness for Godly people, Selah thought as she returned to the hayloft to rest.

* * *

SELAH SAT in the loft sewing a pair of trousers that need a new seam in the seat. That farmer sure was rough on his clothes, and it seemed that he wore his Sunday best out to do the plowing. She had never seen such a thing.

She heard the barn door, and a voice yelled up the ladder. "Selah, you have a letter. Come quickly."

Selah threw her sewing down in the hay not thinking about the scissors as they fell to the floor with a thud. Why was there a letter? Why didn't William come in person? She thought with panic. She slid down the ladder, running to the woman waiting at the door holding out a small folded letter.

Selah took it and unfolded it carefully her hands shaking. It was in her mother's elegant handwriting so much like her own.

Dear Selah,

My lovely sunflower, please do not be sad. Your William has gone home to heaven. He would not give up your note to the overseer and was punished for it. He did not survive.

Please go north and make a new life for yourself. Do not be afraid to love again. William would have wanted it. We will be okay here. Travel safe. God is with you.

Your Loving Mother

"Oh, my God has forsaken me." Selah cried out and fell to the floor. Her sobs could be heard in the farmhouse across the yard. The farmer's wife wrapped her arms around her and comforted her. They sat on the floor of the barn until the moon rose and Selah fell asleep in her arms from exhaustion.

SINGLE GLAZING

The diary turned out to be a fascinating read for Beth. The handwriting was not as difficult to read as Sam had warned. Maybe it was the memory of the girl's face, that made it easy for Beth to hear the story. A trip to the library was in order. Maybe, someone there could help her find some more information. Beth took a sip of her now cold tea. How long had she been reading? She glanced at her phone and noted the time. She needed to get out of the apartment for a while. The air seemed to lack oxygen. She walked out onto the balcony of her flat and checked the temperature. She quickly changed clothes and set off down Main to the waterfront to go for a run and clear her head.

She focused on the pounding of her feet and her breathing to find some peace, but her mind refused to be silent. Why were there more questions? The rhythmic pounding allowed her to clear her head. She slowed to go around a mother pushing her stroller then picked up her pace again listening to her breathing. Brad was not sick. Why were they trying to say he was? She knew that was what they were inferring. At a red light, she continued to jog in place to keep her pace. As she turned up Highway 17, she decided she needed to get away from town. Did they not want her? Why would they choose to block her project so late in the game?

She listened to her feet hit upon the metal of the drawbridge. The change in pitch startled her. A car honked as they drove by. *Yes, I am running on the road. No, do not hit me.* She passed a group of fishermen and then stepped back onto the walkway. She was back into her rhythm again. She stomped on the pavement trying to make the questions go away. But the peace was fleeting. Images of Brad and Martin waving as they turned up the path to the lake appeared. That was the last time she saw him. They had been so happy. Why did he have to leave her?

She listened to her breathing again. The last five years had been hell, trying to pay bills with promises that the funds would eventually be there. Their friends and family had supported her, but eventually, she started selling off all the memories. Everything from the past was gone, and now she focused on her future or at least was trying to.

She stopped and looked around. Where was she? The cars flew by on the four-lane road. She had run all the way to the bypass. She turned around and started back towards Washington. As she ran back up 17, she focused again on her physical activity. She needed to be positive. Brad wanted her to be happy. He would be pissed if he could see the trouble she had experienced. She laughed, and her lungs burned from the extra exertion. He always had a take no prisoners' attitude. He would have marched up to city hall first thing this morning and demanded a retraction and review. But would he approve of Sam? A shiver ran over her. She still loved him. Was there room in her heart for another man? She didn't know. She reminded herself the thing with Sam didn't have to be serious.

She paused under the overpass. Out of the corner of her eye, she saw something move in the trees. The green slimmed water pooled around the railroad tracks in the distance. She started to take off again and then hesitated. She was sure someone was watching her. She squinted into the sunlight shining through the trees. There she saw a head dart in and out. She stepped off the pavement into the grass to investigate. Her heart raced. She reached down and felt for her phone tucked in the waistband of her running shorts. Her running shoes sank into the muck and the hair on the back of her neck prickled. Just then, she saw a figure in the distance run to the next tree. The trees shaded the swampy area from any sunlight that would have helped her see any details.

"Hello? Is someone there?" She waited for a response. "Do you need help?" She climbed over a fallen tree to continue down a makeshift path. "Hello? I saw you get my attention. I'm here to help if you need some." The water was getting deeper, and she was afraid she might lose a shoe if she went any further into the swamp. Beth stopped and shook her head. *What was she thinking?* She turned back toward the tracks to retreat to dry ground.

"No."

Beth turned so quickly she slipped and lost her footing. The foul-smelling water covered her from head to toe. "Shit. Look what you've done." She slung the water and mud off her arms and hands. When she regained her footing, she searched for another view of the person who was watching her. "Are you still there? What do you want?" she screamed out of frustration. Apparently, someone was playing a prank, and she had fallen for it. "I'm leaving and going home."

"No."

Beth felt a gust of wind rush by her, sending a chill over her damp skin. She could see a person standing in the distance in the shadow of a tree. "Do you need to talk to me? I'm coming." Beth worked her way through the overgrowth trying to use the cypress tree knots as stepping stones to stay as dry as possible. As she closed the distance between her and the big tree, she could make out a feminine figure. She hastened her pace determined her baptism in the swamp muck was not in vain. She rounded the huge tree and found no one there. *What the hell?*

Through the Spanish moss-covered trees, Beth could see the lights of Washington's waterfront in the distance. The tree was hollow with a hole big enough to hide a person. She ran her fingers over the rough bark along the edge of the opening and paused, watching a boat drift by on the river. The warmth of a hand fell on Beth's fingers, brushing the skin very lightly and startling her. Beth turned to the inside of the tree and saw her companion clearer now than ever. It was Selah, tucked tightly into the inside of the tree hiding from the light. Her wet dress pooled out of the tree like a dark muddy waterfall. She was shaking from the cold breeze. Beth's own skin had goosebumps as the wind blew off the water and whistled through the trees.

"What do you need?" Beth knew there would not be an answer because this was another one of her stupid nightmares.

"We are in danger. Hide quickly before someone sees you. We should wait until dark before we cross. I saw you on the road. Why would you walk on the road like that? They will catch you and send you back." The petite black woman peeked out of the tree surveying the swamp. "Find a tree and wait until dark. He has his eye on you. We have to be careful."

Beth blinked listening to the warning from the dead woman. "How do you know about the sheriff?"

"I was there. I saw him. The water has bound us, now I must help you, so you can help me find freedom."

"But you are dead." Beth shook her head trying to make sense of what was happening. Turning away from the tree, she grabbed onto a stump trying to gain her balance. The stress was making her crazy. That was the only explanation. Why was she talking to dead girls? Stumbling up the path, she noticed the sunlight fading. She had to make it home before dark to run safely along the road. She hurried through the woods trying to avoid the deep holes that had soaked her on the trip in. She left the girl behind her cowering in the tree. When she was following Selah, she didn't realize how far she had gone. Finally, she made it to the tracks and followed them to the road. A truck blew past her cooling her damp skin. In the wind, she could hear Selah's voice.

"Be careful, he is watching."

SALVAGED BEAUTY

*A*nother vehicle rushed past Beth, as she turned toward the bridge. The moisture in her socks rubbed the back of her feet as she jogged up the side of the highway. She pulled back her hair and adjusted her headband as she slowly built up her speed. The sun was setting, turning the sky a beautiful orange and purple while the swamp took on an eerie misty feel. The earbuds in her ears let her focus on her breathing again, matching the rhythm of her running shoes hitting the road like a drum. She was lost in her thoughts when a horn blared, and lights flashed, snapping her back to reality. She turned around, and there was a truck headed straight for her. *Holy crap!* The truck was driving down the shoulder. Beth jumped into the ditch, barely avoiding the vehicle. It stopped, and the reverse lights lit up. *Oh, my God, they are coming back.* As the vehicle stopped beside her, the window rolled down, and a small hand reached out.

"Beth, what are you doing out here on the highway? You want to get killed?" Beth felt a huge rush of relief. It was Hellen. "Someone is going to hit you."

Beth stood up in the ditch, soaking wet again. "I thought you were going to hit me. You scared me half to death coming up behind me like that. It's already scary enough out here." Steadying herself, she walked towards the truck and told herself she wouldn't be running this way again.

"You want a ride?" She turned to the child in the passenger seat and unbuckled him. "Get in the back and buckle up so Ms. Beth can ride with us." The little boy obeyed and climbed back into the extended cab.

"Do you have a towel or something I can put on the seat? I wouldn't want to make a mess of your truck." Beth opened the truck door and started to climb inside.

"Don't you worry about that. We just went to Dairy Queen. If you get it wet, maybe it will clean some of the ice cream off." Beth started to laugh as she understood instantly what Hellen meant. The seat was covered with soft serve and looking at the kids in the backseat, the rest was on their faces and clothes.

"Okay, I warned you." Beth climbed in feeling relieved that Hellen had shown up. "Would you mind dropping me by the house? I wanted to check on how the cleanup was going."

"Sure. Are you sure you don't want to shower first? I don't know if I would show up in your swamp people costume."

"Right. Okay, well the apartment then. Thanks."

Hellen smiled and turned onto Main Street, the windows rolled down to let the stench exit the truck. She pulled up to the apartment's front door and stopped in the street, putting the vehicle in park and turning to Beth. "Are we still on for another lunch date next week? You have to let me know what day works for you. And no more jumping into ditches."

"I'll let you know after I look at my calendar. Thanks again for the ride. And don't run any more unsuspecting joggers off the road,"

Beth teased with a smile and jumped out of the truck. She inserted the key into the lock and saw out of the corner of her eye the little boy spraying Febreze into the passenger seat. She laughed and waved as she stepped into the hallway.

Peeling off her running clothes, she tossed them in the sink and jumped in the shower. The warm water took the chill off her skin and washed away the stench of the swamp. Sometimes she could be so impulsive. Stupid, that's what she was, plain old stupid. She would have to be more careful. Selah warned her. The ghost said someone was watching her. Surely, she wasn't a suspect in her husband's death. It had been ruled an accident. She needed to stop obsessing. She had answered their questions; now she needed to let it go.

She threw a t-shirt and some jeans on and headed out the door. Walking up Main and then turning the corner, she felt someone's eyes on her. Her gait naturally increased, and she headed up the drive to her house. There were men everywhere; cleaning brushes, hammering, painting. Finally, a little progress. She saw a light through the upstairs bedroom window. Excitement filled her. Stepping into the front room, the building was transformed. Sheetrock and plaster covered the studs. Lights illuminated every room. Her hand caressed the new banister as she climbed the stairs. All the bedrooms were enclosed, and there was a bathroom. An actual bathroom. Amazing. She was anxious to see the kitchen. She dodged a few carpenters and jumped the last step.

A disappointed sigh escaped her when she saw it looked the same, well almost. There was a huge ventilation pipe running from the cellar and hanging out the window. She hoped that Sam had worked some magic and it had moved forward. No such luck. Jose stepped inside the kitchen from the back porch, saw her, and turned around, trying to escape. He put his hand up and shook his head.

"Jose, please can you give me a tour? I want to hear what you guys have done. So much has changed since yesterday. Please."

"Ms. Beth, I have way too much to do, and you're right, we're working our butts off, so you can at least live here. Please don't bug us today."

"Where is Sam?"

"Your guess is as good as mine. He has been making runs to the lumber yard and hardware store all day, so we don't have to stop. Why don't you sit over under the tree and watch the guys work? That will keep from them hanging out in their favorite spot."

"Are you implying they are avoiding me?"

"No implications necessary. They don't like it when you are on site. Okay, I gotta get back to work. Sam will have my butt if he sees me just standing." And with that, he rushed off.

Beth looked over at the old oak tree in the yard. There were three workers leaned against the trunk taking a smoke break. As soon as they spotted her, they put their cigarettes out and grabbed their tool belts. She didn't realize she had made such an impression last week. She walked over and sat down on the moss-covered ground. The light breeze caught her hair and blew it into her eyes. Everyone moved around the work site. It was like a dance to music that no one else could hear, well except for the percussion of the hammers. Everyone had their own project going, but they worked side by side in harmony. It wouldn't be long before she would be in her home. Goosebumps rose on her skin. She couldn't wait. She sent a quick text to Sam.

Beth: The house looks fantastic. Thank you.

Sam: You're welcome. BRT

His truck pulled into the drive five minutes later with a load full of lumber. The men surrounded the bed like a bunch of ants grabbing the supplies and heading into the building. No words were necessary. Everyone knew what was expected, except for Beth. Everyone grabbed their pieces of the puzzle and were gone in a moment. She watched from her post trying not to disturb the synchronization. Sam's face brightened when he saw her under the tree watching. His hand went up in acknowledgment then he returned to the men passing out the supplies. She watched as they listened intently to his direction. She could see why things moved quickly when he was on site. After the bed was empty, he walked toward her.

"Hey, things are really moving along. When do you think, it will be ready for furniture?"

"It won't be long. How about you tell me where you want those shelves so we can get them in place." Stretching out his hand, she grabbed it and stood to her feet. He didn't turn her loose, and it felt right to have his cover hers. They walked across the uneven lawn, dodging the holes made by the equipment. "We will get the landscaping straightened out once the inside is livable. The only thing I can't promise you is the kitchen. We are still waiting for the approval from the city."

"I think it should happen on Wednesday at the meeting. I got a notice in the mail."

He turned toward her with surprise on his face. "You mean you actually went through your mail?"

"I did." He was still staring at her. "Well, long enough to find the notice. The rest is sitting there still waiting." He didn't move, still staring. "Will you stop? I can't help that I hate going through the mail."

He started laughing. "I'm only teasing you. You are the one that feels guilty about the mail. Will you stop worrying about it? Just remind me to hand-deliver my bill."

Beth shoved his good shoulder. His sling was filled with pieces of notebook paper. "What's that?"

"Those are all my notes for the new sump pump in the cellar. Robert and I worked out a plan so that it will automatically pump out the cellar if it floods again." Sam opened the door for her and invited her into the house.

"And who is Robert?"

"He's the guy down at our hardware store. Great guy, really knows how to figure stuff out."

"Ah, I see. I'll have to thank him for my dry cellar sometime." They walked into the front gallery. "I think the shelves should go along this wall. They will look great with pottery."

"You aren't afraid of taking up too much of your wall space? They are pretty big."

"I think they will be great here. I have some smaller pieces that will look nice on shelves. Besides they belong together."

"Yes, ma'am. You ready to see the cellar? They did a great job cleaning it this morning. The fans are still going, but we can go down there if you would like." He grabbed her hand again leading her down the steps to the cellar. The bleach odor made her eyes water. "Doesn't it look great? They pressure washed and disinfected everything. I am going to ask the city if it's okay to waterproof down here. But we can worry about it later. Right now, I'm not changing anything until we get the go-ahead for the kitchen plan."

Her mouth gaped open in amazement. She couldn't believe it was the same room. He turned to her. She loved the wrinkles at the corner of his mouth and eyes when he smiled. "What do you think? Aren't you going to say something?" He waited for her response, but it came slowly.

"It's amazing." Her feet rubbed the cobblestone floor. "It has a floor."

"Yep."

She whirled around giving him a huge hug, and their lips touched. Beth felt tears rolling down her cheeks followed by the brush of his fingers as he wiped them away.

"What are those for?"

"It's home. It's finally a home." She whispered.

His smile grew wider, and his fingers held her chin. A mere breath separated them before he leaned in to take her lips again.

"Boss!" A voice upstairs yelled. Sam's shoulders fell.

"Work calls. We can talk later. You better head back up before the fumes get you."

She nodded and wiped her cheeks.

Sam yelled up the stairs and grabbed her hand, helping her up the slippery stairs. Beth could not believe the difference. She walked around the top floor planning where her furniture would go. All the personal stuff she missed so much. She could be in her own bed in two weeks. Squeezing between the workers as she went downstairs, she saw that Sam's truck was gone again. Sending a short text, she walked up the sidewalk toward her apartment.

BETH: *See you tomorrow. Can't wait.*

DROPPING A STRINGER

September 20, 2014

Sam leaned over the pile of papers on the countertop. The morning light beamed through the window. He could feel his frustration building every minute. He planned to come to the house early before the rest of the crew so there would be a clear plan for the day, but this was turning out to be a real puzzle. He shoved his hand through his hair. Shuffling the papers, he pulled out some graph paper with a sketch on it. An old Honda pulled up the drive, and Sam glanced through the hallway to see Robert walking towards the house. The man was dressed in the same outfit he had worn the day before, and the beard he was sporting had become more and more ragged. A minute later Sam heard a knock.

"Come on in. It's unlocked!" Sam studied the drawing again, waiting for the other man to join him. "Thanks for coming by, man. This has got me stumped. How did we run the pipes down to the sump pump? It made sense yesterday when we were drawing it out. Now I'm stuck." Sam shook the man's outstretched hand. "You can set your bag over there."

"No problem. I know how important the angles are to make this work." Robert grabbed each page of graph paper and put them in order. "You see you have to follow the beam across the ceiling. This is the lowest point on the floor, so you should place the pump there." He pulled a piece of paper out of his pocket, "plus it won't work without this."

"How did I forget a page? I should have had another cup of coffee, I guess. Thanks."

"No problem, I spotted it after you left. You think you could give me the grand tour while I'm here. I would love to see the house in person. We've been working on it from the store for so long."

"Of course. Let me show you upstairs." The two men went up the stairs. Sam was proud of the work they had done on the house and was ready to show it off. "This is the master bedroom. I added the window seat here so Beth, the owner, can look out on the river. I think she will really enjoy it. Across the hall, is the master bath and dressing room. Then a little office." The other man admired the crown molding and other wood accents. They both walked across the hall to the office and were admiring the built-in desk when Sam saw the deputy's car parked out in front. "If you will excuse me. Please feel free to look around. It appears I have a visitor." He left the man standing in the office, took the stairs two at a time and met Deputy Felton at the front door. "Hi, Bill. How's it going?"

"Well, it could be better. I could not be working at the crack of dawn. And I could have some news for you on your case. But all I have, are more questions. Can I come in?"

"Oh, yeah, sorry." Sam stepped out of the way and let the man through. "So, they haven't found anything?"

"Well we found some fingerprints, but no matches. And we've got some bullet casings, but no matches on those either. We have a lot of dead ends so far. Have you thought of any possibilities?"

"No one has come to mind. I mean, I haven't been in a fight since I was in my twenties down at the bar. I don't know anyone who would hate me that much."

"Let us know if anything else comes up. The investigators are done with your office so you can clean it up any time you want."

"Thanks. Well, I gotta get back to work. We are actually making some progress, and I want to be out of here on time this afternoon."

"I'll let you go. By the way, whichever one of your guys has the Honda out there, he needs to get a new registration. His plates are expired. I'm gonna let it go since it's parked on private property but thought you should know."

"Thanks, Bill. I'll let him know. We will get it taken care of." Sam held out his hand and shook the Deputy's.

"You do that. I'll talk to you later." He stepped out onto the porch. "Let Ms. Pearse know that I will be at the hearing on Wednesday to speak on her behalf. It's turning into something incredible."

Sam smiled and shut the door behind him. As he walked back upstairs, he shouted, "Robert, you're on their radar. Might want to take care of those car tags." Rounding the corner, he found the man in the master bedroom staring out the window. "What do you think?"

"It's beautiful. You better get busy if you are going to stay on schedule. I've got to get going. I gotta work today at the store. Give me a call if you need any more help."

"I sure will. Thanks again for coming by so early." Shutting the door behind Robert, Sam grabbed his cell phone and sent a quick text.

* * *

SAM: *Good morning beautiful. See you tonight.*

Beth woke to the chime on her cell phone. She glanced at the screen and saw Sam's morning message. Her smile was almost as bright as the sunlight shining through her window. The rocking chair in the corner of the room rocked to a rhythm that soothed to Beth's restless thoughts. She found it reassuring. Somewhere between the present and another time, Selah rocked a small baby, humming a tune meant to soothe the child but created a dream-like state for Beth as well. Enjoying the tune, Beth curled up under her quilt.

"He was there. Be careful."

The mood was broken. "Who was there, Selah? Where?"

"He was there, at the house. I saw his evil thoughts." The infant disappeared, and Selah was by herself with concern on her face. "Do not let him in again." With the warning, she was gone.

Selah definitely had a way of ruining a mood. Beth pulled her quilt closer around her, wanting the foreboding to disappear. She knew it wouldn't, so she climbed out of bed and pushed herself to get ready for the day. Tonight was her date with Sam. There was something she could get excited about. She walked over to Rachel K's for breakfast. Nothing like a croissant to help figure out life.

Rick smiled at her as she walked in the door. "Long time no see, stranger."

"Hi, Rick. Sorry I've been sleeping in lately. No time for gourmet coffee. Can I get my usual please?"

"Hmm, let me see if I can remember what you have. It's been so long since I have put in an order for you."

"Hush. It hasn't been that long."

The young man laughed. "You're right. I got ya. I was beginning to worry, though. You just disappeared."

"Nice to know I would be missed." Sliding her card to pay for breakfast, she smiled sweetly and winked at him. Rick blushed from the attention. Beth often wondered who would miss her if she just disappeared since Brad was gone. She kept her appointments scarce, so she had time for herself, but it was starting to isolate her. Even though she liked the isolation, she was grateful soon she the gallery would take a lot of her time. She needed to get her rest while she could. Rick soon appeared with her tea and croissant.

"Thanks, I'll be back soon. Promise."

He nodded and smiled, turning his attention to his next waiting customer.

Beth stirred in her honey and lemon and headed towards her favorite bench on the waterfront. The gulls acted like they had missed her too, stalking the buttery pastry flakes as they fell from her hand. As the croissant disappeared down her throat in record time, she realized she never ate dinner the night before. She slowed her pace, taking smaller bites and savoring the buttery roll. No wonder she had been drawn to the bakery this morning. Thinking about what distracted her last night, she remembered the diary. She had begun reading early in the evening and fell asleep with it in her hands. Selah was traveling on a boat toward Washington, and it was taking twice as long as the captain had promised. The young black woman wrote about her days on the dangerous seas on the Shoals, the rocks and waves, traveling at night sometimes to prevent her discovery. The pages recorded, in her perfect penmanship, her suspicions the captain was delaying her arrival to the port because he fancied her. She wasn't sure of his feelings, though. There were also sketches of quilt blocks, projects for the future. She wrote of her dreams of owning a seamstress shop.

Beth thought about when she first dreamed of her gallery. When did it become a goal moving towards reality? She could picture herself sitting at the kitchen table in her Colorado home holding an envelope from the state. She sat there for what seemed to be hours pushing herself to open it. She knew what it was. Why had it been so hard to open it? She finally ripped the end off like a Band-Aid and pulled out her husband's death certificate. It was finally real. The end of her marriage was in print. She felt empty inside. There was nothing more for her there. It was time for a new beginning in a new place. She laughed as tears ran from her eyes. Her thoughts turned to the present and her fresh start among the evil gulls. They dived at her, screaming for her to drop her roll so they could devour the remainder. "Go Away! I don't share." She looked around at the quiet town she now called home. No one cared she was yelling at the gulls. It was the mantra of the town. "Don't feed the birds." Only the tourists ignored the warnings and locals paid for it by putting up with the constant harassment. She absently wondered how Selah dealt with the gulls. Beth pulled out her phone and typed:

BETH:*I'M excited about tonite. But what am I going to do until then?*

Sam: You can come over and help.

Beth: No thanks. I'll leave that to you xoxo.

BETH GLANCED AROUND HER, embarrassed that she was laughing

out loud because of his response. In the distance, she saw a man in a UVA sweatshirt. There was a familiarity to his form that made her uneasy, but she didn't know why. She was making myself crazy. Time to go home and read some more to relieve her over-active mind. She broke the rules and tossed her leftovers into the grass creating a feeding frenzy. The gulls attacked blocking her view of the park.

"You know that's against the law, right?" Deputy Felton startled her standing so close.

"Oh, I'm sorry. I was done and ..." Beth's nerves were on edge, and she was having trouble organizing her thoughts.

He gave her a huge grin. "I'm just giving you a hard time. They can get mean, though. Might not want to make it a habit."

"Thank you." Her shoulders physically drooped as she relaxed.

"Are we ready for the meeting next week?"

"I think so. Do you think there is anything specific I will need for their questions?"

"No, but if I think of anything I can give you a call. Can I get your number?"

"Of course, here's my phone. Just dial your number, and you can save it." She swiped the screen and unlocked the phone before handing it to the officer.

He dialed his number, and his phone started to ring. "Make sure you save my number in case you need me. Sometimes it can be faster than dispatch."

"Thank you so much." Beth glanced over his shoulder scanning the horizon for the man she had spotted earlier, but he was gone.

"Everything okay?" the deputy asked.

"Yeah, I'm just being silly."

"Okay, well you have my number. Don't hesitate to call if you need anything."

Beth took a step back from him, sensing he might have other reasons for getting her number. "I have to get back to the loft. You have a nice day."

"Thanks, you too."

She turned and headed to the loft, anxious to curl up with a story that she found oddly comforting even though she already knew the tragic ending. Did it make her twisted? She enjoyed knowing every detail as it played out to the horrible end. It made her feel normal. She wasn't the only one in the world who experienced tragedy. Bounding up the stairs, she rushed inside to grab the diary and escape for a while.

BLOCK PLAN

*M*arketplace, Washington, NC, March 13, 1860

"Fish for Sale, Fish for Sale." His voice bellowed over the busy crowd at the market. Selah would recognize his voice anywhere. Abram was in the market selling his fresh fish from the sound. His presence in the market was becoming more and more frequent, and Selah suspected he had taken a fancy to her, but she was still in mourning. She would not disrespect William's memory by acting a fool over another man. She was a better woman than that.

"Mrs. Selah, I saved the freshest catch for your Mistress this morning. Look at this beautiful flounder."

He held up the shiny brown fish the size of a ham platter. Selah moved to the front of the fisherman's stall. "Why do you have to be so loud? So forward?"

"I'm not being forward, just a good salesman. The good ones always save their best for their best customers."

"Hmm, I still think you are being forward, but I will buy your fish."

"So, I have won, and you have made me very happy." He turned to wrap the fish in newspaper. Selah admired how his white cotton shirt strained to cover his shoulders. Her memory drifted to their time on his boat as he delivered her across the Shoals to Washington earlier in the year. The splash of the salty water plastered his shirt to his chest as he steered the boat toward the harbor.

"Mrs. Selah, your dinner, ma'am." He whispered in her ear a little too close for her comfort. He leaned far over the table so that he could speak directly into her ear.

She took a step back. "Sir, remember yourself." Her face flushed with shame because of her thoughts. "I told you I am in mourning."

"I know you are, but I am praying that will end soon so that I may court you properly."

Selah looked around her at all the shoppers and pushed him back across the table, quickly placing some coin in his hand. "I don't know when that will be, so you will act right."

"Will you tell me when you do decide to come out of mourning?"

"I haven't decided yet." She tried to picture William's face, his full lips and handsome jawline that darkened every summer with his job in the fields. A tear threatened to escape from her eye. "I don't know if it will ever happen." She turned without a look back and left him to sell his catch, so she could have some peace in her heart.

HAND PLANED

*I*t was getting late, and Beth started to worry Sam had changed his mind. She checked herself in the mirror for the thirty-fifth time, as she struggled with finding something cute and comfortable. A chime sounded on her phone.

Sam: OMW. Sorry had trouble with the hitch

Beth: K

The truck pulled up out front, and Beth locked up the apartment. She rushed downstairs to his old truck pulling a small boat on a trailer. She wondered what he had planned. She hoped she doesn't have to handle worms. She wasn't a girly girl, but Beth hated baiting her hooks with night crawlers. The slime and wriggling freaked her out. She jumped in the truck on the passenger side and smiled at Sam. She wondered what he thought when she saw his smile. He looked very pleased with himself. "Are we going fishing?"

"Yes, but not the normal way. Have you had dinner? I know it's kind of late, but I thought we could grab something as we head out of town."

"Sure, sounds good. What do you mean not the normal way?"

"You will see. Are you up for some Italian?"

"Sounds great."

They headed across town with the boat in tow. She was impressed by the skill he used to park the vehicle in the small parking lot of the local Italian place. They walked across the lot hand in hand into the busy restaurant. Almost every booth was full, but they were lucky enough to be seated right away. High school letter jackets and college sweatshirts were the choice fashion. Beth guessed that Sam had taught most of them or they would be taking a class from him in a year or two. Whispers snaked through the restaurant as they were seated. There was no telling what was being said.

She smiled and touched his hand across the table. "What are you thinking for dinner?"

"I'm thinking something on the light side. Nothing too heavy. We are going to be on the boat. It might be a little choppy."

"Okay, maybe a sandwich. But it all looks so good." A shrill scream came from the corner of the room making Beth jump. One of the boys was tickling a girl. They were starting to get rowdy. Beth saw Sam's silent apology from across the table. "Really, it's okay. They are having fun. It's date night, remember?"

Sam just smiled in response.

"So, tell me about this special way of fishing." A shiver ran over Beth. "Please tell me I do not have to touch worms."

Sam started to laugh so loudly it turned heads. "No hooks tonight, you lucky girl. I am going to teach you the Carolina way to fish."

Excitement filled Beth. She loved experiencing new things. The sandwiches arrived at the table on beautiful Italian pottery. Large sunflower petals bordered the edge with a club sandwich and fries centered in the middle. It was fancy for the simple meals. Beth took a bite and savored the flavors filling her mouth. "It's so delicious. Thank you so much for the suggestion."

"Eat up, so we can head down the road. We have to drive a while to get where we're going. I thought it might give you a break from town." He took a long drink of tea. "Have you ever been on a boat?"

"Not one the size of yours. I've been on bigger ones. You can hardly tell you are on the water."

"But that takes away part of the fun. You can't feel the wind on your face, the bounce of waves. Just wait. You'll see tonight."

Beth could see a sparkle in his eyes. Now she was ready to experience it for herself. "Can we go?"

"Of course." She watched him quickly raise his hand to get the waitress' attention. "Can we get some boxes and the check?" The waitress nodded and set the check on the table. She took their plates to the kitchen to be boxed up and soon returned with a bag ready to take along on their adventure. Sam paid the bill and grabbed the bag before they headed to the truck.

She pulled back her hair and climbed into the cab. When Sam joined her, he started the engine and rolled down the windows, letting the heat of the night escape from the small space. He pulled out onto the highway and headed south.

* * *

BETH WAS AWFULLY QUIET, Sam thought to himself. She looked happy, so it didn't worry him, but he could use some conversation after his busy day. He was running on adrenaline, and it was going on ten pm. "So, what did you do today?"

Beth pulled a stray hair out of her face and smiled at him. "Not much. I had my usual breakfast at Rachel's, walked over to the waterfront and sat for a while fighting off the seagulls."

"You better watch yourself with that bunch. They can get mean."

"I can believe it. I read Selah's diary for a while, then headed to the library. The town history room is excellent. They have all kinds of old documents and people's research. I was trying to find some more information on the property. The librarian helped me search the microfiche for newspaper articles. There were a few bad storms that caused flooding on the street during that time. I couldn't pin down which was the one that Selah was describing. I keep searching the diary for clues, but I haven't found anything exactly yet."

"How is the reading going? I mean are you having a hard time with the handwriting?"

"Nope, it's going pretty well. Her handwriting is beautiful. The water didn't do much damage. Some of the pages were stuck together. I just skipped that part to not lose them. I admire her courage so much. She bought her freedom when she was seventeen years old. So incredible."

"That's really young. How did she earn money?"

"Sewing. There are incredible sketches of her quilt designs throughout the entire book. Sometimes she would color them. Do you think she was the one that made that tiny quilt we found?"

It sounded like she really enjoyed the research she was doing. "Maybe so. Sounds like you are learning a lot. Are you ready for our own adventure?" Sam pulled the truck into the boat ramp area and jumped out to see which ramp would be best for his trailer. There were a few other trucks parked in the lot but not too many to signal a crowd in the marsh. "Hop out and hold the rope for me." Handing it to Beth, he showed her where to stand. "You will watch it float up off the trailer and then walk it to the end of the dock." Eyeing her in the rear-view mirror, Sam watched her follow his directions exactly. He grabbed the supplies for the night, pulling towels, lifejackets, and a cooler from behind the seat of the cab. He checked his watch and saw that it was twenty minutes until low tide. Throwing everything in the boat, he held out his hand to help Beth into the boat. "Here's a cushion for your seat."

"I'm good." She settled onto her bench, without it.

"Oh no, you are going to want this when we get going." He pushed it at her a little harder. "Really, I have mine," he added, showing her as he shoved his under his rear. He jumped from side to side, trying not to bump her. She looked a little uneasy in the small boat. Flipping on the light on the stern, he started the engine. Thank goodness, it started on the first try. He didn't want to worry her. Untying the boat, he pulled away from the dock and headed out to his favorite spot. Beth turned around and stared at him. He could see her eyes go big as saucers. "Will you relax?"

"But can you see? It is totally dark. I can't see a thing. What if you hit something?"

"I can see just fine. Just sit back and enjoy the trip. I'm taking you to my secret spot. The moon shows me the way." Sam waved toward the sky. He took note of the leaving wake zone sign and yelled: "Hold on!" The boat jumped at the command of his wrist, and he watched the wind blow through Beth's hair and the spray of the water sparkling on her skin in the moonlight. He heard a shrill squeal and her laughter just above the noise of the engine. Her hands flew to each side of the boat. He was thrilled she was enjoying herself. She turned and looked into his eyes. Despite the darkness, there was magic between them. The light of the boat ramp disappeared behind them as lights of boats in the distance appeared ahead.

*　*　*

THE WIND FELT SO good in Beth's hair. She could not believe that they were fishing in the pitch black. How did he know where to go? The spray of the water cooled her skin, and the waves knocked the boat, jarring her body. Thank goodness, he insisted she has a cushion. Her butt would likely still hurt in the morning, that's for sure. The moonlight shined on water like a beacon to wherever he was taking her. He slowed the boat and stood up, making it wobble with his weight. She squealed when he stepped out of the boat. Surprisingly the water was only shin deep. He stood beside the boat tying the mooring line around his waist. She watched him strap on a PVC pipe across his chest. "Oh, my God, I haven't seen a fanny pack since the '80s." He reached in and flipped a switch lighting the sand underwater. "It's a flashlight!"

"Yep, this is the battery pack. I'm very proud of this." Under the water, creatures scurried across the sandy floor

"Are you going to tell me what we are fishing for? Is it those conch things?"

"Nope, we are flounder gigging."

"What?"

"Flounder gigging. Basically, we or I walk along looking for flounders, and when I spy one the right size, I stab him with our gig."

"And what is my job while all this is going on?"

"You, Ma'am, are in charge of the boat. And since I'm down an arm, I need you to operate the net to get the fish into the cooler. Here's your net." Sam handed her a small fishing net on a long handle. Beth ran it through the water, dragging it along the bottom.

"Do I get to keep anything I catch?" A blue crab darted just out of reach of the net. She was hoping she would catch a bunch and then they could eat them Sunday. It couldn't be that hard.

"We will have to see. There are rules for certain fish. Now the flounders have a strict limit of one per person, and they have to be pretty big."

"Okay, I'm ready." Beth was so excited. She would show him how good she was.

"Almost." Sam handed her a headlamp. "Just don't blind me."

Beth turned on the lamp on her forehead and looked at Sam. "Like this?" laughing at him squinting.

"Yes, like that, you brat."

Beth laughed and turned her attention to some pink glowing eyes in a trench. "And where are you going to be?"

"Over here." Beth panicked when she heard his voice. He was several yards away. She felt reassured the rope was still tied to his waist. She just barely could make out his form with a bright light on his head. There was a beam of light under the water as he strolled along the shore. The shoreline was covered with marsh grass swaying in the light breeze. Her spotlight cast shadows among the reeds. A large dead tree rose from the reeds in the middle of what appeared to be an island. Such a beautiful and spooky place. The breeze strengthened and created a rustling sound.

Beth leaned over the edge to shine her light into the water. A conch slowly crept along the bottom leaving a trail in the sand. Then she spotted some more crabs. Maybe she could catch one if she moved the net slow enough. The crab seemed to sense the net and shot off into the grass. Her face frowned with determination. She was going to try one more time. She leaned over the side of the boat to get a better angle. Suddenly she lost her balance and fell back in the boat. It was moving through the water by itself. She shook her head trying to gain her composure and realized Sam was pulling it by his end of the rope. When she looked in the direction she was moving, she heard a splashing. She couldn't quite make out what was going on, but there was tension on the rope pulling her along.

"Get your net ready." He yelled as she finally arrived alongside him. He had his spear pressing it under the water. "I'm going to lift it up, and you need to scoop the fish in the boat." Beth saw him struggling to keep the spear in place. The weight of the fish seemed to be too much for her one-armed fisherman. Adrenaline filled her veins as she waited for his cue.

"Now."

Beth scooped the fish as quickly as she could, determined not to lose it. It was huge.

"Oh, my God, Sam it's so heavy. I'm going to drop it."

"Just sling it in the boat."

Beth used some momentum and swung the net into the bottom of the boat. The fish hit the side with a loud thud. Sam jumped in and opened the cooler untangling the flounder and putting it on the ice.

"I got it. I got it." Beth screamed. Her voice echoed over the marsh. She grabbed Sam and gave him a huge hug and kiss. She could feel him deepening the kiss and let the moment take her. The boat started to rock with the movement of the waves, and Beth lost her balance, breaking the magic.

Sam smiled down at her, his light blinding her. "So, we caught a fish. Did you catch anything?"

"No, they were all too quick. What are the pink eyes that I keep seeing?"

"Sweetheart, those are shrimp. If you are super stealthy, you can catch them, and we could have some to go with our flounder."

Beth's hair bristled at the sound of the endearment. She wasn't quite used to the southern habit of calling everyone sugar or honey. "Why do y'all do that?"

"What's that?" he asked casually.

"Call everyone sweetheart or darling. I know it's something I need to get used to, but I just don't understand why everyone is a sweetheart."

"First, I like you. That is why I used it. Second, I don't call everyone sweetheart. I don't know why other men use it to put women in..."

Beth's eyebrows rose, and her face turned red. With every one of his words, she felt her temper rising.

"Wait a minute, that didn't come out right. I meant to say I don't know why men use it in a negative way. It should be nice to hear. You might want to get used to it."

"But I don't like it. Well except when you say it." She blushed at the thought of how much she liked it when he called her sweetheart.

"If you like it why are you so upset?" His mouth twisted with what looked like amusement.

"Are you laughing at me?"

"Yes Ma'am, I am. You are being such a Yankee."

"I am not a Yankee." She punched him in his good shoulder. "I am just as Southern as you are."

"I beg to differ." He jumped out of the boat and started to pull the boat toward the shore of a small island. The beach was just big enough to park the john boat so she could get out. He held out his hand and helped her out onto the sand, throwing the blanket and other supplies beside her feet. The sand gave way as her feet hit and she lost her footing leaning into him. He was all business, though. "Grab your net." Beth reached into the boat and retrieved the fishing net. "Shine your light down there along the edge. See if you can find some blue crabs."

"I tried to catch some, but they are too fast." Her voice trembling "I'm no good at this."

"Here, let me help." He wrapped his good arm around her waist and walked her down into the water. The warm water felt good on her feet as it soaked through her sneakers. He guided her hands as they parked the net behind a crab. Then he startled the crab with his foot causing it to run straight into the net.

"Oh, my gosh. We got it." Beth's voice echoed in the night. She jumped up and down in the water, splashing him with her excitement

"That was just one. Calm down so we can have some more."

"Oh, right." Beth instantly started to scan the water which was cloudy with silt.

"Wait a little while, and the sand will settle. Here you can see under the water." He lightly moved his flounder light under the water's surface. Her headlamp's glare disappeared, and she could see the sea life scurrying into the camouflage of the seagrass. Beth chased another crab, but it escaped. She let out a frustrated cry, and Sam turned her around. "Patience. You have to have patience."

"But I'm tired of being patient." Her eyes sparkled in the moon-light. Her lips pouted, and she tried to look like a typical two-year-old not getting what she wanted.

Sam grabbed her arm and slowly guided it through the water. "Like this. Slow. Move with the current, so you don't startle them" She leaned against him, and they started to sway with the breeze that cooled them. His arm began to turn her around, so their bodies melted into each other. Her arms went around his neck pulling his face down to hers. Slowly his hand caressed the small of her back, her body responding, arching toward him, so there was no space left between them. The water disappeared, her feet were on a beach, the kiss deepened, and he lowered her down onto a blanket. She never knew such tenderness existed. Was this what it was supposed to be like? Her head became fuzzy for a moment, and she thought she saw Brad lying next to her touching her. *No. I can't,* she told herself and then she made herself say it out loud. "Br, I mean Sam. I can't. I want to, but I'm not ready. I'm so sorry." A tear rolled down her face.

Sam looked down at her. His thumb wiped the tear away. "Beth, I'm not trying to rush you. Just get comfortable and lay beside me. I have no expectations, and technically this is our first date. I love spending time with you, that's enough."

"Thanks." She snuggled up close to him and put her head in the crook of his arm. Her nerves calmed as she watched the stars twinkle. The sky was so clear there seemed to be a million of them. "Sam, what do you want? You know, for your future."

"I don't know. I always thought I would get a position at one of the state schools. But turns out I love my renovation work. I don't know if I could go full time into research, I prefer the hands-on aspect of teaching."

"Do you think you will ever move? I just couldn't imagine ever leaving this place, now that I have made it my home."

"Have you made it your home?" He looked down at her smiling with an upturned brow.

"What do you mean?" she asked.

"I haven't seen you truly move in yet. You are still living in your temporary apartment," he teased her. "When am I going to see a moving truck?" He ran his hand up and down her arm lightly stroking it.

He was distracting her. "When you give me the go-ahead, the moving guys are on their way." She ribbed back.

"Really, just one word from me and you are here permanently?" He asked, amusement in his voice as his lips brushed her ear and trailed down her neck.

Goosebumps rose on her skin. "Yes." The word barely escaped her mouth.

"Call them," he responded and pulled her close. The breeze cooled them as they laid under the stars; both dreaming of what may be.

CRACKED FOUNDATIONS

September 21, 2014

Beth looked at Sam under heavy eyelids. The golden sun was starting to rise in the distance. They both fell asleep on the sand, and despite their wild surroundings, slept peacefully. The waves slowly rolled up on the shore, and the rhythm lulled her back to sleep. A light breeze brushed the skin of her arm as it peaked out from under her blanket. The gulls and pelicans dove in the water offshore looking for breakfast. When a fiddler crab scurried past her face on the open sand, she restrained herself so she wouldn't wake Sam. It was so quiet she could hear her own thoughts screaming at her. Why couldn't she just enjoy life? Things were perfect last night, and she drew it to a screeching halt. She was lost in that thought when her stomach growled so loudly she grabbed her abdomen, hoping Sam didn't hear.

Sam laughed. She felt his body shake next to hers, suddenly she was aware of how good he felt next to her.

"Someone's hungry."

"Oh no, you heard me."

"Who couldn't." Sam looked around and saw the sunrise. "We better get back. We'll stop on the way for some breakfast." Beth's stomach growled again. "Before you eat me. Although you look good enough to eat this morning." He leaned over and gave her a kiss. He hopped up to his feet and offered her his good hand. She stood up brushing the sand from her back. "I could help with that." He pulled her close reaching around her and brushing the sand off her bottom, then giving it a teasing spank.

"Ouch." Beth looked up at him with squinting eyes. "You better be careful, I might spank you back." The corners of her lips curled up into a smirk.

"Hmm, I better get us somewhere public, so you can't hurt me." He grabbed the anchor and pulled the boat closer to shore. "You are going to have to wade out. The tide has come in, and it's deeper than it was last night."

Their surroundings were not as haunted as it appeared last night. There were sport-boats and barges floating by as they collected their supplies. Such a public place. Her thoughts went back to the intimacy she had experienced with Sam the night before. Her face heated and blushed, she couldn't believe she had acted so carelessly. She didn't want him to think she was a tease.

Sam looked over and saw the expression on her face. "What's wrong?"

Beth opened her mouth to explain her disappointment in herself, and his cell phone started to ring. His hand in his sling came up signaling that he was going to take the call.

Really? He should learn to let it go to voicemail. Especially on a day like this. But before she could judge, she remembered the last time she ignored an important call and let it go.

She didn't mean to eavesdrop, but she couldn't help but wonder what was so important early on a Sunday. Sam answered the call, and instantly a look of concern flashed on his face. She could only make out some of the conversation.

"Thanks for calling... No, it's no bother" He looked at Beth and winked. "That's good news...an expensive gun wow ...Okay if you need anything else...Thanks, Bye."

"What was that about?"

* * *

"It was about the office at the school." Sam regretted mentioning it as soon as he said it. How much should he share? This was going pretty well, and he didn't want to ruin it and scare her.

"What happened at the school? You never did tell me." Her face looked up at him with wonder.

God, she was beautiful this morning.

"Well, I didn't want you to worry. My office was in terrible shape when I got there the other night. The sheriff seems to think that it was a personal attack." That was enough to answer her question without giving her reason to be scared.

"Who would want to hurt you?"

"I have no idea, and now they know what type of gun they are looking for. "

Her eyes were huge. "A gun? They used a gun at the school. That's crazy. Sam, you should have told me."

Shit. He'd said too much. Why did he tell her? Sam ran his fingers down her cheek and grabbed her chin, tipping it up so he could kiss her. "You don't need to be adding anything to your plate right now. I don't want you to worry about me. Take care of the house and the gallery. This is going to be resolved soon, and I can put my office back together for the new school year."

"But what if you were there? You could have been hurt."

He sensed concern and what he thought was anger in her voice.

"You can't keep things like that from me just because you think I have a lot going on. You have a lot on your plate too." She brushed the sand off his arm.

He could tell she was trying to be brave, but her face was etched with worry. "Enough about that. How is the art hunt going?" Yes, he opted for a distraction. He didn't want to argue with her right now. Last night was too perfect to ruin this morning. He grabbed the blanket and folded it. Sand flew off the plaid fabric. He casually tossed it in the boat and organized the rest of the supplies, so they had room for themselves. Popping the top of the cooler, there was still plenty of ice for their catch from the night before.

She updated him on Martin's new acquisitions of the week. Her face beamed as she described the pieces. The tension he saw before disappeared. Good. Her hands moved in the air as she motioned showing him on an imaginary wall how the pieces would fit on the main display. He helped her get in the boat, and she didn't pause for a moment. He started the motor and moved across the river. He could only hear every other word, but her excitement was infectious. The boat bounced on the waves; spray covering them with the brackish water. It didn't take them long to arrive at the boat ramp. It was very busy with sportsmen ready for a Sunday morning of fishing. They waited for their turn slowly trawling in the no wake zone. When there was room, Sam reluctantly interrupted her.

"I'm going to need your help again. You ready?" He pulled alongside the dock and quickly tied off the boat. He jumped up out of the boat and leaned down to help her. She grabbed his hand and stretched to put her foot on the dock. "Nope, turn around and put your butt up here." Beth did as he suggested and could easily sit down on the walkway.

"Wow, that was better."

"Stay with the boat." He ran up the dock and retrieved the truck and trailer. He could see her watching him back down the ramp lining up the trailer with the waterway. Setting the parking brake, he was on autopilot. He jumped in the boat again unloading the important cargo onto the dock. He decided it was best to leave the cooler secured to the seat. Untying the boat, he guided it toward the trailer. She was still watching him, moving out of his way when he needed. "Can you carry some of the stuff to the truck while I get the boat attached."

"Sure."

He watched her struggle to fill her arms so she could make fewer trips. Sam was less conscious of her eyes now that he was busy. He hooked the straps and cranked the handle to pull the boat up onto the trailer. The boat traveled smoothly through the water and was soon on the rollers. In one leap, he was out of the bed and back into the truck. He pulled the truck out of the way and joined Beth on the dock to finish loading the rest of the gear. After organizing the bed, Sam started the truck. "Are you ready for some breakfast?"

Buckling her seatbelt, she smiled at him. "Absolutely."

Sam leaned over on the console and grabbed her hand as he steered the truck onto the highway.

* * *

THUNDER CRACKED, and flashes of lightning illuminated the large oak trees. The rain made Beth's shirt cling to her body as she looked around the now-familiar yard. Her first instinct was to run to the shed like she had so many times to save Selah. Screams came from inside the small wooden shack. Waves crashed against the bulkhead across the street filling the yard with water. She knew what would come next. Light from the window shined through the lace curtains of the main house's large side picture window, and a slight movement caught Beth's eye. A woman peeked out, watching. Beth ran into the house. In the main room, the older woman dressed in a black dress with a stiff lace collar crossed the floor quickly and placed a large ring of keys in a desk drawer before sliding it shut.

"Now you will do as you're told," she said as a smile appeared on her face.

The look caused shivers to run up Beth's spine. *How could she do that? Didn't she know how dangerous it was out there?* Beth ran to the woman's side.

"You can't lock her in there," she screamed. She stood in front of the woman, but she ignored Beth's pleas. "Please unlock the door." Beth reached out to shake her but couldn't grasp the stiff taffeta of the woman's dress.

"You will not leave us," the woman smugly stated before going back to the window, her dress floating over the wooden floor.

Beth followed her, watching over her shoulder. The shed started to sway and collapse. Wood splinters and boards filled the water in the yard. A gasp escaped the woman's mouth. "No! The baby!" She ran to the door and down the stairs to the yard, Beth close behind her. "Not the baby," she yelled.

* * *

BETH WOKE SCREAMING, "The baby, the baby."

The loud noise of the truck hitting alert strips brought her back to reality as Sam pulled the truck on the shoulder of the road. The truck jerked to a stop, and Sam pulled her into his arms. "Shh. Shh. It's okay. You're all right."

"The baby. There was a baby." Tears ran down her cheeks.

"What do you mean? You just drifted off to sleep. You were dreaming." Sam held her tighter.

"No, there was a baby. In the shed."

"But Beth, you were only dreaming." Sam's hands brushed her hair out of her face. His eyes connected with hers.

"It was so real. The shed collapsed, and she said there was a baby." Beth had trouble catching her breath in between sobs. "I couldn't save her; Selah died because I couldn't save her. What if there was a baby too?"

"You aren't making sense, honey, calm down. You had a nightmare."

"Don't tell me to calm down. You weren't there. It's my fault."

"You can't take that on your shoulders. She died two hundred years ago; that isn't your fault. It's part of history. You can't change that. I think you need to lay off the diary for a while."

She pushed against his chest forcing him back to his side of the cab. "How can you say that? It matters to me." Emotion filled her voice. Her eyes were looking at him, but she couldn't see through her tears. "How much farther?" Tears continued to roll down her face. Her breaths came in gasps as she tried to calm herself.

"Not much longer. Look, I didn't mean to upset you. I had a good time last night and didn't mean to ruin it." He turned on the blinker and checked for traffic. She felt the truck accelerate and laid back in her seat.

"Can you just take me home? I don't feel well." She turned her face toward her window. She watched the trees blur as Sam pulled onto the highway. She told herself not to fall asleep. She couldn't return to the horrible nightmare. If she couldn't save Selah, then she would have to stay awake for now.

TUCK POINTING

*S*am looked down at his students' papers blindly.

Compare and contrast English architecture of the Tudor and the Stuart period and how it correlates with the social mores of the day.

He needed to catch up on his school work. There were some thinkers in this class, but some were struggling. But his thoughts were elsewhere.

What was he supposed to do? Beth had only been dreaming. Couldn't she realize it wasn't real? She had been so upset. He only wanted her to relax and enjoy the rest of their trip. She made him drop her off at the curb in front of her apartment without a hug or a kiss goodbye.

Oh man, he'd blown it. But maybe it was for the best. He could finish the job and help her open then concentrate on other things. He shuffled the papers in front of him again. The letter from the North Carolina State University slipped out of the pile; his invitation for a position. Maybe he should take it. But having just discussed why he wanted to stay there with Beth made even considering the job offer cowardly. It was impossible. *Concentrate, man. Concentrate.* It must be the pressure of the opening and the city council meeting this week. That's why she acted that way. He pushed it out of his mind by telling himself he would call her later to check in. Grabbing the next essay, he sat back in his office chair twirling his ink pen between his fingers.

The small Tudor houses of Mill Street, Warwick are an example of the end...

Ugh. Why should this be the end of something great? He felt stupid. He threw the paper and pen across the room and ran his fingers through his hair. He went to the sleek entrance table where he had dropped his phone and keys earlier. Picking up the phone, he dialed Beth's number half expecting her to let it go to voicemail while hoping she wouldn't.

RED-LINED PLANS

*S*elah sat in her rocking chair and watched Beth cross the bedroom to the closet and flip on the closet light. Beth's hands flew up in the air.

"Where is my freakin bag? I can't believe this. And what are you staring at?"

She looked right at Selah. The rocking chair stilled.

"You are making me crazy. I don't need your stress and my stress, your loss, and my loss."

"I'm here for you, to keep you safe."

"Safe from what? I'm not in danger. The only thing you have done is scare the shit out of me and make me paranoid. I've got to get out of here."

"You are in danger. He's watching. You need to listen."

"I'm going to my Mom and Dad's and get away from this craziness." She looked under the bed. "Now, if I can just find my bag."

She picked up her music box and pushed the buttons to make it chime.

Selah shook her head. Beth was so stubborn.

"Ah, I remember. The day of the last inspection, I dropped it in the front room, right by the front door. I'll just run real quick and get it."

"No, you can't go over there. He…"

"Nope. No more about what *he* is doing. I'm leaving town for a while. You and whoever 'he is' can find someone else to watch."

"But, Beth you are my friend, and this is danger…"

"Go away, Selah. I don't need you here." Beth turned to the closet, held clothes up in the air, and laid some on the bed.

Selah sat still, trying not to be noticed. She had a lot of practice being invisible in a room. Based on the clothes in a pile, it looked like Beth was planning to leave for a few days. She wondered if Beth was ignoring her or couldn't see her anymore. The later made her sad. She had grown accustomed to being in Beth's presence and really enjoyed her company.

"Okay, now to the house." Beth grabbed her keys and rushed out the door, throwing the deadbolt behind her. Selah could hear her footsteps on the stairs.

Beth's music box started to play and danced on the bedside table. The vibration pushed it over the wood surface. Selah tried to grab it, but it fell through her hands to the floor. Something was wrong. Beth was not thinking straight. Why did she leave her box behind? Why won't she listen? The box continued to vibrate on the Oriental rug. Selah paced around the room. Suddenly, she stopped and faded from the room.

* * *

BETH SLOWLY STROLLED down the street. The fresh air cleared her head a bit. She turned the corner to the house, and it stood dark and empty. A fog had settled in as the sun set and blanketed the waterfront. It felt strangely eerie without all the usual activity. Goosebumps rose on her skin as she took in the yard. An Easterly breeze blew the steam as it rose from the ground. As she grew closer, the hairs on the nape of her neck prickled and a shiver ran through her. Something wasn't right. Her brain told her to turn and run, but she shook off the warning. She was imagining things, she rationalized. Her bag should be in the front room. She'd just grab it and go. Maybe she should start the car first. Nah, she'd be quick.

Selah stepped from the front door with a moses basket tucked under her arm and a huge smile on her face as she hurried around the side of the house. Beth walked to the left of the front yard and watched her disappear into the mist. She refused to fall for the ghost's antics again. She always ended up soaked when she followed her.

"Go Away," the familiar voice said, "You shouldn't be here right now. Leave. Leave, now."

"You don't have to tell me again. I just need my bag. I'll be quick. I told you to go away," she shouted toward the mist. Her shoes sounded heavy on the wood planks as she stepped onto the porch. She reached for the door and realized the front door was cracked open. Slowly she pushed the door.

"Hello? Anyone there?" She tried the light switch, but nothing responded. She moved farther into the house. It was pitch black.

Her eyes widened as they started to focus in the darkness. She couldn't believe the front room. All she could do was let out a piercing scream. She couldn't catch her breath as the sound disappeared into her throat. *Why would someone do this? Why?* Suddenly, an arm reached around her and covered her mouth. She felt rough beard as a muffled, "Shut up, ungrateful bitch," rang in her ear. A strange chemical odor filled her nostrils. Her throat started to close, and everything went black.

* * *

SHE DIDN'T PICK up her phone. Sam had started pacing. Should he drive over and apologize in person? Why won't she pick up? A text, maybe she will respond to a text.

SAM: Worried about you, need to apologize, please call.

HE DIDN'T WAIT for a reply and instead grabbed his keys and his phone. His palm felt a vibration, as it rang startling him. His heart jumped thinking it was her. He hit the button. "Hey, I've been trying to call you."

"I haven't got any calls from you," a male voice said on the other end of the line.

Confused, Sam looked at the screen and saw that it was Bill. "What'cha need? I was waiting for a call from Ms. Pearse."

"I was calling to let you know that there was a dispatch out to the Water Street house. I'm on the other end of the county, so Tim is headed over."

"What kind of call?"

"A noise complaint. The neighbors heard a scream. We get the calls for noises in the night all the time. Usually turns out to be an opossum or a cat. Maybe you can head over in case he needs in the house."

"Sure, no problem." Sam was already in his truck turning the ignition.

"Call me if you need backup. I'll bring the trap."

This was the perfect excuse he needed to drive into town. It would give him a reason to stop by the apartment and fill her in on the exciting trapping expedition.

He pulled on the main road and sped into town. No sense in making Tim wait for backup. The ten-minute drive seemed like an eternity. Sam pulled into the drive and noticed that the house was completely dark. There should have been one or two work lights burning. He'd talk to the guys about it in the morning. Tim's squad car pulled in behind him.

"What took you so long? I thought I would have to go in alone."

Tim looked puzzled. "I just got the call five minutes ago, over my radio. Came right over."

"No problem, man. I'm just giving you shit. How you want to do this?"

"I'll walk the outside perimeter just in case. Then we will check the inside. Keep an eye on the front if you don't mind."

"Okay. Yell if you need me."

Tim nodded and disappeared around the side of the house. He would have to get the alarm system working sooner than later. It would make him feel better. He heard a rustling in the bushes and Tim soon appeared covered in leaves.

"Nothing strange. Some large footprints but with your guys working here; that's not a big deal. Let's go ahead and check the inside."

Sam put the keys in the door and turned the knob. "That's odd. The deadbolt is thrown."

"You guys don't typically lock that?"

"No, we just lock the door. It's a separate key. Beth, Ms. Pearse, has a key and me. I didn't make extra's."

"Okay. I'm calling for backup. An animal didn't throw the deadbolt. We will wait to go in. Get back in your truck."

The deputy motioned toward the vehicles and grabbed his radio from his shoulder. He slowly walked back to the truck, passing Beth's car. What was he going to do? Just watch? No way. He stopped and turned but caught Tim's gaze.

"Get back in the truck," the deputy said more forcefully this time and pointed to it.

"But I…" Sam tried to explain his desire to help.

"Now."

"Okay, okay, I'm going." Sam turned back around and rushed back to the cab. He could hear the sirens in the distance as they came into earshot. He slammed the door and peered through the windshield. Looking from window to window, he nervously watched for any movement in the house. It was getting darker by the minute, and the fog that blanketed the property played tricks on his eyes. One minute he saw a figure upstairs and then the next, there was nothingness. He tried to call her cell again, and it went to voicemail again. He slapped the dash of the truck. "Where is she?" He hoped that she was just mad and not picking up, but he had a bad feeling. There were no signs that she had even been at the house. Her car was still parked in its usual spot since she preferred to walk around town. He was probably being stupid.

The squad cars arrived in the lot and filled the sky with psychedelic red and blue flashes against the mist. The other deputies met with Tim at his car and Sam watched as they split into two groups. One went around the side of the house, and the other went in the front door. It felt like time slowed down as he watched them force their way through the deadbolt lock. Sam flinched as the door facing splintered into a million pieces. The brand-new front door that he had perfectly matched to the original hung at an awkward angle. Flashlights on the deputies' heads flashed in the windows, reflecting off the walls. Sam tracked the lights as they traveled quickly to the second floor.

Sam was so transfixed by the action inside the house that he was startled when Tim knocked on his window.

"She is not in the house," Tim said. "There is some vandalism inside, though. Have you had any contact with Ms. Pearse today?"

"Not since this morning," Sam responded.

And what time was that?" Tim asked.

"Around eleven, I was on my way to talk to her when I received the call about the house."

"Why not just call?"

"She's not picking up her cell. Honestly, I'm worried," Sam admitted.

"We will check the apartment. You can head on home. We will call you if we need you. Do me a favor, don't leave town." Tim requested

"Really, Tim. What's that supposed to mean?" Sam looked at Tim questioning him.

"You were the last person to see Ms. Pearse, and we may need to talk to you." Tim tried to reassure him.

"Can you at least ask her to give me a call if she is at the apartment?"

"Sure, no problem."

Tim hurried over to his squad car, his fingers pressing the button on the side of the radio on his shoulder. Tim's face turned to one of concern, and he looked right at Sam's gaze. He mouthed. She's not there. Sam's shoulders fell as he felt a weight land on them instantly. She was missing. Beth was gone.

"I have to go. You need to go home. Call the guys and let them know, no work tomorrow. We have a crime scene."

Sam watched as the junior deputies taped the house with police caution tape. They may as well tape his heart. It must be the same person that had destroyed his office. Why didn't he give her more warning? What if they had her? He tried to shake off the feeling but couldn't. A chill ran up his spine. Oh God, what will they do to her?

He climbed into the cab and shined the headlights into the house. There was no one inside, and he could see into the main room. Everyone had been ordered out so that no evidence would be disturbed. Sam saw writing on the wall, and his fears became more real. It was only part of the message, but he guessed the rest. "UNGRA BIT" Instantly, he called Bill's phone. *He better get his ass here or have a really good reason not to.* The cell phone on the other end rang with no answer. Where the hell was he? He needs to be here handling this, not some junior deputy.

"Bill, you need to be here. Someone has taken Beth, and there were threats painted on the wall in the house. Where are you?" Sam's voice was loud and forceful. Probably not the best way to ask for help, but damn it, why wasn't anyone answering their phones?

ALIGATORING

*S*eptember 22, 2014

Beth woke with a massive pounding in her head. Everything was dark, and all she could hear was the lapping of water. She tried to move and realized that her hands were taped tight together at her waist. The dampness in the air clung to her skin. She struggled again trying to twist free, her brain foggy. She tried to remember how she got where she was, but she couldn't think straight. She knew she was in a boat and there was someone behind her steering. *She was in a boat. Details, remember the details.* Suddenly, the burning returned to her nostrils, and the darkness overcame her again.

* * *

EXHAUSTED, Sam went by Mom's Grill for coffee and conversation. Martha was always a comfort no matter how preachy she got. Soon as he stepped into the small store, Martha came around the counter and wrapped her arms around him.

"You poor baby. Samuel, come here and have a cheese biscuit. Tell me what happened last night at the house. I won't tell you 'I told you so.' Get your coffee, and I'll meet you at the table. Tabitha has the grill."

"There's not much to tell. Someone trashed it, and now Beth is missing." Sam sighed.

"We heard the sirens and wondered what was going on. They never use those sirens. I'm telling you it's that house. You should just walk away right now. You haven't heard anything from the girl?"

"Beth. Her name is Beth, and no I haven't heard from her. We argued yesterday morning on the way home from fishing, and I thought she was ignoring me."

"You took her fishing? It must be serious." Martha tried to lighten his mood.

"Then the thing with the house. I should have listened to my gut."

Tabitha brought over a cheese biscuit, and Martha shoved it at Sam. "Eat something. Does the sheriff know anything?"

"Not yet. Not that I know of, anyway. Bill won't call me back. No one will talk to me. They are treating me like a criminal, and all I want to do is help. I need something to do. I can't even work at the house now." Sam ran his fingers through his hair. His face showed worry and tiredness. "I tried grading papers, but I can't even see the words. I'm so tired, but it's impossible to sleep." He took a sip of coffee.

"You could fix the shed door for me. It just won't close right. You can handle that with your cast, right?" Martha looked over at Tabitha and gave her a wink.

"This thing doesn't slow me down much," he bragged, raising his cast. "Shed door huh?"

"Yep should keep you busy for a while. Plus, you will be here in town if anyone needs you." She grabbed Sam's good hand. "You need to stay away from the house. The police will find you if they need you."

"Thanks, Ms. Martha. I'll look at it and head over to the hardware store. I'll have it fixed before you head home this afternoon." Sam grabbed his biscuit and coffee and headed out the door. Busy work was exactly what he needed. He had the feeling that Martha could have fixed the door herself, but he didn't mind. He took some measurements and headed the hardware store for some new hinges.

* * *

THE SMALL BEAM of sunlight breaking through the ceiling of the concrete room hurt Beth's eyes. It would disappear and then come back. The call of a gull was faint, but it was still there. She had been in the dark for so long. She tried to focus her eyes and collect her thoughts. Someone had her, and she didn't know why. Her body started to shake. There was nothing on the walls except for soot and ash. The floor was swept clean but had centuries of dirt ground into the surface. She was on a dirty mattress, her hands still bound. Rope cut into her wrists and ankles. The musty smell of the damp air lingered, and the complete silence enveloped her. Her mouth was covered with duct tape, so she couldn't even talk to herself. The mind was an evil thing when she was left alone with her memories.

Stay positive. I must stay positive. Someone will miss me. The house was a mess. Someone will look for me. The message was meant for me "Ungrateful Bitch." Painted in Red. Who would do something like that? Would Sam even care? I was so hateful to him. He was right. It was just a dream about the past. I need him to care. Please look for me, Sam. Please.

161

The silence was broken by the sound of scraping in the corner. A bright light turned on and shined directly on her. A figure dressed in black crossed in front of the lamp creating a large shadow over her. Gloved fingers slowly pulled the duct tape from her mouth. The pain was excruciating. Tears slowly rolled from her eyes, and she started to shake.

"Please don't hurt me."

The figure placed a notebook on her lap with writing on it. At the top, it said, "You will read this for the camera, and you will not be hurt." Manhandling her up by her wrists, the person shifted her, upright, so her back was against the wall. It then returned to the space behind the light. Beth could see a small red light on a camera. When the figure pointed to her, she started to read.

"I am Elizabeth Lewis Pearse, and I am being held for ransom. I have not been hurt. Do not contact the police. I will be returned for 2 million dollars. Further instructions will follow in 24 hours. If you involve the police or do not pay, I will be killed."

The camera and light turned out, and the darkness returned. Beth screamed, "Help, Help me." A quick, gloved hand covered her mouth with tape to quiet her and slammed her back on the mattress. She heard the footsteps as they disappeared, and she was left with her thoughts again. She listened for any sound in the darkness. She would have welcomed Selah's company at that moment. A small pitter-patter appeared, and her mind began playing tricks on her. Mice. Not her favorite animal. The chill in the air brought goosebumps to her skin. The temperature was dropping, and she had nothing to cover herself with, not that she could move from her position to grab it. All she could do was doze off.

TYMPANUM

 he hardware store was a quick trip from the grill. Sam only needed a couple of two-inch hinges, and the door would be sturdy as new. He knew Robert would hook him right up. The bell rang as he walked through the door and he saw the owner at the counter. "Hi, Mike. Where's Robert?"

"The heck if I know. I haven't seen him in a couple of days. If you see him, tell him to get his butt back to work." The older man grimaced as he moved from behind the counter. "It was good to have him around."

"I know what you mean. I need a couple of hinges. I got it if you don't mind. Go ahead and stay here."

"Thanks, help yourself."

Sam browsed the aisle of hardware looking in the bins and locating the hinges. He tried to remember if there was anything else he needed, picking up some wood screws. "Hey, Mike, do you have any screw bits for these decking screws?"

"Check on the end of the aisle by the smaller packages."

"Got it."

Sam wandered back to the front counter, "I think this is it. I might be back this afternoon."

"Okay. How are you holding up?" Mike asked while he rang in the items. "I heard what a hatchet job they made of the front door at the house. You gonna need a new one?"

"Yep, if you'll order the same one."

"No problem. It will be $5.65 today."

"Here you go. I'll see you later." Sam grabbed his bag and headed out the door. The elderly owner hopped back on his stool at the counter. Hopefully, Robert would show back up. He had been a huge help over the last few months, and good help was hard to find. Sam wondered where he'd run off to. He was really good at his job. Sam drove over to the Grill and got busy with the shed. He took the doors off and laid them flat to make sure that they were not warped. His cell vibrated, and when he looked at the screen, he felt relieved. Bill; finally calling him back.

"Hey man, where you been?" he answered.

"Hey to you too. Sorry, like I said last night, I was busy. What'cha need?" Bill asked.

"I need someone to tell me what the hell is going on. I need you to tell me if Beth is okay. You have to know what is going on."

"I can't tell you."

"You can do better than that."

"Soon as we know more and when I can share it with you, I will. Have *you* heard from Ms. Pearse?"

"No, I still haven't heard anything. I'm worried. Call me if you hear anything, will you?"

"Will do if I can," Bill emphasized the 'can.' "They still might call you in for more questions. We are trying to put together a timeline."

"No problem, just call me. I'll be right down."

"I have to go."

"Okay. Hope to talk to you soon with good news." Sam disconnected and went back to work. Soon the shed had fully functional doors that would lock. He knocked on the back door of the grill, and Ms. Martha poked her head out the door to inspect his handy work. She turned and gave him a big hug.

"Samuel, very fine work. What do we owe you?"

"Not a thing. It was my pleasure. Besides, it kept me from going crazy."

"At least let me give you a biscuit."

"Okay, tomorrow I will drop by for coffee and a cheese biscuit." He knew it was useless to resist her. She gave him another tight squeeze, and he packed all his tools in the truck. He couldn't help himself and drove by the Water Street house. It was busy with police, probably experts from Greenville. It seemed like too many cars for a little vandalism in his opinion. Something big was going on, and he had no idea what. It was killing him.

WROUGHT IRON STAGGERED PICKETS

*S*eptember 24, 2014

Fingers ran through her hair in soothing strokes and relaxed her for a moment. She forgot where she was. A lullaby tune hummed near her ear, coaxing her awake. Beth opened her eyes and as they focused she recognized a familiar face. Selah. She must have heard her wish for company. Beth's head lay on her lap, and Selah brushed the tangles out of her dark hair. Beth started to struggle.

"Shh. Save your strength. You are so hard-headed. I told you not to go in the house. When are you going to listen?" Selah whispered. She continued the motion and the lecture. "I had a sister just like you. Lizzy just wouldn't listen. Got in trouble with the Master's son, she did. Now she's in heaven with his baby. You've got to listen. He's got you now, but he won't hurt you. He's got too much to lose. Just bide your time."

Beth tried to answer her, but the tape dammed her voice. She wanted to scream, "Who is it?" Nothing escaped. She couldn't breathe; her chest hurt from her lungs trying to push the air in and out of the restricted space. Her eyes bulged with exertion.

"Shh. Calm down. There is nothing to fear right now. I am here, and I won't leave you." There was a sound of chains and a scraping of metal across the cement floor. And Selah was gone.

"I'm here," whispered her voice of comfort.

Beth lay trembling on the blanket, afraid of what was coming despite Selah's reassurance. What would they do with her? Soon the figure loomed over her, dressed in black as before. She could not see their face because of a black mask. They sat her up as before with her back against the wall and placed the pad of paper on her lap. They ripped the duct tape off her now raw skin around her mouth. She licked her lips and could taste the metallic liquid of blood.

Rising and turning their back to her, they went across the room and turned on the spotlight. Beth was blinded once again. Hours in the dark caused her not to see with the light present. How long had they left her alone? She had no sense of time. The person stood in front of her casting a shadow, bending down they lifted a coffee cup to her mouth. The warm liquid warmed her throat as she swallowed its contents. Chicken soup, just the broth, though. After she finished the whole cup, they gently washed her face with a baby wipe. The gentle touch was so different from the way she had been handled earlier.

Walking back to the light, the red light on the camera turned on, and the hand in the light pointed at her. On cue, Beth started the read her voice hoarse with dehydration.

"I remain unhurt. The funds are to be placed in the off-shore bank account that you received in this email. I will be released when the funds are confirmed. I remind you there should be no involvement with the police. The police activity at the house is disconcerting. Do not risk my life. Just pay them."

The camera and light turned off. Beth started to plead, "Please don't hurt me. I need to pee. Please, let me go out and use the bathroom." The large hands of the kidnapper soon replaced the tape and laid her back down on her side. She would not give her captor the satisfaction of wetting herself. She tried to hold it, but it was no use. What was going to happen to her?

* * *

THE GRAVEL under Sam's feet shifted with his gait as he ran up the shoulder of the road. The music that played on his phone did little to distract him. It had been forty-eight hours since Beth disappeared and still they would tell him nothing. *Damn them.* They had interviewed him several times. Asking him about their date and the argument. They asked him about her planned trip to Virginia. She hadn't said anything to him about going anywhere. Besides her car was still at the house. He tried to concentrate on his breathing instead of her disappearance. A call broke through the music, and he looked at the number. It was an international number that he had never seen. He picked it up.

"Hello, Sam Howards speaking."

"Bonjour, this is Martin Pommier. I am Beth's art dealer. Monsieur Howards have you heard from Beth?"

"No, but she told me that you are close friends."

"That is correct."

"She has been missing since Sunday. No one has seen or heard from her."

"I have just received something via the computer that I think you should see. I am flying to the States right away. Can you pick me up at the airport?"

"Of course, which airport are you flying into?"

"I was going to ask you which would be the most convenient. I am at the airport now in line to buy my ticket and check in."

"Greenville would be the closest."

"Okay, done. I will text you my itinerary as soon as I know the details."

"Okay. What did you receive?"

"I can't talk now. I will see you soon."

The phone went dead. Sam stood in the middle of the road. He bent over and grabbed his head with both hands. Straightening, he let out a yell that echoed through the woods. The blackbirds left their perches in the pines. He felt so out of control. This was why he didn't get involved with women. He didn't like this feeling of vulnerability. He felt useless. He needed to find something to do and quick.

"Siri, call Bill." The cell dialed the deputy, and to Sam's surprise, Bill picked up. "Hi Bill, it's Sam."

"Hey, what'cha need?"

"Is there any way I can start cleaning up the house. I need something to do. I'm not in the mood to grade papers now."

"Let me check and see where they are on the site, and I will get back to you."

"Thanks. Just give me a call."

"Will do. Look, I'm sorry this is rough on you. We have to be sure." Bill said.

"I know. I just want to find her." Sam responded.

"We all want to find her, Sam."

"It doesn't feel like it."

Silence hung heavy on the other end of the line before Bill answered. "Sorry, you feel that way."

"Just hurry up and do your job." Sam was pissed.

Bill offered a curt, "Will do," and disconnected.

Sam turned back toward home, his stride brisker than he took on the way. He turned the music back on and made time. As he turned up the drive, a text arrived. Martin's itinerary. He was coming in at four in the morning. *Crap*. He'd have to get up early, so he hoped he'd get some sleep tonight.

He headed into the house and over to his desk. The stack of papers seemed overwhelming. He was not doing a good job keeping up with his teaching responsibilities. He needed to change that, and this could keep his mind from thinking of what may be happening to her. He sat down and grabbed the first paper with his red pen. Some of his students complained he requested all papers be turned in on paper. He liked the feel of the paper. It added a tangible feel to the student's abstract ideas. Papers were now overtaking his desk, and he regretted not having digital copies of the two hundred papers he needed to grade. Time to bite the bullet. He put on some music and started grading.

Two hours later and he had made considerable progress. Proud of himself, he decided to get cleaned up and make some lunch. Deciding to make a sandwich, he went to the fridge to collect all the fixings. As the door closed, the hanging calendar caught his eye. Today was circled, and in the memo, he'd listed the town council meeting about the house. He couldn't let them postpone it. It would affect the gallery opening. He decided to go and represent Beth and the gallery. He could at least do this for her. He finished eating his sandwich standing at the counter.

DUROMETER

*B*eth laid on the mattress, dirty and ashamed. Her captor had left her no choice but to soil her clothing. She wondered how long they planned to keep her here. She had only had broth for sustenance. She wanted to hear someone's voice, anyone's. They still had not said a word. The only communication was the notebook to give her orders on what to say for the videos. The gulls were now silent, and there was no noise from the outside world.

Selah comforted her, but she reminded herself that Selah couldn't help her. She wondered if other people could see her ghost companion. Maybe she could get Sam a message. When Selah appeared next, she would ask. But how? She couldn't talk. They had made sure the duct tape was secure, and there was no chance she would call out. The skin on her lips and cheeks showed the scars as proof of the person's unkindness. Maybe she could talk them into leaving the tape off the next time it was removed. It was an idea. All she could do was lie here and think. She was driving herself crazy. She knew she was near the water; they did bring her here on a boat, right?

She thought it was only one person. The figure was the same size in their black outfit. It was hard to tell, but it seemed like a man. The man that grabbed her at the house had a mustache. She felt it next to her ear. So, it was a large man. What else did she know? Her mental list was getting longer. The figure returned with her cup of broth. When the tape was removed, her sores were worse. Blood dripped onto the mattress.

"Can you please not tape my mouth again? I don't think I can handle losing another layer of skin."

The man lifted the cup to her mouth. The broth tasted so good. Pretending it was a fine glass of wine helped her enjoy it, but her stomach told her that it was needed.

"I promise I won't yell or scream. It hurts so bad," she pleaded.

He seemed to agree because he didn't replace it before he left. There was no video this time. The message was sent she supposed. There was a small beam of light coming from the ceiling signaling the start of another day in her dungeon. He left just as he did every time, pulling the gate shut and locking the chains. She waited for a while and then whispered, "Selah are you there? Selah?"

"I am here. Aren't you smart? You got him to leave the tape off. Good job."

"Selah, can you take a message to Sam? Can you talk to him?"

"No, you are the only one who can see me. I don't know why."

"I was hoping you could show him where I am. I'm starting to feel desperate. Nothing seems to be happening."

"Things will start moving soon. Your man Sam is brilliant. He will figure it out. I was at the house after you were taken. He was rushing in to save you before he knew what was wrong."

"Selah, who has me?"

"The one who watches."

"But who is it?"

"He doesn't use his name."

"I just want to scream, but I know if I do, he will tape me again. I don't think I could handle the duct tape again. I'm starting to lose faith, Selah."

"Keep faith, Beth. Whatever you do, keep your faith." Selah brushed her raw cheek. Beth flinched from the pressure. "Do not let him take your spirit."

Selah ran her fingers through Beth's hair and held her gently in her lap. Beth fell asleep with the soothing motion. "Rest, rest, sweet one."

GUN CONSISTENCY

A laugh snuck out. Sam was thankful he was alone. He just couldn't help it. One student had obviously been watching too much cable TV. The afternoon had been a productive one, and a stack of graded papers with constructive criticism sat on his desk as proof. He needed to get his office squared away so he could have office hours. Some of the students were in trouble, and their writing needed someone on one discussion. He would work on it tomorrow.

There was no call from Bill this afternoon, so he guessed the house wasn't ready to be released. His watch reminded him it was time to prepare for the meeting. He gathered up the plans and the business proposal Beth had given him when he was considering the job. He shouldn't need anything else. Hopefully, the council wouldn't question her absence, but he knew it was likely too much to hope for in such a small town. He knew her disappearance was the hot topic of the week.

Riding into town, he drove by the house. The police tape was gone, and a temporary door had been fitted on the front. It looked like the police were finished. Why didn't Bill call? That wasn't like him. He'd ask him tonight. Taking the turn to the town building, Sam noticed the lot wasn't very full. Bill's truck was there. *Good.* Looked like all the council members were there. That's what's important.

Balancing all his props, he swung the front door open to the building and was immediately greeted by Bill.

"I didn't know if you would be here with Beth missing and all. Shouldn't you be out looking for clues or something." Sam confronted him.

"Well, 'hello' to you too." Bill's face showed the strain of the week's events.

"I'm pissed you didn't call, the house looks good to go. I need to get started on the cleanup so she can open on time."

"I'm trying to be as optimistic as you are, but we don't know if she's still alive. You need to face the facts."

"How can I if you guys won't tell me anything?" Sam erupted louder than he had intended, and it called attention to them. "I could help, you know."

"Let's get through this meeting and get the final plans approved, then we will go have some coffee and talk."

"Sounds like a plan," Sam agreed and took a seat in the middle of the meeting room.

The meeting went smoothly. Sam went over the original plans and the adjustments. The cellar didn't change most of the house. He had pictures of the completed rooms of the house and the hand-drawn sketches of the cellar cover. No one questioned why he was doing the presentation instead of Beth. They were impressed with his attention to historical accuracy. One member stated the house will be a "genuine historical document of Washington's Antebellum past." Sam swelled with pride and, as he looked around the room, he wished Beth was there to share the moment. The plans passed unanimously.

She should be here. Sam's heart sank as he remembered Bill's words, *'We don't even know if she is still alive.'* She *was* alive. She *had* to be. He would know if she was gone. He had to keep his faith. Just one clue. It was all they needed. After the meeting concluded, he shook all the council member's hands and thanked them for their time before he searched for Bill. Where did he disappear to? Sam hung out watching everyone slowly disappear and then went out to the lot.

"Damn it."

Bill's truck was gone.

Sam dialed his number, and of course, it went straight to voice-mail. "Hey man. I don't understand why you are dodging me. Thanks for coming tonight, but I really wanted to talk to you. Call me back."

Sam swung by the sheriff's office on his way back to his house. Tim was at his desk working on paperwork.

"Hey, Tim. How are you doing?"

"I'm exhausted. This case is killing me. So much paperwork for a missing person. Hopefully, she will show up soon."

"So, she's officially missing?"

"Yep, the sheriff ruled it a missing person case. The house has been cleared of evidence. You can start work again. I wanted to apologize for what a mess the officers made when they went in."

"Thanks, man. I appreciate that. How bad is it? I haven't seen the inside yet."

"There was some graffiti on the wall, but that's about it besides the door of course," Tim winced.

"The door was enough. I'll start work tomorrow. Is there any reason to worry? You guys didn't find anything that showed she was hurt, did you?"

"Nothing at all. We are staying in contact with her parents in Virginia. They said they received a text from her saying she was headed there. We are hoping she is on her way there and got delayed for some reason. Her car setting in the drive is the sticker. Let us know if you hear anything."

"Will do. Gotta go. Keep me updated."

"Will do," Tim said passively as he turned back to his computer.

Sam headed out to his truck. He would get started on the house tomorrow after his trip to Greenville. Martin was coming in early enough. As he drove down the waterfront, he noticed Jose's truck parked at Down on Main Street. A beer would be good. Plus, he'd give Jose the okay to start work tomorrow.

Sam strolled in the back door squeezing past the wait staff in the back hallway. A waitress smiled up at him as he walked by. Sam had always been on the eligible bachelor list, his good looks and family money pushing him to the top. As he emerged from the hallway, the music was just as loud as the laughter filling the bar. It was busy for a Wednesday night. Beers were flowing, and Sam noticed his buddies surrounding the pool table in the corner. This would distract him from his concerns, at least for a while. Too much time had passed for Beth to still be on her way to her parent's house. Three days was way too long.

The waitresses tried their best to catch his attention, but he didn't care. The break of the rack of balls caught it instead.

"Nice break Mike. What have you been up to this week?"

"Hey man, nice of you to show up." Jose slapped him on the shoulder.

"I never get invites anymore."

"We got tired of you telling us you were busy."

"Okay. Fill me in on what's happening around town." The guys opened their mouth, Sam grabbed a stick and added, "that doesn't include me." The men laughed, and Jose aimed a shot for the far-right pocket.

"Oh man, I finally took delivery of my boat. She is so sweet. We should go out this weekend," Mike started while waiting for Jose to finish his turn at the table.

"This is the speedboat, right?" Sam took a swig of beer before he took a shot of the four-ball balancing his stick on his cast.

"Yep. The perfect ski boat. You need to get you one." Mike said.

"Why when all my friends have one?" Sam laughed looking up from the table.

"I know you've had your eye on that one down at the yard for a while," Jose chimed in. "It's been sitting there waiting for you. I could borrow it while you're working."

"I would never see it." Sam laughed. As he dropped the 8 ball, he added, "besides I don't have time for it right now. It hasn't moved in four years, it's not going anywhere. It will be there when I'm ready."

"That's where you're wrong, Sam. That beauty was picked up last week when I was down at the shop arranging delivery for mine."

"Did he finally sell it for the dry dock fees? Someone got a steal."

"Nope, the owner finally showed. The last name was Pearse, I think."

Beer spewed out of Sam's mouth, the spray spotting the table felt. "What? Ah, damn it. Sorry." He grabbed some napkins to dry the table top before it damaged it. A waitress rushed over to help him. Sam didn't notice in his daze. "Why would she need a boat?"

Jose laughed loudly.

Mike answered. "It wasn't Beth. It was a guy, but it didn't look like he could afford a boat. Yet, they were treating him like he was made of money. Warren asked him what he had been up to. He just said that he was traveling and couldn't contact them. It was bizarre."

"A guy?"

"Yeah, a guy. What's wrong with you? He didn't have a trailer with him. He had them drop it in at the launch, and he drove away down the river like he was headed somewhere important."

"Sam here," Jose said with a finger pointed at Sam, "has been looking for his girl this week. He thinks someone has taken her. Why I have no idea. It sounds like a bunch of kids tearing shit up to me. I think she just decided she's had enough of this small town and headed for some excitement."

"First, she's not my girl. We've only been on a couple of dates. Second, she's in the middle of a massive project, she wouldn't take off, no matter how bored she was."

Mike had a look of shock and amazement on his face. "Did you say a couple of dates? You went on a date?"

Sam knocked him on the shoulder. "Shut up. I date."

"When was the last date this man went on, Jose?"

"I honestly can't remember." Jose's face grimaced as he tapped his forehead like he was searching for a thought. "Maybe since you dated my…"

"Will you guys shut up? It's not like her to drop everything and head out. She cares too much."

"About you? No way." Mike shook his head laughing, "How could she put up with you? We barely can, and we've known you forever."

"I'm not that bad."

"Yes, you are." Both men agreed in unison, giving each other fist pumps.

"What did this Pearse guy look like? Just curious." Sam tried to stay as casual as his friends.

"He looked like a bum, hadn't shaved in weeks. His clothes weren't clean. I don't know, a guy who couldn't afford much of anything and then he left in a damn expensive boat."

"Sounds like you're jealous, dude." Jose laughed.

"Shut up."

"Boat envy," Sam agreed. "How about some real info, man. Tired of hearing he shouldn't be able to afford the boat he has. Hair, eyes, height, you know something that would help me recognize him if I saw him."

"I didn't get a really good look at him. He was our height, probably about our age, dark hair. Sorry, don't really remember much besides the boat. Why are you so grumpy?" Mike shrugged.

"Okay, this is nice and all, but I have to get up early. Beth's art dealer is coming in."

"Are we finally going to be hanging some art in the house?"

"We have to get it cleaned up first, and a front door hung. Meet me at the house at seven. We'll make a plan. Make sure all the guys report by nine."

"Okay boss." Jose took another beer from a pretty blond waitress and arranged another rack of balls. Sam gave the waitress a twenty and waved goodbye to the staff behind the bar. Heading out the back door, there was no moon in the sky, and the stars were brilliant against the clear midnight blue. It was a beautiful night, and all he could think of was her. He prayed she was safe. He jumped into the cab and headed toward the big empty house he called home.

Z-BAR FLASHING

*S*eptember 25, 2014

The trip to Greenville wasn't too bad. At three in the morning, there weren't many people on the roads, so he was right on time to meet Martin at baggage claim. Sam didn't like how secretive he had been about the information he was bringing. It was going to be bad news for sure. People didn't fly around the world to share good news in person. Truth be told, he wasn't sure he was up for more bad news. This week's worth had already worn his resolve thin. The light turned green, and Sam made the turn into the airport. He had no idea what Martin looked like. Sam parked the truck and made his way through the parking garage to carousel number four. He saw a man collecting his leather suitcases and trying to balance them on a cart. Sam suspected this was his passenger. Sensing Martin's frustration, Sam slowly approached him.

"Excuse me, are you Mr. Pommier?"

"Oui, Monsieur Pommier. Martin. You must be Sam." He held out his hand.

Sam's hand swallowed Martin's smaller one. The difference in the two men's sizes was considerable, and the other people at the baggage claim stared as Sam started to tuck bags under his arms. "Here, let me take some of those. We will restack the big ones on the cart."

"Merci."

Sam took four of the smaller ones, while Martin pushed the cart beside him. "My truck is parked out this way. How was your flight?"

"Miserable. I thought I would get some sleep, but it was impossible. So many crying children. I hope you don't mind. I brought extra bags because Sophia and the children will come for the opening. This way she doesn't have to handle the bags and them."

"I was beginning to wonder." Sam gave the man a sideways glance.

"I can only imagine." Martin chuckled. "I have a lot to share with you, but we should wait till we get somewhere private."

"We can go to my house. That way you can shower and rest too."

"Thank you, I can already see why Beth is so fond of you."

Sam unlocked the truck and threw the luggage into the bed.

The ride home was just as uneventful as the trip over. Sam kept the radio low, and there was no conversation between the two men. Martin dozed off finally achieving some of the peace and quiet he sought all night. When the truck pulled into the drive, he had been asleep for half an hour.

Sam turned on the lights as they entered his house and he took the luggage to one of the guest bedrooms. When footsteps didn't follow him down the hall, Sam walked back to the foyer area and found Martin staring at the Miró above the fireplace.

Sam walked up next to him. "You are welcome to stay here as long as you like. There is a bathroom through that door there. Are you hungry? I know the time difference…"

"No, I'm fine for the moment." Martin walked over to the kitchen island and unpacked his briefcase pulling out his laptop. Sam followed him into the kitchen.

"I have something you need to see." He turned on the laptop, and the computer seemed to take an eternity to boot up. "I apologize for being so secretive, but I didn't know who was listening to my phone." Martin pulled up a video and hit play.

Beth, dirty and scared, was sitting in a dark room with a bright light shining on her. Sam's blood started to boil. He knew someone had her, why didn't anyone believe him? Now here was proof. Sam studied her surroundings, but nothing stood out as identifiable. She was reading a note. They were asking for $2 million. Sam noticed the sores on her face. They had hurt her. He couldn't stand it.

Turning to Martin, he demanded, "Who are they? Do you know?"

"I don't know, but they know about her business, details no one knows. It would have to be someone who knows her." The emotion started to break through his businessman demeanor. His French accent became stronger. "I just don't know."

"Did anyone else get this?"

"Non. It came to me specifically. That is peculiar to me."

"Do you have access to that much money?"

"Yes, I have unlimited access to her funds for art purchases. The pieces she wanted were very expensive so no one would raise the alarm if I withdrew that amount of money."

"Really?"

"Yes, Beth's acquisitions have been very significant over the last year. I have had a hard time keeping them quiet so the prices would not inflate."

"I have some friends in the Sheriff's office that could help us out."

"Absolutely not, they are already nervous. I will send the money, and they will release her. Simple"

"It's not that simple. What if they demand more money? You already said they know about her business. They know there is more money. We need to have help."

"You trust these men?"

"Yes, I do. I have known them since we were children. I will make some calls. You should get some rest."

"Okay." Martin closed his laptop and set it on the bureau on one side of the room. "Thank you for your help and letting me stay in your home. You certainly have a sense of style. I was admiring your painting above the fireplace."

"The Miró?" Sam laughed. "Beth loves that painting."

"I bet she does. I've been searching for something very similar for her gallery. She has a specific theme she is following for the art, and I am struggling to find her a Miró."

"I'm sure you will find one."

Martin looked at Sam. "I'm sure I will as well."

Sam closed the door behind him, pulling his cell out of his pocket to start making calls. He started with Bill and gave him a chance to redeem himself for the last week.

* * *

THERE WAS no sun to stream through the crack in the ceiling this morning. The drip of the rainwater made a puddle in the middle of the room. Beth laid on her mattress and listened to the splash of the drips. She let the rhythmic noise hypnotize her. She could hear a heavy rain in the distance. Another storm. Would the rain never stop this summer?

"Selah, are you there?"

"I'm here."

"Will the rain ever stop?"

"This will end. It will end soon."

"I have to get out of here. He is going to kill me. I know he is."

"Be patient, it is not time."

"No one is coming. I don't think anyone has even missed me."

"They are looking."

"No, they aren't, it's been too long."

"Keep your faith."

"How can I? I don't even know where I am or if anyone will come."

"Shush, listen to me when I tell you, timing is everything, and faith is all you sometimes have.

"I was on a beach, waiting for my next conductor to show me the way. I knew I had to get to Washington, but I had no idea where I was or where my next stop was. There was a small fishing hut weathered and barely standing. It was my only shelter and, in the corner, was a barrel of fresh water and fishing gear. I dislike fishing, and I was determined not to fish. My stomach was growling, and I knew I was going to starve to death waiting. I had traveled all this way just to die on the beach. I missed my mom and my family. I left them at the plantation, and it was my fault I was so alone. I went in the shack and sat on the ground and prayed. All I could do was pray. I refused to give up hope. I knew God's timing was perfect.

"I sipped the water and prayed. In three days, my conductor arrived. A beautiful man with a smile that could warm your heart. His name was Abram, and before he took me on the next leg of my journey, he built a fire and cooked some fish. The best meal I ever had. After I was warm, he packed the boat, and we set off across the shoals. You see, you have to believe everything will happen in God's time."

"But, Selah, I have to find a way out. Help me."

"The time will be here soon, have patience." And she was gone.

The gate scrapped across the floor, and her captor brought her daily broth. The warm liquid sated her stomach, but she knew it wouldn't last for long. It did take the chill off her body for the moment. After she was finished, he didn't disappear as he had before. He pulled a blindfold out of his pocket and put it over her eyes. She listened carefully as he moved across the room. She felt the metal of the scissors before she realized what he was doing. He started to cut the sleeves of her t-shirt splitting the fabric up to her neck. He followed the same path on the other side. He was removing her clothing. Beth started to struggle against the rope binding her hands. *He is going to rape me.* Her pulse raced. "No, No, you can't," she screamed. He instantly covered her mouth with his hand.

"Shh, I'm not going to hurt you."

She stopped; stunned. Her brain tried to process what she had heard. Her captor had not spoken to her before this, but the voice was one that couldn't be. It belonged to a dead man. Maybe he was a ghost.

He cut her shorts and panties off removing the filthy clothing. She laid there in shock as he cleaned her exposed skin. It didn't make sense. She started to say something, and a finger moved to her mouth. She wanted to hear his voice again. He slowly unbound her hands and cleaned the raw sores the tape and rope had made. A fresh shirt went over her head, and the rope was retied with tape overtop to make it extra secure. The process was repeated with her ankles, and her shorts were replaced with a pair of jogging pants. He moved the blindfold purposefully making it impossible for her to see what was next. As he finished, she whimpered.

"Brad?"

He shook his head and put his finger to her mouth again. He laid her down in her usual position, removed the blindfold, turned, and left.

"Brad." She said louder, her voice cracking. She must have imagined it. She had finally gone insane. Or maybe they were dead together.

The confinement had surely pushed her over the edge if she believed her dead husband had returned and was holding her hostage. As the chain and lock clanged against the metal gate, she started to give in and lose hope. Her captor was winning.

ABOVE GRADE

*S*am's truck pulled into the driveway, and Jose was already waiting to tour the property. The temporary door the deputies had put up was an eyesore and reminder. It would be replaced as soon as the new one arrived. Jose had propped it open, and Sam figured he'd already been through the house.

"Hey man. How does it look?"

"Not too bad. We will have to repaint. I was looking at the red the vandals used. We should be able to cover it up with some good primer. It is filthy inside from all the foot traffic. The guys can clean up today, and I will take a couple to paint, and we should be back on track tomorrow."

"Okay let's make a detailed punch list. Tomorrow I want the alarm guys in here and complete by the end of the day." Sam looked at Jose questioning whether he should tell him what he had learned earlier.

"You think that will give them enough time?"

"They don't have a choice. I want this place secure before the weekend. Martin is here, and he will want to start placing things soon. We need to have it ready."

Jose's eyebrows raised in surprise. "Yes, sir."

"Sorry, just trying to make sure the house is ready when Beth gets back."

"So, you've heard from her?"

"No, but it's my job to make sure everything runs smoothly in the meantime."

Jose rubbed the back of his neck with his palm. "You've given up your kidnapping idea, right? Boss, she's probably just taking a break. I'm sure she's fine."

"I'm sure you're right," Sam agreed but told himself she wouldn't be fine until he got her back. *Whatever it costs.*

The men did a quick run through. Jose was right about the walls. The red paint used to write the insult to Beth made Sam furious. His face turned as red as the paint as he stood in front of. It would be easily covered, but the image was seared into his memory. White footprints marred the dark stained wood floors. "Be careful when you guys mop these floors. This dust will scratch the finish. Do a good job sweeping, first." Jose nodded, and Sam looked around for anything else that needed to be done. He wondered where the fine dust had come from, there was none on the property. They hadn't used cement on this job at all. They both walked back to Sam's pickup.

"Okay, you've got this, right?"

"Got it."

"I'll be around town. Call me if you need me." Sam shut the door to his cab and backed out of the drive. He gave a little wave and left Jose to handle the least of his worries for the day. He headed to Mom's Grill to grab some breakfast and meet Tim to fill him in. Bill, damn him, didn't pick up his cell again. It was starting to get old.

He rounded the corner and Tim's truck was parked in the side lot. Sam would talk to him before they went in and placed their order. Tim stepped out of his truck when Sam parked beside him.

"What is so important that we have to meet here?"

"Beth's business partner got a ransom video. Somebody has her. The kidnapper said not to contact the police, but you are the only one I trust now."

"No Shit? Where's Bill? I thought you were going to call him."

"I did, and you see who thought it was important to be here."

"Ah man, there must be a reason. Bill wouldn't ignore a call."

"I don't know. He's been ignoring quite a few of mine lately. I can't seem to get five minutes with him."

"I'll get with him. He will want to be in on this. Besides he's fond of Beth, always talking about her and the art."

"Really? I hadn't noticed."

"Yep, in fact, I thought he was going to ask her out until you were seen around town with her. I guess you have to move quickly if you see a good one around here."

"I guess." Sam's mind wandered thinking about the events that happened the last two weeks. Things between Beth and him did move quickly, but she slowed them down the last night they spent together. There was nothing wrong with it. After all, they had their whole lives in front of them. Or did they. Things had changed this week. Sam's future was not as sure as he thought, and Beth's life was definitely not as certain. He physically shook his head.

"Hey man, you there?" Tim stood in front of him waiting for him to answer a question that Sam didn't even hear. "Let's get some breakfast." He put a hand on Sam's shoulder, and the two men went into the small gas station.

Ms. Martha gave him a big smile as he came around the corner. "Hi, Samuel. Tim." She gave Tim a nod. "You want your regular?"

"Yes, ma'am."

"Tim, we don't see you very much. You should stop in more often."

"Yes, ma'am. Your cooking is so good I have to watch myself and my waistline. I'm not as active as Sam here, who can eat here every day."

"Sweet talker."

"Just being honest, Ms. Martha."

"I'm going to need an extra biscuit for a friend who's visiting. Make it the best one you have. He's from out of town, and we want to impress him."

"Samuel, are you implying I wouldn't give you the best?"

"Of course not." He smiled at the older woman, giving her a wink. She grinned and wrapped up an extra biscuit.

Handing the bags over the counter, she commented, "You boys be good now. We don't need you getting into trouble."

"No ma'am," they both said in unison and headed over to the cashier to pay for breakfast.

As Sam got into his cab, he yelled over the top, "Meet you at the house." Tim nodded and started his truck. As the trucks headed out of town, the rain started.

The storm grew worse. Sam could hardly see through the windshield. Another bad one. This summer had been the wettest he'd ever seen, and now the Fall was taking on the same theme. Hopefully, they wouldn't have any hurricanes. Sam knew not to hope too hard. They always seemed to show up when he needed clear weather. The bigger the project, the bigger the storm. They still needed to get the landscaping done at the gallery. He would make a final list this week so the crew could knock it out. The truck started to slide in the high water as he turned onto the highway. He slowed the truck and paid closer attention to the road. It wasn't a long trip, but high water could be dangerous. They pulled into his drive, and he waited for Tim to pull up beside him.

Sam rolled down his window. "We need to be quiet when we go in, Martin had a long flight, and he didn't get much sleep." Tim gave him a thumb up, and they both jumped out of their trucks and made a run for it. They were soaked through when they made it inside. Sam went to the back and got a couple of towels. "Here you go."

"Thanks." Tim grabbed one and dried off. "So, what's the plan?"

"We will get with Martin when he is up. I saw Mike and Jose at the bar last night. Mike mentioned that a Mr. Pearse picked up his boat down at the boatyard last week. I didn't say anything to Martin this morning, but I think it could be something."

"You think he's related to Beth?"

"Maybe."

"I'll go by the boatyard, see what I can dig up."

"Martin said that the person who has her knows way too much about the business to be a complete stranger."

"That would explain a few things."

Sam heard some stirring in the back bedroom. "Sounds like Martin is up. We'll give him some time and then you can watch the video."

A text came in on Sam's phone. He skimmed it and then locked his phone.

"Anything from Bill?"

"No. Jose. What is going on with Bill anyway? He seems so distant these days."

"He had a lot going on with his parents for a while; took leave. But I thought all that was over. Oh, he has that play. Got permission to grow out his beard."

"He's just not available. It's driving me crazy. I'm going to swing by his house."

"I don't know if that's a good idea."

Martin walked into the kitchen. "What's not a good idea?"

"Ah, nothing. Good Morning. Martin, this is my friend Tim. Tim, Martin. Tim is a sheriff's deputy and a good friend of mine. He's agreed to help. I got you some breakfast." He handed Martin the brown bag with his cheese biscuit in it.

"Merci. Coffee?"

"Fresh pot over there."

A breath of relief escaped Martin's lips. He grabbed a mug from the counter and filled it with the dark liquid. As he took a big whiff, he let out a huge, "Ahh. Now that's what I needed."

Sam smiled. "Can we look at the video now? Tim might catch some details I missed."

"Okay. I'll get my laptop. Might want to make another carafe."

"Will do." Sam went over and refilled the coffee pot to brew another pot. Martin disappeared down the hall and soon returned to the counter with his computer. He already had it booted up, so he pulled the video right up. Tim sat right in front of the monitor studying the video, slowing it down to watch the movements and the shadows on the screen.

"Looks familiar, doesn't it?" Sam commented as Tim rewound the video to watch it again.

"I can't quite place the smooth cement wall. The lighting is artificial so wherever they have her is dark with no windows, maybe underground. Can you hear any ambient noise?"

Sam placed his head closer to the speakers closing his eyes. "Seems like it's been masked."

"I agree. Of course, there is no guarantee they kept her close. At this point, she could be anywhere."

Sam turned to Martin who was refilling his cup. "Has there been any other word?"

"Nothing. I am prepared to pay the ransom. I have lost one friend, I will not lose another. Sophia would never forgive me."

"If they contact you again, tell them you are getting the funds ready. That will give us some time."

"What are you two going to do?"

Tim looked away from the screen into Martin's eyes. "We have a few leads we are going to check out. We will keep you updated. Sam said your family is coming. When?"

"Next week, Sophia was going to help Beth unpack her things from Colorado."

Sam shifted his weight and asked, "So the movers are bringing her furniture?" The surprise in his voice could not be hidden.

"Yes. They arrive on next Friday and Sophia and the boys come Monday. Beth called me Sunday, and we arranged it."

"The alarm system will be one hundred percent this weekend. Hopefully, this rain will stop."

"At least the house will be secure then," Tim commented.

"My thoughts exactly," Sam agreed. "Okay Martin, we are headed out. You stay here and online. Let me know if you hear anything else."

"Okay, I'm going to call Sophia and check on them. They think I am getting ready for the opening. I did not tell them Beth is missing."

"Our secret for the moment."

"Exactly. No need to worry her. Besides, if she knew, she would want to come right away, and I do not want her to be in danger as well."

"That's your call. We'll talk to you later." Sam and Tim headed out to the trucks parked out front.

Tim ran to his truck and jumped in the cab still managing to get drenched on the short run. He rolled down the window and pulled his truck parallel to Sam's. "I'll head out to the boatyard. If I find out anything interesting, I'll call you."

"Sounds good. I'm going to Bill's first. Then I'm going to head out to Brick Kiln Road. Maybe the old abandoned kilns will have something. I just wish I could think where I have seen that room before."

Tim gave a wave and then Sam headed down the driveway and onto the highway.

ADHESIVE FAILURE

*T*he rain made it difficult for Sam to see the driveway. His wipers couldn't keep up with the downpour. As Sam drove up the narrow gravel lane, he knew no one was home as soon as the house came into view. It looked like no one had been there for a couple of weeks. Bill would never allow the shrubs and garden to become so overgrown. Even with all the rain, Bill kept his property squared away. This was not like his friend at all. What was going on?

Sam stepped outside the cab and walked up the steps to the front window. The small cape cod cottage was dark inside. Sam peered through the windows to find the living room littered with pizza boxes and takeout containers. He walked around the porch to the kitchen window and saw the kitchen in the same condition. His heavy footsteps sounded loud as he came around the corner. A crack of thunder boomed, and he froze. A rustling noise came from around back.

Sam leaped over the railing and landed in the leaves on the back lawn. His feet sunk into the soft, saturated ground. Pausing, he heard the noise again coming from the shed. Slowly, he walked across the yard stepping carefully so he would not alert whoever was in the shed. As he peeked through the small window in the back of the building, he saw his friend bound and laid on his side. Bill still wore the clothes from council meeting on Wednesday night.

He tried the door, but it was locked. The door gave way as Sam leaned in and rammed it with his good shoulder.

He pulled the duct tape off his friend's mouth.

"Thank God you came! A crazy man tied me up. I found out he was the one who shot up your office." Bill was almost ranting he talked so fast, and Sam wanted to hear everything, but first, he needed to get him untied and comfortable.

"You need to relax. Calm down, Bill. I will listen to everything, but first, let's get you inside."

Bill flexed his hands as Sam untied his hands and feet. Sam rubbed his friend's hands to get the circulation back in them. "Can you walk to the house?"

"I think so." He leaned on Sam's good arm as they walked to the house.

Bill took a seat on a bench on the front porch. He started to explain that he had been following his investigation of the vandalism at the school and witnesses reported seeing Robert, the guy working for Mike, Sr. at the hardware store, at the school that night.

"When I went to question him, he got really hostile and pulled out the gun. He looked crazy. Next thing I knew it I woke up here, tied up. It's been at least a couple of days."

"Sorry I've been burning up your phone."

"Have you seen him?"

"Nope, no one has."

"Damn it, son of a bitch. I knew I should have questioned him at the station. Stupid."

"It's not your fault. You didn't know it was him for sure."

"You better be careful. He hates you. It is very personal with him. He kept raving about how she was his and no one else's. Over and over. He is absolutely insane."

"You don't think he has her, do you?"

"What? You mean she's still missing?"

"Officially a missing person by the department. Plus, we haven't reported it, but her business partner got a ransom note, demanding money. So, someone has her." Sam tried to fill him in on the last twenty-four hours.

"You think I could get something to drink. I am so thirsty. The key is behind the shutter there." Sam grabbed the key and went inside to get Bill a glass of water. His friend sat in a chair on the porch, hunched over, hands holding his head. There was a nasty gash on the side above his ear.

"Are you okay?" Sam asked, the glass only inches from his friend's hands. "Here's some water."

Bill looked up at Sam. "He's going to kill her." He grabbed the glass and set it on the floor as Sam's hands started to shake.

"What? How do you know? Martin's going to give him the money, and he will turn her loose. Right?"

"I just have a feeling."

Sam ran to the truck. He grabbed his cell and dialed Tim. Panic filled his chest. *Oh, my God what if they didn't get to her in time.* Bill stood up using a support column to get his balance. The glass of water still sitting on the floor. He tried to walk down the stairs, but his equilibrium was gone. Debating whether to go help Bill to the truck, Sam told Tim how he had found Bill tied and gagged.

"Bill says this guy is mean."

"Well, I got some info on your boat owner. Warren says he is the original owner, a man named Pearse from Colorado. Says he's our age. Apparently, the money was no object when building the boat, brown hair has a little gray now. Couldn't remember the eye color. Mike was right; Warren says the guy looks homeless now."

"Did he remember what he was wearing?"

"Let me ask... Hey, Warren, what was the guy wearing?" Tim yelled in earshot of the phone.

"He says khaki shorts and a UVA sweatshirt." Tim was back on the phone.

"Shit." That wasn't what Sam wanted to hear, but he knew it was coming.

"What?" Tim asked.

"I think it's Robert. I even had him in the house. Gave him the grand tour, Damn it."

Bill made it to the truck. "What's going on?"

"Oh, sorry man. Tim got some info about our guy. Let's head back to my house and fill in Martin." He turned back to the phone call. "Tim, we will meet you back at my house."

Sam helped his friend into the cab. He was a little worse for wear from his experience. Sam wondered if a trip to the hospital to get Bill checked out was in order. He could have a concussion. He knew Bill was dehydrated. Sam glanced at the porch and saw the full glass of water sitting next to the Adirondack chair. He needed to get Bill somewhere safe so he could recover. He turned to his childhood friend beside him and saw someone that had aged ten years over the last two weeks. Why hadn't he asked for help? He never shied away from it before.

"All set?"

"Yep. Let's go. I'm ready to get this guy." Sam saw a glint of, what was that? Fury. Yep, straight up rage simmered in his friend's gaze.

As the truck fired up, he echoed his sentiment with a, "Me, too." He might have driven a little fast, but he was ready to end this.

As he took the turn onto the main road, his cell rang.

"Hey, what's going on?"

"Well, we figured out what was all over the floor," Jose announced proudly. "It's lime."

"What?"

"I said lime," Jose repeated.

"Why would lime be there?"

"I have no idea. We have some at the office ready for the landscaping, but we haven't brought any here yet."

"Okay. How's the cleanup going?"

"Almost finished. Mike called from the store, said the door is in."

"Pick up the door and get it installed. Have you heard from the alarm guys?"

"They will be here this afternoon to get started. Hey, do you want them to work through the weekend? It will be extra if they do, you know.

"Yeah, I know, but we need it up and running. I'm tired of worrying about who's in the house." Sam looked over at Bill who stared out the window.

"Okay, I'll let them know."

Sam pulled into his driveway, "Call me if anything else comes up. I'm working at the house right now."

"Will do. No worries here." Jose disconnected.

Bill finally spoke up. "You have a lot going on. Do you have time to deal with all this? The sheriff should be handling this."

"No, we can't get him involved. You'll hear why in just a bit."

Tim's truck pulled in behind Sam's. The rain was still steady, and the men had to dash to the front door.

They burst through with a holler, shaking water all over the tile floor and surprising Martin who was perched up on a chair examining Sam's fireplace painting. His chair started to teeter his hands out in the air swaying. Tim was the first to react catching the stylishly dressed Frenchman.

"Oh, mon dieu. I hope you don't mind. It has intrigued me since I first saw it."

"Not at all, help yourself. Bill, come and watch the video and tell me what you think."

Martin's eyebrows anxiously went up at Sam's invitation to the stranger.

"Sorry, Martin this is my friend Bill. Bill, Martin. He is the other friend I was telling you about." Martin climbed down off the chair and extended his hand.

"It's nice to meet you. The video is open and ready. I've been hoping to catch some other details, but Beth just appears dazed."

Sam sat at the kitchen bar and turned the laptop, so the three men could see it. "Martin, does Beth have any relatives in Colorado?"

The man almost tripped over his own feet. "What?"

"Does she have any Pearse family that would come here?" Sam repeated.

Martin's eyes were large and full. "Not that I know of. Brad was an only child."

Tim pulled a piece of paper out of his pocket. He unfolded it and placed it flat on the counter. "Take a look at this guy for me."

"Where did ..." Sam started, but Tim interrupted with an explanation.

"I talked Warren out of it. Told him it was for a critical investigation. He was reluctant, spouting customer privacy and all. But gave it up. I told Marine Patrol to be on alert for the boat, but I doubt they will see much in this weather."

It was a printout of camera shot showing a middle-aged man in khaki shorts, a UVA sweatshirt and Sperry's standing on a yacht. It was Robert, no doubt about it. Martin walked over to see what the men were looking at. When he saw the photo, his hand gripped hard onto Sam's shoulder.

"Where did this photo come from?" Martin asked half in French and half in English.

"A local boat shop. The guy disappeared around the same time as Beth. Then attacked my friend Bill and locked him in a shed." Sam watched Martin carefully. "Who is this, Martin?"

"That..." Martin's voice shook with emotion. "No, it can't be." He shook his head. "I am not sure. Looked familiar for a second but it cannot be who I think." He glanced over at his wrist. "Oh my goodness, the day has disappeared. I better call my wife. If you will excuse me." He opened the door and nodded at the men as he pulled it shut behind him.

Sam watched the door shut. "Something shook him up."

ANGEL LIGHT

*S*eptember 26, 2014

The tide was coming in, Beth could hear the waves
lapping on the shore. She focused her eyesight in the dim light of
an overcast day. Her dingy mattress was damp, and the waves she
heard seeped into the room she had been in for days. The tide
never entered the room before. The storm must be a strong one.
She heard the strong ping noise of metal snapping against something. The wind blew hard outside. *Ping, Ping.* A flagpole maybe.
She focused, could that mean someone was close? Should she yell?
The water was getting deeper. She thought of the cellar and how
the water would fill the small room during a storm. She must be
close to the water. But where? Was she going to drown? If it filled
the room, with her hands and feet bound, she would not be able to
swim. She started to struggle with her ropes and tape. She had not
tried to free herself since the first day. The chaffing on her wrists
and ankles bled with the new-found strength she found. The
restraints were looser than before. Maybe he felt sorry for her
because of the sores. She would not drown like the people she
loved.

"Selah, help me. I have to get loose. The water is coming."

"It's time, Beth. Jerk your wrists. The knots are coming undone. Get loose, and I will show you the way."

Beth worked the ropes at her wrists. She could feel the warm trickle of what she guessed was blood on her palms. There would be time later to deal with that. Her sitting position didn't help her chances as the water grew deeper. She was running out of time. The salt water loosened the duct tape, and the rope fell away. The water was up to her shoulders as she reached to her ankles removing the tape and the rope. The room was filling fast. Her wounds burned from the salt in the brackish water and her stiff muscles protested after lying in one position for so long. They didn't want to work. She wasn't strong enough to walk against the water pouring into the room.

"Don't give up, Beth. Sam is waiting."

Beth pictured Sam on the beach shaking the sand from the blanket. He had held her that night with no expectations, only dreams of the future. *Their future.* She had to fight. With her newfound strength, she swam toward the rusty iron gate. There was no way she could break the chain. She latched on to it as the water flowed around her legs. There was an opening at the top. It didn't cover the whole door only four-fifths, and she thought she could possibly squeeze through the top. *I will squeeze through.* The rough metal sliced her fingers as she climbed the gate. The water was already chest-high when she made it to the top. Sliding her leg through the opening, she pressed herself against the stone curvature of the entrance. She pushed herself through, the top of the gate scraping her abdomen and cutting into her, proving she didn't fit as well as she thought. *I will have one less croissant if I make it out of this mess.* Tears ran down her determined face. She gave one more push, and her other leg followed her body as she fell into the water on the other side.

The current pushed her into the metal gate, liquid choking her as she tried to rise above the water line. She swam through the water to the wall of the structure, until she heard the ping again.

"Follow the sound, Beth. Follow the sound." *Ping, Ping.* She went up and out a small opening into a wooded area. The water was up to her chest now. The tide worked against her. A crack of lightning followed by thunder confirmed the severity of the storm. It was raining so hard she couldn't see. *Ping, Ping.* She followed the sound as she tried to swim through the brush and trees, stopping once in a while to gather needed strength to swim against the current. The wind whipped her wet hair and face. She tried to see what was in front of her, but it was impossible.

She emerged from the woods and saw lights. Elation filled her. It was the lights of the waterfront, the flagpoles on the sailboats clanging in the distance. *Ping, ping.* She was almost home. She swam toward the lights, the water fighting her. The tide pulled her up-river. A wave crashed over her and forced her under. Water filled her lungs as she tried to cough and regain her breath. She reached upward, and she saw a bolt of lightning flash across the surface. A hand reached for her, wrapping strong fingers around her sore wrist. Beth saw a uniform as she got pulled her from the water before everything turned black.

MOMENTIVE

A pause symbol sat in the middle of the laptop sitting on the island top. "Well, what do you think?" Sam turned to Bill to hear his reaction. Bill had a concerned expression on his face, a cross between bewildered and angered.

"And you say he received this in a direct email?" Bill asked again.

Sam wondered why Bill kept coming back to that question. "Yes, that's what he said. It was sent directly to him with no contact information."

"I bet the office could get the address and information from the email," Tim offered.

"No department involvement." Sam refused. "This guy says no police involvement, and that's what we will stick to. Understood?" He turned back to the screen. "The walls of the room look familiar, but I can't remember exactly where."

The front door opened. Martin looked like he had regained his composure. "I apologize for stepping out." He joined the other men at the counter.

"No problem. Everything okay at home?"

"Yes, Sophie is trying to get the boys to go to sleep since it's late there." Martin smoothed his hair to one side and straightened the scarf at his throat.

"We've been trying to come up with our next step. Have a fresh cup of coffee." Sam handed him a mug. "Has the jet lag hit you yet?"

Martin shook his head, and Sam glanced at the screen behind him as an email notification flashed.

You are Warned was the subject lined.

"Martin, you might want to check..." Cell phones started ringing and vibrating. The men looked at each other and then their devices.

Tim was the first to say, "It's the office." Then they all answered the phones.

"Hello," Sam listened to the dispatch operator.

"Professor Howards you are needed immediately at the hospital. Ms. Pearse has been found and is asking for you."

"Thank you for calling. I'm on my way."

"Martin, get your jacket. Beth has been found and is at the hospital. We're going." Sam grabbed his keys and jacket and headed out into the storm; Martin in tow. "She's been found. Take everything to the office. Show the Sherriff everything." He yelled over his shoulder. The two men on their cells hopped off the stools and the front door slammed shut behind them.

* * *

THE STERILE SMELL of hospital antiseptic filled Beth's lungs. It was a welcome relief after the week she had spent in filth. There were beeps and blips throughout the room. She could feel the tubes and wires surrounding her, tethering her to yet another bed. This time a safe one. She was so tired. Her heavy, laden eyes refused to open. *Sam.* When would he come? Did he even know? Would he care? People spoke in the corner of her room, but she couldn't focus on their words. The room went fuzzy, and she slipped into darkness once again.

* * *

SAM SAT by the hospital bed and held Beth's hand. A nurse slipped in to check her vitals and fluids.

"Did they say she asked for me?" Sam inquired.

"Are you Sam?" The nurse inquired seeming not to want to disappoint him. When Sam nodded, she looked relieved. "Then, yes. When they first brought her in, she was asking for Sam."

"Can she hear me?"

The nurse nodded. "It helps a lot if you talk to her. She's been through so much."

Sam turned back to Beth and began stroking the skin on her arm above the bandaged wounds. "I'm here, sweetheart." And then he laughed. The nurse turned to him with a funny look on her face. "I know you don't like it when people call you that, but you will just have to deal with it until you wake up and tell me to stop," he teased, tempting her to wake up and meet his gaze.

He laid his head beside her on the bed. "Beth. Wake up. I'm here, and you're safe. I'm waiting for you." Her fingers tightened around his hand, and a tear formed at the corner of his eye. Grown men don't cry, he told himself. But he had always told himself they don't fall in love either. Today he had done both.

BUILDING LINE

riday afternoon, September 26, 2014

Sam's cell vibrated in his pocket waking him from his nap. He straightened up in the hospital room chair and ran his hand through his rumpled hair. Beth slept, unaware of his abrupt movements. The doctors claimed they didn't know how long she would remain in this state, but her body would use the time to heal. Sam checked his phone and found a voicemail from Tim. The poor reception in the hospital sent all calls to voicemail. They were still looking for Robert, no luck yet. And Beth's parents were on their way from Virginia. *That's good. They need to be here with her.*

He stood up and stretched. His body had stiffened while sleeping in the chair, but he needed to be close in case she stirred. He peered at all her bandages and scrapes as he face flamed with anger. She didn't deserve to be treated like that. Why did Robert do it? Because he didn't want her to be with Sam? He'd sent a message with the damage at the office, but Sam hadn't listened. Instead, Sam had put her in danger. It was his fault. His anger turned inward. Why didn't he listen?

An older couple poked their heads in the room. The woman wore a polo top and khaki pants, and the man was dressed similarly. They looked like they had just left the country club but with a touch of tiredness.

"You must be our Beth's Sam." The woman moved toward him with outstretched arms. "I'm Marie, and this is Tom. We're Beth's parents from Charlottesville. Thank you for taking care of her." She wrapped her arms around him and squeezed. He guessed this woman had never met a person she didn't like.

"How was your trip?" Sam asked, aiming for polite conversation.

"It was long, but Tom has a lead foot, so it wasn't as bad as it could have been. Has she been asleep this whole time?"

"Yes, ma'am. The doctors say her body will know when it's time to wake." Sam repeated what he'd been told.

"She looks so peaceful. You know she was coming up to Virginia for a little break last week when she disappeared. She said the stress was getting to her." She started to sob. Her husband gathered her in his arms to comfort her.

"Ma'am, it will be okay. Beth is a strong woman. If I have learned anything since meeting your daughter, it is that she can do anything she sets her mind to," Sam reassured. "If you don't mind, since you are here, I'm going to run home and change my clothes. I will be back very soon. I don't want to miss her if she wakes. The nurses have my number if you need me."

Sam needed a breather. Beth did not need negative energy around her right now, and all he could think of was how he wanted to wrap his hands around Robert's neck.

BLISTERING PAINT

*T*he hospital halls were full of people, and Sam knew he had to escape. His rage boiled, and it wouldn't take much to set him off. He hadn't felt like this in a long time. Too many people. The air was stifling too. He had to get out of this sterile place. His gait quickened as he saw a familiar person step into the elevator. Was it his imagination? He ran to the elevator buttons, pushing them over and over, willing the doors to reopen.

"Take it, easy buddy." A male nurse told him. "You don't want to break it."

"Stairs?" Sam asked breathlessly.

The orderly pointed three doors down. Sam sprang toward them. He was only on the third floor. He would have to hurry if he was going to catch him. The sound of his shoes hitting every other step echoed through the stairwell. Sam's breathing struggled to keep up with his will to beat the bastard to the bottom. He rounded the curve and ran smack into Bill. What the hell was he doing here? He looked as surprised as Sam. He opened his mouth to say something, but Sam pushed him out of the way and broke through the fire door to the bottom floor. Just as he did, a man in a blue and orange UVA sweatshirt pushed the exit door to the hospital. Sam watched as he put his hood up despite the comfortable temperature outside.

Sam couldn't be sure it was Robert. His adrenaline had taken over, there was no thinking now. He ran across the vestibule and pushed through the rotating door. He looked to his left and then his right. No one, the man had disappeared. He walked over to the building and squatted to catch his breath.

He was so close, he almost had him. Robert must have been there to check on Beth. He would ask Bill for some protection for the room. "Ah, man. Bill." Remembering the friend he had literally run into in the stairwell, he rose, turned, and went back inside the hospital to apologize. Sam hoped Bill was there to finally get himself checked out. Sam walked back over to the staircase entrance. Not finding Bill, he poked his head through the door, but only heard footsteps and then a door above open and close.

He'd get with him later. Sam grabbed some coffee from the vending machine and turned to go back to his truck. His cell phone started to ding like crazy as messages started coming in now that he was finally out of the vacuum of the hospital building, giving him some bars. He slowly walked to the parking lot, pausing to check for traffic, his eyes still on his phone. Martin was making calls for the movers and the art transporter. Tim was on the water. Sam looked at the clouds and ran from the safety of the pedestrian cover through the rain. He hoped his friend was safe on the water. Anyway, he would call for an update later. Jose was getting things done, and it sounded like the yard would be postponed until after the movers finished.

Sam rounded the corner of the truck to get in the cab. He looked up from his phone and cursed. Flat tire. He needed a damn break. Just this once. He walked over to the tire to check it, and the anger flared again. He let out a yell. "Damn you, I will get you if it's the last thing I do." People walking through the lot turned and stared. He kicked the tire and dialed Tim.

"Hey, man."

"I know you're busy, but someone slashed my tire."

"I think we both know who did it. I better send some guys."

"Okay, I'm headed back up to Beth's room. I think he was in the hospital. Is there any way you can get some protection over here?"

"We've got a lot going on searching for the place where she was held."

"Yeah, I know. Just see what you can do."

Sam turned and went back up to Beth's floor. As he rounded the corner at the nurses' station, he heard a familiar laugh coming from Beth's room. It was Bill. What was he doing up here?

"We are so glad Beth has found such good friends here," her mother said sweetly. "It's so nice of you to watch over her after her ordeal."

"It's no problem at all, ma'am. I would do anything for her. She's quite the girl, but of course, you know that. I can see where she gets it from."

Sam entered the room in time to see Beth's mom blush at the compliment. Good grief. Sam was going to have a sugar spike from all this. "Sorry to interrupt, looks like I won't be going anywhere for a little while."

Bill looked both surprised and perturbed.

"Seems I have a flat tire."

"Oh dear, we have Triple-A, would you like me to call them for you?"

"Maybe later, thank you. I came to check on my girl." He glanced at Bill, whose jaw started to twitch.

"You were in an awful hurry to leave five minutes ago," Bill commented. "Where were you headed?"

Sam looked him in the eye with a warning glance, "You know, chasing ghosts. We do that a lot around here." He smiled at Beth's parents. They didn't seem interested in the men's conversation. They were too busy fussing over Beth, as it should be. Bill shifted in his chair in the corner of the room uncomfortably. Sam knew he had caused his friend to feel like an interloper, but he didn't care.

FLEMISH BOND

*B*eth's parents hovered over her motionless body. It seemed surreal. Was she dead? She had asked that question way too many times in the last week.

A hand grabbed hers, and she saw Selah next to her. "No, my dear friend, you are not dead. Only resting." Selah's smile warmed her and a sense of peace wash over her. "So much love in the room."

"Yes, there is. Why is the deputy here? Is he investigating?" Beth saw the warning glance that Sam gave Bill. There was anger in his eyes. She had not seen that before.

"He is watching as he always does."

"Why?"

"Because he covets what he cannot have. I have seen it before, Beth. You have to be careful with that kind of love. Sometimes it turns to hate."

Beth watched Bill as he shifted in his chair. He was uncomfortable, but he looked determined to stay. Sam stepped over to the bed and took her hand gently. He brought it to his lips and whispered something. She looked back at Bill, and his eyes flashed dark. Selah was right, she could see the evil building. He was dangerous, but Sam didn't know. She needed to tell him.

"Selah how can I warn Sam?"

"He will know when it's time. All in good time." Selah turned loose of her hand and moved around the bed. "I like your parents. They are very devoted to you." Beth smiled at her comment. They were always supportive but not helicopter parents. She had put them through so much in the last five years.

"I hope they are okay. I don't want them to worry about me."

"They are fine, Beth. They know how strong you are. They are just waiting for you to give them a sign."

Her mother sat by the bed holding her hand, running her fingers through her hair and brushing it from her face. Beth remembered the touch of her fingers from when she was young. She would curl up beside her mom and lean in. Words were never necessary. Peace washed over her with every brush of her mom's fingertips. She moved her fingertips ever so slightly in her mother's palm.

"Oh, Tom! She moved. She moved her fingers." Tears filled her eyes as she leaned across Beth's body and patted Sam's hand. "Did you feel it? She just lightly brushed my hand." Her eyes searched Sam's wanting him to agree with her.

"She knows you're here." He said reassuringly.

Beth was so thankful that Sam was here for her parents. He was a good man. She watched Bill stand up from his corner post.

"Well if you will all excuse me, I have a kidnapper to catch. It was very nice to meet both of you. If you need anything, you have my card." Bill shook their hands and then nodded in Sam's direction, "Sam."

Sam looked up at him, "See you later. Call me if there are any breaks."

"Will do." Beth watched him step out of the room.

Her mother turned back to the sleeping Beth and patted her hand. "You are so lucky to have such nice important friends. No wonder you love it here."

"Beth has definitely made a reputation for herself." Sam smiled.

Beth knew what he was smiling at. She remembered how shocked she was to learn that she was the gossip topic around town and how townspeople were making up stories about her. He had been so honest and open with her that night. He had turned into her confidant, someone she shared her dreams with and then there was the argument. She looked at him as he held her sleeping body's hand. She thought he didn't care about her after their argument, but did she give him a fair shake? She didn't tell him everything. His opinion was on the basis that she was having nightmares about Selah's diary. He probably thought she was a raving lunatic. She hadn't been completely honest with him. Would it change things if he knew she was keeping something from him? Would he still be here by her bedside?

Sam's phone buzzed, and he glanced at the screen. "If you folks will excuse me, I have to go see about my truck. I am just downstairs if you need me." He leaned down and kissed the sleeping Beth on the forehead and whispered something in her ear. The room began to grow dim, and Beth's vision was fuzzy.

"Selah, what is happening?"

"It's time to rejoin your family, dear."

Beth began to stir in her bed. "Sam, Sam." Everything was dark, but she could hear her mother's voice.

"I'm here, Beth. It's mother. Honey, go and see if you can catch Sam before he gets in the elevator."

Beth's eyes wouldn't open. Her lids felt like they weighed a ton. She tried to move, but her arms wouldn't work. She felt her father's shadow as he walked out of the room. When he stepped back in he said, "He's gone, already on his way down, I suppose."

Beth moaned.

"Shh, darling, He will be back, and you can tell him yourself when you're awake."

Settling, Beth fell asleep again.

SCREEDING

$\mathcal{H}$e didn't have time for this ridiculous nonsense. He had been saying that a lot lately and he wasn't in the mood. Sam rounded the corner of the entrance to the hospital and saw the sheriff's cars out by his truck. As he got closer, Tim met him about one hundred feet from his truck.

"Man, I thought you said you had a flat." The men walked toward the rest of the deputies, "Not two."

Sam let out a frustrated grunt. "What?" They rounded the truck and Sam saw both of his driver's side tires slashed. "There was only one when I called."

"They must be watching you somehow," Tim said thinking out loud.

"I thought I saw Robert when I came out to the truck to leave. I tried to chase him, but he disappeared when I came out of the building."

"Sam, you have got to let us do our job. You are putting yourself in danger."

"You aren't doing enough. Beth has been in jeopardy since my office was destroyed. Your office has done nothing to protect her. Bill called me a couple of times with minimal information. Like the gun that was tied to the bullet."

"Wait, what bullet?" Tim was astonished.

"The bullet found at my office," Sam offered to clarify. "Bill called me Sunday morning and said that it had been tested and they knew it was from a Glock."

"But he wasn't involved with the investigation at the college. I worked with an officer from Greenville. He did a few student interviews, and I let him call you, so you would know what was going on."

"No. You were the one that was doing the interviews when I got there. Why would he make up his involvement?" Sam shook his head trying to make sense of everything.

"Sam, I'm telling you the truth." Tim grabbed his friend's arm. "Bill was not involved with the case. I shouldn't say anything, but he has been on limited casework since his leave. He's been mostly doing traffic duty unless we need extra deputies for something."

"Like the night at the college," Sam completed.

"Exactly." Tim nodded. "I would not lie to you. I don't know what Bill has told you, but we were cautious with everything we found at the school because of the location. The sheriff's department didn't need a media frenzy about the college. We considered it vandalism and nothing more."

"Thanks, Tim. I wonder why Bill would make up information like that."

"I have no idea. I'll look at the truck, see if there is any evidence.

You can take off. I know you're anxious to be with Beth. How's she doing?"

"She's still asleep. The doctors said it's not a coma."

"Well, that's good news."

"I just wish…" Sam's thoughts drifted off.

"What's that?"

"Oh, nothing." He shoved his hands in his pockets and looked down at the pavement.

"It's going to be okay. We'll find this guy." Tim reassured him.

"I know you're working hard. I'm going to head back up. Text me when you're done with the truck. Can you do me a favor and have someone check on Martin? I'm kind of stuck here."

"Sure. I'll get with the garage in town while I'm at it."

"Thanks. I'll see you later." Sam headed back up to Beth's room. As he went up the stairs, he wondered why Bill was behaving weirdly. Maybe the thing with his parents was too much stress. It was strange having him in Beth's room earlier. He acted a little over-familiar with her parents. There was more traffic in the stairwell this time. Sam passed orderlies and nurses as he stomped up the stairs. Doors opened and closed echoing loudly. Was anywhere quiet around here? He texted Jose to come and get him. He would worry about the truck later. It was in good hands with the local mechanic. Jose typed back quickly; he would be over in half an hour. Sam could spend some more time with Beth. It upset him to see her in the hospital bed. She looked so helpless. Her physical injuries were superficial and would heal quickly. It was the mental ones he worried about. He had no idea what she had been through, and until she came around, he wouldn't.

He still felt guilty about giving her a hard time about the dreams. Why wasn't he supportive when she was upset? Instead, he was calloused and didn't listen to her. He would have to apologize when she woke up. Or better yet, he had an idea. He needed to go to her apartment for something.

TRANSOM LIGHT

*T*he light outside began to dim, signaling the ending of another long day in the small hospital room. Beth's mother and father were relentless with their attention. She knew they were there by their constant requests of the nursing staff. Beth wished she had the strength to give them the hugs and reassurance they deserved. She was aware but asleep and very confused. She willed her body to wake up to no avail. So many times, over the last few years, her mother was the one to reassure her. Now it was her turn.

Beth's fingers moved and tightened around her mother's hand as she heard her mother thanking someone. She couldn't see who it was.

"Thank you so much for all that you have done. You saved our daughter. Thank goodness you were there when she was in the river. I don't know what I would have done if I lost her." She heard the emotion in her mother's voice. But who was she talking to?

Her mother moved away from her chair by the bed. Beth's eyes slowly parted, and she saw her mother hugging Deputy Felton. Beth couldn't believe the shocking sight. This was news to her. He was the one that pulled her out of the water?

"Mom," Beth struggled, but the word escaped.

"Oh, my gosh, she's awake. Look, Bill, our darling is awake."

Beth's mother rushed to the bedside along with Bill. Overwrought with emotion, her Mom gave her a big hug making Beth groan with pain.

"Oh, honey I'm so sorry. Look, honey, your special friend is here." He took her hand, and Beth pulled back into her bed. He was way too forward for their acquaintance relationship. She wasn't strong enough to remove her hand from his, but she didn't reciprocate his grasp either.

"Deputy Felton, thank you for being here. Did I hear right? You were the one that pulled me out of the river?"

"Yes. I had been searching on the river for a while. The storm and tide were getting so strong, my boat captain wanted to go in and wait for a break in the weather. But I said 'No, my Beth is out here, and I need to bring her home.'" He gave her that big smile of his.

The hair on the back of her neck prickled with warning; the same warning she had felt when she entered the house that night. Something wasn't right, but she had no idea what it was.

"Oh, darling isn't that sweet? You have so many great friends here. Thank you again, Bill, for taking care of her."

"It's no problem, ma'am." Bill smiled down at Beth. That smile reminded her of him in her dream with Selah. What had Selah said? She remembered she needed to be careful around him. What did she say?

"Thanks, Bill." She couldn't look him in the eyes anymore, so she turned to her mother. "Mom, where's Sam?"

"He had to step out, dear. There was some trouble with his truck, and he had to go down to the mechanic's."

"Oh, okay. Can Dad call him, please? I need to talk to him."

A nurse came in and started checking her pulse and all the tubes connected to her. "The Doctor needs to see you first before we start having a social hour, young lady."

Why was Bill here then? Beth wondered. The nurse continued to check computers and write things on her chart.

"I brought your phone in case you need me. I'll put it right here on the table. The sheriff will want to interview you as well," Bill said as he gazed at her with … *What was that look?* Goosebumps rose on her skin.

"Are you cold, honey?" the nurse asked.

"A little," Beth answered hiding the chill she was getting from Bill's stare. He went to the corner of the room and retrieved an extra blanket. As he spread it over Beth's lap, he spread the edges down to her feet facing the door. Beth watched him making sure the hem was perfectly straight, and something hit her panic button. Maybe it was his smell or the shape of his head, but suddenly her adrenaline was flowing, and her pulse increased as everyone could see on her monitors. She couldn't breathe.

Her nurse pushed Bill out of the way and started checking connections and her oxygen level. "You have to calm down." Beth nodded but couldn't catch her breath. "I need everyone out so I can check her," she ordered. She put her hands on each of Beth's parents directing them toward the door. Bill was standing in the way and was herded along with them out into the hall. The nurse closed the door behind them and turned back to Beth. As soon as the door shut, Beth's pulse normalized.

"Honey, you are safe." She looked Beth straight into her eyes. "You're safe, I promise you." Beth nodded with comprehension. Her breathing became steadier.

"Thanks," she squeezed out in a hoarse voice.

"Honey, is there anything you need to talk about? I know you have been through a lot, but we didn't see any evidence of assault when you were brought in."

Beth's head started to swim. She didn't want to remember what happened. If she could push it to the back of her mind where she kept all her horrible memories, she would be content.

"Beth," the nurse tried to bring her back from wherever she escaped. "Beth, is there any reason we should do a rape kit?"

Beth shook her head no. The nurse turned to the monitor as the alarms started to go off again.

"Are you sure?" she turned back to Beth.

"I was not sexually assaulted," Beth declared as if the nurse needed to be convinced. "I was restrained, left alone for however long it was. I don't even know how many days it was. Do you know?" Beth's eyes begged. "Do you know how long I was there?"

"I don't. They haven't told me. I can tell you, I've been on your case for two days here. You have been in this room since you were checked in from the ER." Beth listened intently. "You were dehydrated, and your body temperature was low. You had scrapes and cuts plus abrasions on your wrists and ankles. Nothing broken."

Beth pulled the bedding up over her chest. Remembering how cold and wet she was pushing through the rushing water, goosebumps rose on her skin.

"Are you still cold? I'll get another blanket."

"Thank you. Can you let my family know that I'm going to rest for a while?" The nurse smiled and nodded in agreement. "And," Beth hesitated, "can you make sure that my mom and dad are the only ones allowed in without checking with me first."

"Of course, Sweetie. Now you get some rest." She patted the bed and closed the door behind her.

Beth carefully turned in her bed to face the window. The raindrops coated the window panes blocking the view of the parking lot. She grabbed the remote for the television and turned up the volume to block the sound of the water hitting the glass. There was a talk show on, and she could care less. She closed her eyes and listened to the voices, anything to block out the sound of the water.

MITER JOINT

*S*aturday, September 27, 2014

The smell of oil and sound of torque wrenches filled the garage, and Sam was growing impatient. The clerk fought with the computer, trying to locate Sam's account and Sam wanted to jump over the counter and pull it up himself. *Tap, Tap, Tap.* The clerk held his keys hostage until the bill could be settled and it tortured him. *Tap, Tap, Tap.*

"Oh, here it is," he exclaimed.

Sam let out a sigh, making the clerk look up at him.

"Sorry, Professor Howards, they didn't put it under your name. It was actually under the sheriff's account."

"No problem. How much is it?"

"That will be $569, please. Do you need an extra copy for your insurance?" The clerk offered, trying to be helpful.

"Insurance?" Sam pulled his card out of his wallet and handed it over.

"The sheriff's office said your truck was vandalized. You should be able to file for reimbursement."

"I never thought of that. Thank you."

"No problem." He slid the card through the machine and handed it back with Sam's keys.

Sam's phone started to ring, and he fumbled the keys as he tried to grab his receipt along with everything else. He glanced at the screen and hit the button. His heart pumped with anticipation because it was a Virginia number. He figured it was Beth's parents with news. The doctors were supposed to give them an updated report this afternoon.

"Hello, this is Sam." He bent down, shoving his wallet in his pocket and picking up his keys and receipt again.

"Hi, Sam, this is Beth's dad. She's awake and is asking for you."

"What?" He dropped everything again, and his receipt floated away across the grimy floor. He shook his head in frustration.

"She's awake."

"I'm on my way." Sam chased the receipt, waved to the clerk and disconnected. He jumped into the truck and started the engine. His phone rang again.

"Hello, this is Sam," he repeated, not bothering to look at the screen.

"Sam, this is Martin. The movers are almost finished. Everything is a disorganized mess here. Do you have anyone that can work on placing the boxes in the correct rooms, so Sophie can unpack them?"

"I'm sure that Jose and his wife would be glad to help."

"Jose here at the house?"

"Yes, ask him if they can help."

"Okay, thank you. Also, Sophie and the kids will be here tomorrow. Is there a car service I can arrange to pick them up?"

"I think there is a taxi service from the airport. I will Google it and send you the number."

"I can do that, don't bother."

"It's not a bother. It will be good to have Sophie here for Beth."

"It will be good to see them together." Sam heard a massive crash in the background. "Talk to you later." And Martin was gone.

"Oh boy." Sam put the truck in drive and threw his phone in the passenger seat. He watched cars drive by, people on their way to work or to the grocery store with no idea that there was a dangerous man on the loose. He pulled out and turned toward the hospital. He drove through town making a note of all the vehicles. He chastised himself. Since when was this his job? Tim told him over and over to leave it to them, and he had been busy at the hospital, but now he needed to feel useful. He parked as close to the building as possible. He was nervous. Would she want to see him? They said she was asking for him. That was a good sign, wasn't it?

Sam went through the revolving door, his nerves still on edge. He saw Robert around every corner. Where was he hiding and why? Sam would make him pay for what he did to Beth and Bill. The man was pure evil and needed to be found as soon as possible so Beth could sleep easy.

Sam put on a stoic face and walked down to the nurses' station. The nurse immediately jumped up and stepped in front of him. "May I help you, sir?"

"I'm going to see Beth Pearse. She's expecting me."

"Your name, sir?"

Sam saw Bill in the hall waiting room reading a newspaper. How long had he been there? "Sam Howards."

"Of course, come this way." She escorted Sam down the hall to Beth's room. Knocking on the door, she opened it and announced him. "Sam is here, Beth."

Beth looked up and smiled. Her face lit up when her eyes focused on his. "Hey, Mr." She held back, uneasy about how he would react. The nurse stood at the door waiting for Beth to tell her she was okay. She didn't look away from him only said, "Thank you, Susan. I'll be okay."

"You have your button if you need anything."

"Yes, I have it right here."

Sam stood over her. "Hey, beautiful."

"Oh no, don't say that. I look terrible." She motioned to her face with her bandaged hand.

"You look like you're one of the crew now." He smiled big and held out his cast. He was trying to not show her his unease, but he worried he was failing miserably.

"Sit down, will you? I need to talk to you."

Oh, no. Here it comes. She's going to tell him to get lost. No doubt that's why Bill is waiting in the hall. Sam grabbed the chair and slid it closer to the bed, so he could be near her, if only for a little while. "Okay, what should we talk about?"

"I need to apologize to you. I haven't been entirely honest with you."

"Don't you worry about anything right now. You need to lay here and relax."

"I have done nothing but lay down. I need you to listen to me." Beth pulled in a breath. "When I was tied up, I thought about how I treated you the last time I saw you. I am so ashamed of how I acted. It wasn't your fault that you didn't understand why I was upset."

"Shh, it doesn't matter now. You are back safe. That's all that matters."

"Sam, it was Selah who…"

Sam immediately cut her off, "No, you shouldn't apologize. I didn't listen to you when you were trying to explain. I should have shut up and listened. I'm sorry, sweetheart." Sam leaned over and grabbed her hand. "When you were gone, I couldn't function. It showed me how special you are. I left you so many messages and then …"

"What? You aren't mad at me. But you didn't come. I waited for you, and you didn't come and get me."

"I was searching for you. Believe me, baby. I had my friends out looking for you. We didn't have anything to go on and then Martin brought the video from France."

"Martin is here in Washington?"

He nodded. "That opened some possibilities and Tim, you remember the deputy that came to the waterfront that night?"

"Oh, my God." She turned red at the memory.

"He found some evidence to start looking on the river." Sam smiled at her modesty. Was it wrong not to tell her about their suspicions about Robert? The timing wasn't right. He would wait till she had her support system here, then he would tell her. "That's how the marine patrol was on the river."

"Is that when Bill found me?"

"Bill didn't find you."

"What? But he said…"

"No, he was with me when you were found."

Her head went fuzzy. "I don't understand. So many people…so many people looking for me?" She was amazed. "I thought…" Her voice faded.

He ran his fingers across her cheek and pulled her chin his way as he neared her lips. "You were missed." He kissed her, gently at first, then waited for her to respond. He felt her kiss him back. It was as if the kiss awakened something inside of her. She deepened the kiss raising up to meet him. He didn't want to put her in pain, so he held back letting her control it. Sam found it difficult to control his passion, but he knew it was better for her. He had missed her kisses.

She pulled back and looked at him.

"Welcome back, babe." He gave her his biggest smile.

"Thanks. So, tell me what has happened. I hate being stuck in here. It's annoying watching the world go by and not able to do anything."

"Let's see. Martin is here, but I already told you that. He has taken over the gallery. You will be right on schedule to open. The movers delivered the furniture today, and we will have you unpacked by next week. I just let Martin run the show after we finished with the house."

"That's amazing."

"Yep, your new home." He grinned and brushed his lips over her bandaged knuckles. "The town is getting ready for the festival at the beginning of next month. Your gallery is all the talk."

He watched her eyelids droop as he continued to talk. Pulling the linens up under her chin, he settled in to tell her all the happenings around town: the new band playing at the bar downtown, the new librarian, the record number of entrants in the dragon boat races, anything he could think of to distract her from her trauma. Soon she was dozing with her hands in his. He laid his head on her stomach. She winced, so he moved upward taking his weight off her. He allowed himself to relax and enjoy her company. The nurse popped in to check on things. She gave him an approving look when she saw him holding Beth's hand.

"She's been asking for you since she got here, you know?"

"Really? But she was so still when I was here before."

"She is having a tough time trusting people after what she's been through. She needs to feel safe. Just be here for her; that will be enough." She nodded at Sam, pushed a few buttons on the monitor and left closing the door behind her.

Sam brushed the hair from Beth's face and whispered, "I love you, Beth. I will always be here for you no matter what." He kissed her cheek and laid his head back down. Her hand came up to rest on top of his head, and he heard a whisper barely escape her lips, "I love you too."

LATH AND PLASTER

Sunday, September 28, 2014

Beth heard the kids before they popped through the door. The nurses were telling them to hold it down, but it was useless. They were yelling in French for Beth going from door to door.

"In here guys." She tried to yell, but her voice wouldn't cooperate. She tried again. "In here." They were right outside and pushed through the door, pulling Sophie behind them. "Sophie." Beth squealed with tears in her eyes. "Thank God you're here." A rush of relief flowed through her. She pushed up from the mattress with her hands out for her dear friend. Sophie ran to the bed.

"Look at you. You look terrible. What have they done to you? And you are so skinny." She hugged Beth tightly. "So, tell me what happened."

Beth watched the two boys run to the window to look out at all the cars. "I will tell you later when there aren't little ears around." Beth smiled and used her eyes to point at the boys climbing on the chairs. "How was your flight? I can't imagine getting these two to sit still for that long."

"Oh, mon dieu, thank goodness for iPads. They brought their favorite cartoons with them."

"What are your favorite shows, Phillipe?"

"I like PJ Masks. "

"How about you, Jean?

"Mine is Babar. "

"Those sound fantastic. We should have movie night one night, and we can watch them together when I get home."

"When are you going home?" Sophie asked.

"The doctors will decide tomorrow. I'm hoping it will be tomorrow afternoon. Sam said the house is ready."

"Not quite. I have a few more things to do before it is one hundred percent, but it will be ready enough tomorrow. I will be up with these two all night, so I might as well finish up. Text me as soon as you get time, so I can drive up and wait."

She gave her friend another hug. "Thank you for taking care of the move for me. I just couldn't even think how I was going to get it all done after this happened." Beth held up her hands. The boys started to stare at the monitor and analyzing the switches.

Sophie watched them and whispered to Beth, "I better get them out of here before they do something like turn off your oxygen."

Beth laughed. "Okay, I will see you tomorrow. Thank you so much for coming." Giving Sophie one last hug, she didn't want to let go. Sophie grabbed each of the boys by the hand and hurried them from the room. She was right to rush them out before they could get into mischief. If anyone were to push a button, those two would without a care in the world. She laughed to herself. She would see Sophie tomorrow and then they could have a long talk.

Beth looked through the half-open door down the hall. When was Sam coming back? He said he had some things to get ready for her homecoming, but he didn't say how long he would be. The hallway was busy with people moving from one room or another. The nurse had kept her word, and she didn't have any unwanted visitors. She kept the list short on purpose. Bill had tried to come back, but she didn't want him here, and the nurses knew it. Sam, her parents, and now Sophie were all she wanted to see. She sent her parents out to sightsee, so they were not stuck in the room with her. They deserved some play time now that she was out of danger.

The police would want to talk to her. Eventually, she thought. She would have to repeat all the horrible details she made herself remember. All the things the man did to her; the sounds, the smells. She still wasn't certain what he looked like or who he was. There was a time she'd believed she heard Brad's voice. But it wasn't him, it couldn't be. He was dead.

Most of the tubes and cords were disconnected now so she could move around the room freely. She got up and looked out the window. Sophie was having trouble getting the boys in the rental car. They were running up and down the islands in the parking lot. Beth giggled out loud. It felt good to laugh. She stretched her arms and bent over stretching out her back. Oh, she was so sore. The doctors should be in soon to evaluate her for release. She was ready to be home curled up on the couch with Selah's diary. Selah did not visit as often here in the hospital. There were too many people around, and Beth had plenty of support.

She felt his gaze on her back first and as she turned around Sam's filled with excitement despite his tired, unshaven appearance.

"You're up. Fantastic."

* * *

SAM COULDN'T BELIEVE his eyes. She was up and out of bed, wearing sweats. He watched her as she laughed and stretched looking out the window. Only one tube was attached to her arm. She looked so much better, rested. But was she ready for all the news he had to share with her? He crossed the room and wrapped his arms around her. She felt so good against him.

"What's so funny out there?"

"Sophie is trying to control the boys. They are doing everything they can to not get in the car." Beth gazed up at him. "How are you?" she rubbed his bristly chin with her fingers.

"I'm doing okay. I came to tell you I have to go to Raleigh for a few days. Sophie and Martin will be here to help you. The house is ready. I wanted to be there when you saw it for the first time, but I have an appointment I can't miss."

"I understand," she said. "You need to take care of business." Her arms tightened around him.

"Are you going to be okay?"

"I'll be fine," she reassured him. "I'll miss you."

Sam leaned down and kissed her. "I'll miss you too. You're something special, ma'am."

"Thanks. Do you have to leave right away?"

"Yep. I'll be back on Tuesday though." Sam watched her movements, searching for any little reason to stay in town. He didn't want to leave her. The thought of her returning to the place she'd been abducted without him was breaking his heart. All she had to do was provide one iota of resistance to his trip, and he'd cancel.

"I'm sure there is plenty for me to do. Martin can help me with the hanging."

"You need to rest. Just because they say you can go home, doesn't mean you can go full speed ahead. Hellen said she can help as well, so give her a call if you need to."

"I will, I will. Will you stop worrying? I'll be fine. I might look a little rough at my opening, but I'm healing."

"Don't say that. You're beautiful." Sam watched as she turned pink with embarrassment. He loved it when she blushed.

"Can't you stay just a little longer?" she asked.

He smiled. "Okay. Get back into bed, and I'll stay." He couldn't resist. He was putting off the news he would have to tell her when he got back. There was no need to rush her pain. No one had seen Robert in days, so he was probably long gone. He helped her up into the hospital bed and set on the edge.

"You know, both of us fit on here." She glanced over at him then patted the space beside her.

"We've done it before, haven't we?" He chuckled. She moved over even further to make more room for him. He pulled the covers up over both of them and wrapped her in his arms. The heat between them was intense, and he couldn't concentrate. His mind fogged with thoughts of what he wanted to do with her. It was different this time. He didn't want to do things to her but with her. The passion that filled him was so strong, but he knew now was not the time. He needed to reign it in and let her rest.

She snuggled in close to him, her head on his chest. Her hands snuck beneath the bottom of his shirt creating circles of heat on his skin. "You are supposed to be resting, young lady. If you keep that up, you are going to get us kicked out of here," he warned.

A slow smile spread across her face. "You are the one that wants me to rest, I said no such thing."

Sam's body shook as he laughed to himself. Her fingers roamed just under his waistband. His breath caught. "Beth, sweetheart, I am a strong man, but I don't know if I can stop if we get started again. I have respected the time you need. The other week we put the brakes on because you weren't ready, and it almost killed me. But I survived."

She put a finger to his lips. "Shh. This past week has taught me something. We aren't promised a tomorrow. Besides, I want you."

"I want you too, but this isn't the place." He kissed her forehead, smiling at her pout. "I promise when I get back, we will have our time. Now, I have to go. Do you want me to call anyone for you?" Sam slipped her hand out of his clothes and got out of bed.

"No. I'll be okay. I'm just waiting on the doctors right now. Sophie and Hellen both offered to get me when I'm ready. I'm going to the waterfront house, right?" Beth looked excited by the possibility.

"It's all ready for you. Take your time and be careful on the stairs." He said.

"Thanks for finishing everything. I was worried things would fall apart." She beamed.

Warmth filled him. "Beth, I would never let that happen. You've worked too hard for this." He hesitated. He could stay long enough to get her home and make sure she was settled in. *No.* He should get going before he got stuck in traffic. Sam leaned over and pressed another long, deep kiss to her lips. "I'll be back as soon as I can," he whispered against her lips. He released her, determined to stick to his schedule.

As he crossed the room, Sam asked, "door opened, or closed?"

"Open, please."

Sam thought he saw her eyes tear up. He swung the door open wide so she could see the action in the hallway.

"I'll call once I get to Raleigh. Text me when you get settled in at the house and let me know what you think."

"Yes, sir." Beth teased.

He knew he was being bossy. "Sorry, habit."

"S'okay. I'm used to hearing your bossy voice." She laughed.

It was good to hear her laughter. He paused and memorized the sound to keep with him. This was going to be a long week.

* * *

A NURSE KNOCKED and poked her head in the door. "You have a visitor. A Ms. Hellen, she isn't on the list, but I thought I would ask before I told her you were resting."

Beth looked at the nurses' station and waved at Hellen. "Hellen can come in. She's my ride home." Beth smiled. Hellen didn't wait for the okay and pushed past the nurse into the room and gave Beth a huge hug.

"Hey Lady, I see you're finally awake. You look one hundred percent better than the last time I was in."

"You came to visit?" Turning to the nurse, Beth gave her a smile. "Thank you for bringing her in. "The nurse nodded and left the ladies alone.

"Yes, it was when you first checked in. Sam snuck me in to see you. I was so worried. You know those men didn't even tell me you were missing. I could have killed them when I found out."

"I'm sure they didn't want to worry you."

"Actually, Jose admitted that he thought you left town for a break. That Sam was overreacting. I gave him hell for it."

"Well, that was the plan. I was headed to Virginia when I was taken. I went to the house to get my bag so I could pack." A feeling of uneasiness settled in on her as the memory of the night surfaced with gooseflesh on her skin. She rubbed her palms against her forearms and shivered.

Hellen grabbed Beth's hand and squeezed. "We don't have to talk about it if you don't want to. It must have been horrible." Her voice dropped an octave. "Has Tim been by yet?"

"Mom said he tried to come by while I was sleeping, but I haven't seen anyone officially yet."

"They probably wanted to make sure you were ready."

Beth shook her head. "I have a feeling something is going on, but they are keeping it quiet."

"Well, I don't know anything. Apparently, they are good at keeping secrets. So, are you going home to the waterfront house?"

"Yes, definitely. I'm ready to be in my own house. Honestly, I was ready three weeks ago, but I didn't say anything. No sense in putting pressure on the guys when there weren't any walls."

Hellen laughed. "I guess you're right. It's good to see you've kept your sense of humor."

"I've decided I wasn't going to give up anything else to that creep, whoever he is." Beth lifted her chin and raised an eyebrow.

"Good for you." She gave Beth's hand another squeeze. "I'm going to plan on staying with you a few days if that's okay. At least until Sam gets back."

"What about the kids?"

"Jose has it under control. Besides I'm looking forward to some girl time." She laughed. "It will be like a mini-vacation."

"Not for Jose. But, I'm excited for us!" Beth hoped her smile relayed how much she appreciated her. Hellen really made her feel missed and grateful to have her back. Beth couldn't explain why it meant so much to her, but after feeling so alone, this was exactly the cure she needed.

"Oh, I have a surprise for you." Hellen pulled a small brown bag from her purse. It was from Rachel K's.

"Oh, my gosh, Hellen, you didn't." Beth peeked in the bag and pulled out an enormous buttery croissant.

"I knew you were on hospital food for a while. I figured, you probably needed some empty calories by now."

Beth shoved a big bite in her mouth and found buttery heaven. "Thank you so much," she said with her mouth full. Covering her mouth with her hand, she added, "Sorry."

"It's okay. I would have smuggled in tea, but I didn't want to risk getting tackled." The two ladies laughed. "By the way, Rick says 'hi.' Apparently, he misses you." She wiggled her eyebrows and smiled wide. "What is that all about?"

Beth blushed. "Oh, that's nothing. I usually have breakfast there in the morning. He's only being sweet."

"I would say he's sweet on you, but whatever you say." Hellen winked at her.

"Will you stop it?" Beth giggled.

"I'm going to go check and see when you're getting sprung." Hellen went out to the desk and bugged the nurses.

Beth wasn't used to getting so much male attention. She was ready to be home and back to normalcy.

IS IT PLUMB?

Monday, September 29, 2014

Beth eased herself out of the front seat of the minivan. Every muscle in her body ached. The ride from the hospital was pure torture. She broke out in a sweat as she looked at the picture postcard. Visions of her last night here flashed in her mind, and she grabbed Hellen's hand. The house was beautiful. Full flower pots decorated the front porch, giving the house a warm and welcoming appearance from the street. The large tree in the side yard now held a tire swing, and underneath bright yellow toy dump trucks sat in the shade. It was the epitome of 'home.' Hellen followed Beth's gaze. "The boys thought Sophie's kids might need something to do while they were here," she explained.

"Thank you. I'm sure everything won't fit into a suitcase." Beth searched the yard for Sophie, who said she would be there when they arrived. Then, she heard squeals from across the street. Ahh, there she was. Sophie was at the dock trying to control the boys who both had created make-shift fishing poles from sticks and string. But it appeared the boys were more interested in playing whack-a-mole on one another than catching anything. They were a handful.

"Can you help me get into the house before the terrible two attacks?" Beth joked.

"Of course. Are we headed all the way up? "

"Yes, please. I am exhausted." She slid from the minivan, taking a beat to get her balance.

Hellen held onto Beth's arm as she walked over the uneven ground in the yard. They took the stairs nice and slow into the house. The front room was newly painted, and the classic picture hanging system was hanging from the ceiling waiting for the paintings that belonged in each place. Martin had already placed the placards beside the spaces for each piece. They really would be ready for the opening. They walked through the hall to the stairs to head up to her living quarters, and Hellen moved a chain with a sign that said "Prive." Nice touch, Beth thought. She held onto the banister and slowly climbed to the second story.

Her eyes filled with tears when she emerged into the sitting room. There were her things. The comfortable couch sported her favorite quilt thrown over the arm. The TV in the corner on a country hutch. Photos from all her travels covered the walls. Every frame held a memory that made her heart swell with emotion. They continued through the room down to a hall that led to the bedroom. There was a door with a ribbon on it and a sign that said, "No Entry Without Me, Sam."

"Oh, he is mean," Beth said, looking at Hellen.

"No peeking." Hellen laughed. "He made me promise that I would keep an eye on you."

"We don't have to tell him."

"Oh no. He has threatened me with bodily harm if you set foot in there. It's a surprise." She grabbed hold of Beth's arm. "Come and see your bedroom. You are going to love this." Hellen opened the double doors to her bedroom. The large room had her bed with bookcases on each side of it and then the wall at the front of the house there was a massive window with a window seat that faced a view of the river. Beth's mouth dropped open.

"Beautiful, just beautiful." Looking at Hellen, she knew that she agreed. "He did such a great job creating a place that's separate from the gallery."

"Yep. Hard to believe that your business is downstairs. Come on, let's get you into bed." She pulled back the quilt and helped Beth out of her shoes. "Don't forget to send him a text. I'll be downstairs if you need me. The intercom is right next to the bed."

Beth snuggled down under the covers, her covers. She took in a big sniff and exhaled. It was heavenly. She watched the sailboats on the river as they took advantage of the bright day. A cold sweat broke out on her skin. What if he came and got her again? What would she do? *I'm safe with people who care about me.* Visions of water swirling around her filled her mind. The oxygen left her lungs, and her vision grew dark.

The next thing she knew Hellen and Sophie by her side.

"Beth? Honey, are you okay? You must breathe for me. Slow, deep breaths." Beth focused on Sophie's voice. She had her hand in a vise grip. She was safe, and her friends were here. It was okay. "Breathe Beth, just breathe. That's it. Great job."

Beth's phone rang, and Hellen picked up. "No, now is not the right time. Give us an hour to get settled in." She quieted while whoever was on the other line responded.

"Damn it, Tim. We just got home from the hospital. She hasn't even had a chance to talk to Sam yet." Her expression darkened. "I said one hour." She hung up the phone. "Damn men. So bossy." She turned back to Beth who was taken back by the way Hellen had spoken to Tim. "How are you feeling now? Better?"

Beth nodded her head, "Can we close the curtains please?"

"Of course." Sophie crossed the room and pulled them shut. "Bonne?"

"Oui, c'est bonne. Can I get some privacy to call Sam?"

"Yes. We will be downstairs. Tim will be here in an hour, but don't worry I will sit with you if you want. Tell Sam 'hi' for us." They disappeared behind the doors. Beth dialed his number, and it rang. She looked at the time and told herself he was still driving and probably couldn't pick up. She texted him.

BETH: *Miss you. I'm home, and the house is amazing. TY Call when you can.*

SPLAYED LINTEL

$\mathcal{T}$raffic was bumper to bumper, and Sam was pissed off. This was going to throw off his meeting tonight. He needed to call the Dean of the History Department, but he would wait until he was in a better mood. His phone rang. Beth. He wanted to pick up but knew his mood would make her feel guilty if he talked to her now. The time he had spent with her this morning was worth the headache tonight, but his brain didn't believe his heart at the moment. A text came through, and he glanced at the screen. Good. She liked the house. Hopefully, the girls had kept her out of her new study. It was a special surprise.

He hit his brakes and banged on the steering wheel. This was ridiculous. He hit the button and told Siri to call the NC State History Department. The administration assistant picked up after a couple of rings.

"Hi, this is Sam Howards. Can you pass on a message to the Dean please?"

"Of course, Professor Howards."

"I'm stuck in traffic, so I will be delayed. I should be there around eight. I know that will be too late to meet so perhaps he will have some time before the symposium starts tomorrow."

"I will check his schedule and let you know."

"Thank you. I will be here in traffic until further notice."

"Thank you for letting us know, sir."

Sam hung up the phone. He knew that this would not make a good impression, but he also knew he wasn't going to accept the job offer. There was a more important reason for him to stay in Washington. He would give his presentation at the symposium in the morning, wow the other academics with his research, and then go back to his renovation business and the community college. He would live happily ever after if she would have him. He dialed Beth and breathed a sigh of relief when her sleepy voice came on the line.

"Hello. How's my girl doing?"

"I would be doing better if you were here."

"I miss you too."

"Tim will be here in a little while to question me. I wish you were here.

"You will be okay. Lean on the girls if you need them. That's why they're there."

"I had a panic attack, looking out at the river. What if I can't be close to the water again? I live on a riverbank for God's sake. What am I going to do?"

"We will get through this. I will be right beside you. It's just going to take some time. Are you okay, now?"

"Yes. Hellen and Sophie helped me. But Sam, I don't know if I'll get better. What if I'm broken?"

"You are not broken, you are just hurt. It takes time to heal."

"What are you doing right now?"

"I'm driving; more specifically, sitting in traffic. Oh, I wanted to let you know that I have Selah's diary. Martin got it for me when they were packing up the flat."

"Oh. What do you need it for?"

"I'm going to be with some experts this week, and I thought they could help me find some more information on her family."

"That would be fantastic."

"I'll bring it back safe and sound. I promise."

"When will you be back?"

"I'm shooting for tomorrow night. It would be boring for you. It's just lots of lectures on different periods of history. I will come back full of new information and refreshed."

"It actually sounds interesting."

"Next time I'll bring you along if you're up to it. Gotta go, we're moving again."

"Sounds good. I'll talk to you later."

"Text me if you need me," he said before disconnecting.

Sam wished he could be there for her interview with the sheriff. He was worried about her now. If she had a panic attack looking out of her window, what would happen when Tim asked her the difficult questions about her abduction? All he wanted right this minute was to wrap his arms around her and hold her close so she would feel safe. He traveled with the rest of the traffic, passing a stranded car on the side of the road with a wrecker which was the cause of the jam. Now maybe he would be there in time to get some dinner.

He started to mentally review his presentation for the next day. He was the first presenter so technically he could skip out on the rest of the symposium, but he knew he wouldn't. He was looking forward to seeing his colleagues and hearing their presentations. This was the one time a year they met at State. Historians from all over the country attended every year to share their thoughts with others in the field. Sometimes, his papers were controversial because of the field he chose for work, but history symposiums didn't typically break out in fistfights so he would survive. He did every year.

"Preserve to document or replace to enjoy: Living with History by Samuel Howards, Ph.D." A smirk appeared on his face, and Sam laughed out loud, this year there may be fists thrown, and he would be the main instigator.

* * *

Someone was standing over her bed. Beth looked up and tried to focus. Hellen nudged her awake.

"Beth honey, you need to wake up and have some medicine. Tim is here waiting for you."

Beth blinked at her, trying to focus but the dim light in the room made it difficult. "Hellen?"

"Yes. Time to get up. I'll bring Tim in here. Close your eyes. I need to turn the lights on."

Beth shut her lids and waited to see the lights. She heard the click of the switch and slowly opened her eyes. They weren't too bright. Just enough to help her see.

Hellen walked over to the dresser and picked up Beth's brush. "You might want to use this."

"Do I look horrible?"

"Not at all, just a bad case of bed head." Hellen smiled at her. "Tim won't care. He's totally professional."

"But he's a friend of Sam's, right?"

"Yes."

"Well, I don't want him reporting that I look terrible. Sam will be upset."

"Will you stop? You just got home from the hospital. Tim is by the book when it comes to his job. I doubt he will share anything with Sam. Relax, I don't want you having another panic attack." She patted Beth on the shoulder and turned toward the door. "I'll be right back."

A few minutes passed before there was another knock at the door. Hellen poked her head back in the room. "All ready?"

"Yes."

Her friend opened the door and brought a chair with her to the bedside. She was followed by the tall, blond deputy. He held out his hand for Beth.

"Deputy Tim Whitaker. I won't keep you long Mrs. Pearse. I just wanted to see if I can get some details about the period of time while you were missing."

"Of course,"

The interview was not as long as Beth thought it was going to be. She described the trip over the water in the boat and the cement room that she was held in. She told Tim about how the kidnapper's treatment of her changed after what she guessed was a few days. She wasn't sure. They never spoke to her, only gave her notes except for that one time, but she was sure that was her imagination.

"And what did he say? You told me you were sure that it was a man."

"Yes, a man. He said he wouldn't hurt me. It was quick like he was panicking. He was taking my clothing off, and I thought he was going to rape me. I started to struggle, and he said, 'I'm not going to hurt you.' Or something to that effect."

"Do you think you could identify the voice if you heard it again?"

"Yes." Her mind drifted to the thought that she would never forget that voice; the voice of a dead man.

"Ms. Pearse, are you okay?"

"Yes, thank you. Sorry. Do you know when Sam will be back home?" She refocused on the deputy.

"As far as I know he should be back in a couple of days. He has his presentation and the job interview."

Beth physically jerked from the comment. "Job interview?"

"Yes, the University offered him a position. The interview is probably just a formality, really."

"He didn't mention an interview," Beth commented.

Tim grimaced. "I hope I didn't spill the beans. I'm sure he will tell you all about it when he gets back."

Beth nodded her head but wondered if he would say anything.

"I think that is all I need. If we need anything else, I will give you a call to schedule another interview." Tim stood up and shook her hand again. "Thank you for your time. Should I send Hellen or Sophie in for you?"

"Hellen, please," Beth requested. She remained in her bed still unsure of herself outside of her bedroom.

Tim nodded and pulled the door shut behind him.

MODIFIED TRIGLYPHS

When Sam pulled into his hotel, he was exhausted. He didn't hear anything from Beth, and he hoped that was a good sign. Tim knew what was going on so he would be easy on her. He wouldn't make it an interrogation. Sam checked in at the front desk and took all his research and luggage to his room. He was supposed to have dinner with the Dean, but since it was late, he would settle for a quick bite at the hotel bar. He would bring his notes with him to go over his presentation for in the morning. Grabbing his packet, he headed out the door.

In the bar, he ordered a sandwich, fries, and a beer. The presentation he was giving was his standby, but it had turned into a controversial one in the academic world. It was based on his business. The scholars fought him saying that all historical preservation should preserve the old, but his opinion was that if he could maintain the integrity of the location and historical record but replace and make the space more livable, it made the survival of the historical location more likely. Sam saw too many buildings torn down because of safety reasons and so the preservation was lost forever. It broke his heart.

The kitchen was quick, and Sam wasted no time in the bar. He needed to be on his toes in the morning. A good night's sleep was a necessary evil. His colleagues were respectful, but they would push his buttons and try to rattle him so he would not make his case. He needed to stand firm. This topic mattered to him, and he had to ensure that funding would be approved for future projects. He texted Beth when he returned to his room.

SAM: *Good night, hope your day was a restful one. Call me if you need me.*

Right away came the reply.

Beth: Is now good?

Sam: Sure.

THE PHONE RANG ALMOST INSTANTLY. "Hey. How was your day?"

"I should ask you how your drive was." She responded.

"It was uneventful, just too long. I'm exhausted." Sam shared with her. "How was your interview?"

"Not too bad. Officer Whitaker is very nice. I shared as much I remembered. He told me to write down anything that pops into my head later. He said they have an idea who took me. I just don't know if I would recognize him if I saw him again."

"Do you remember much?" He asked trying to be supportive, but his anger over what had happened made it hard for him to hold his temper.

"The only thing I remember is a beard against my ear when he took me first. I was in the cement room for several days, but there was no way to keep track. I'll just have to think about it and write it down for him. Anyway, enough about that. Did you touch base with your colleagues tonight? Tim said that you are quite known out there at the University. What's this job interview that you didn't tell me about?"

"Oh, it's really nothing. I was late so it will be rescheduled tomorrow. But enough about me. If you need to talk about anything, we can. We don't have to talk about my stuff. It's routine really." Sam was embarrassed that Tim had bragged about him. He wondered what else his friend had shared with her.

"I want to hear about your presentation tomorrow. All the juicy details. I'll let you get some sleep."

"You need your sleep too. Don't blame it all on me."

"I have been doing nothing but sleeping. I will be glad when I can get out in the fresh air."

"Get one of the girls to walk outside with you. Enjoy some sunshine while we have some."

"I will. Call me tomorrow when you have time?"

"Okay. Sweet dreams."

"Thanks, good night," she responded and disconnected.

Sam sensed some stress in her voice after he mentioned 'sweet dreams.' Maybe he should have stayed. If she was still having nightmares, she would never get enough rest to heal. He took a breath and reassured himself she had plenty of support.

At four o'clock, Sam finally gave up and got out of bed to work out. His brain would not turn off. He pulled on his sweats and headed down to the hotel gym. The room was deserted, and the treadmill was just what he needed. He listened closely to the news during his run and was surprised to hear they were tracking another storm. It was currently a week out, putting it ashore around the time of the festival. That would be a shame. The rain this summer had already caused enough problems with the tourist industry in town. If Smoke on the Water rained out, it would be hard for local business to recover. He hoped the storm would turn.

Sam pushed himself hard, quickening his pace to burn the rage he was dealing with since Beth had been found. No one should have to deal with what she had gone through. Tim was trying to track down Robert and prove the man's identity, but it was proving difficult because Robert had covered his tracks well. It was as if he completely disappeared or had never existed at all. Sam ran faster hitting the button to increase the incline. His breath began to strain, and he couldn't think of anything but regulating his breathing. He didn't like the negativity that was taking over his mood. Turning off the treadmill, he reached for his iPhone and texted Beth.

SAM: *Are you up? Thinking 'bout you.*

HE TOOK a huge drink of his water and wiped the sweat off his face.

The answer came back quickly.

Beth: *yes, missing you.*

Sam: *Me too.*

Beth: *Are you going to tell me what's behind the hall door?*

He laughed and gathered up his things.

Sam: *Nope, you have to wait.*

Beth: I could just walk down the hall *and peek.*

Sam: You could, but you won't.

She'd gotten her sense of humor back. That's good. Sam stepped into the elevator and pushed the button for his floor.

Beth: You're right, but I really want to. How is your meeting going? Are you having fun hanging out with all your fellow history geeks?

Sam: That's later.

Beth:Good Luck

Sam:Thanks, now go back to sleep.

ARRIVING AT HIS HOTEL ROOM, he tried his card key, and it wouldn't work. He tried again, and the red light told him the key wasn't going to open the door. He turned around and headed back down to the lobby. Glancing at his phone, he noted the time and told himself he had about two hours until he needed to be on campus. The hotel lobby was empty, and Sam hit the bell for service. There was no one to be seen. Maybe if he knocked on the office door. He walked over to the door and found it wide open. The clerk was asleep with his head on the desk. Sam knocked hard enough to wake him but not to startle him. He began to stir, stretching his arms.

"Hey, dude, what'cha need?"

"My key's not working."

"Oh sorry. Let me make you a new one." The young man took Sam's card keys and swiped them through the machine. "What room number do you need?"

"659."

"And your name?"

"Samuel Howards."

"You're here for the symposium. I'll be over soon as I'm off here."

"Are you in architecture or history?"

"Both I'm looking forward to your presentation. Here you go. I'll see you later then."

"Make sure you ask a few questions. It will help me out."

"Sure thing."

Sam gave the clerk a quick nod and then headed back upstairs. He would have to hurry if he was going to grab some breakfast.

TRUSS CLIP

*T*uesday, September 30, 2014

The lecture hall was one of the larger ones, and it was filling up fast. Sam had chosen his gray suit with a smart looking tie to match. The only thing that made him stand out from his colleagues was his steel toe work boots. He did it to prove a point. He was different from the rest of the academics in the room. He used his knowledge in the field every day of the year. He organized his notes and tested his pointer. He scanned the room and noticed the young hotel clerk about halfway up the theater seating. Good, he knew there was at least one supporter in the crowd.

"Professor Howards, so good of you to join us." An older man held out his hand, and Sam gave him a firm handshake.

"Dean Stewart, thank you for attending my lecture." Sam was unsure why he was here.

"It's my pleasure to introduce you today. You ready to get started?"

"Thank you, yes sir." Sam smiled and turned to his papers and notes. His nerves began to set in.

The Dean stepped up to the microphone. "Can I get everyone to take their seats, please? We will be starting in five minutes."

There were no empty seats, a full house. *Oh boy.* He smiled.

The Dean returned to the mic and unfolded his notes.

"Ladies and Gentlemen, I would like you to welcome you to the 20th North Carolina State University History Symposium. We have prided ourselves on being the stage of which every idea is listened to and respected. The groundbreaking discoveries that have been announced at this event have introduced the academic world to new thought and use of that information. We believe that history is not just the past, but it is our future.

Our opening lecture is just such an example of this. It is my pleasure to introduce Professor Samuel Howards. Professor Howards graduated from Stanford University with a master's in architecture. He then attended Columbia University to receive his Ph.D. in History specializing in Historical Architecture. He currently teaches in Washington, North Carolina and runs his own historical preservation company. Please join me in welcoming Professor Howard to the platform." The Dean stepped to the side and motioned to the microphone. Sam stepped to the podium and started a speech he had given hundreds of times, but this time was very different. He was nervous.

"Thank you, Dean Stewart, for the most gracious introduction. I am here today to talk about living with history and how we can make it more accessible to the masses in a holistic way. Architectural Preservation has been in a dilemma for centuries. Do we tear the old buildings down? Do we let them crumble around us? Do we fix or replace? There is always a more appropriate method in every circumstance. I am here to argue that in most cases if we replace with historically accurate modern materials, the historical properties will survive for many more generations to enjoy."

A disgruntled roar came from the crowd in the room. Comments came from every direction.

"I will be glad to answer questions and respond to comments after I am finished. Let's take a look at some properties that support my theory." Sam hit the button, and the power point presentation began. He ran through numerous properties around the world showing families living in historically relevant houses with a modern lifestyle. The hour-long presentation held his colleagues' attention although grumbling could be heard here and there.

"In conclusion, I would add that if we can make this type of preservation affordable to the masses, there will be historical buildings for generations to come. I will now open the floor to questions." Sam took a deep breath, readying himself for the naysayers. He pointed to a gentleman to the right.

"Is it not true, that when you speak of replacement with modern materials, you are actually diluting the historical value of the property?" the man asked.

"I would disagree with that. With properly researched replacement materials, they can be historically accurate as a repurposed material from another location." Sam answered.

"So, you have no concerns that a future researcher, say in one hundred years, would mistake a Federally styled metal door as an original piece of the construction." Concern registered in the man's voice.

"Of course not."

"Then would you not make an extra effort to find a proper replacement from the era." The man stated bluntly.

"That would be cost prohibitive for most homeowners." Sam rebutted.

"If one chooses to be a historical property owner, then the cost should be considered a responsibility." The men surrounding him nodded in agreement.

"The reason we are losing our historical buildings to decay is the government can no longer afford to pay for upkeep. If we provided an affordable alternative to families who are willing to live with the tourist curiosity of their property, why not give it to them?" Loud applause arose from the audience. The young hotel clerk stood while clapping and others joined him while the traditionalists refused. Sam could feel the division in the room and knew it would never change. The new generation were the ones he was talking to. They were the ones that would make a difference.

The Dean stood up and walked over to the podium, his hands clapping high above his head. He motioned toward Sam and clapped again, urging the audience to continue their praise. He shook Sam's hand and leaned over to his ear. "Lunch is on me."

Sam nodded and bowed his head politely. He gathered up his papers and excused himself from the room as the applause continued. He could hear the Dean announcing the next speaker, and he pulled out his cell phone to call Beth.

ROUGH FRAME

The light snuck through the crack in the drapes creating a line across the bedroom and up into Beth's eyes making it impossible to continue the nap that should have ended hours before. The sound of boys playing in the yard interrupted her dreams, changing her mood to a happier one. The dreams, or rather nightmares, had continued. It wasn't about Selah, though. It was Brad invading her sleep. His drowning repeated over and over in her mind. She was sure the voice she heard during her captivity was his but was it real?

So much in her life didn't make sense right now. She was ready to start the next part of her life, but the past wouldn't go away. She needed to let go. She had friends here in Washington to help her make it happen and someone who cared about her. But he would be leaving. He told her he wanted to stay, but how could he pass up such a great job in Raleigh?

Her phone rang, and she glanced at the caller id, showing Sam's number. He said he would call after his presentation. She rolled over and hit the screen.

"Hi. How did it go?"

"It went fantastic," he answered. "You should have been there. I really shook things up."

"Is that what you wanted?" She asked, "to make waves?"

"You know me, the rebel." His laugh caressed her ear through the phone.

"Oh, yeah; a real James Dean."

"I wish. But I did have the grumpy old men grumbling through the whole thing. The Dean was very impressed with my research; invited me to lunch."

"Are you going?" She was curious about what would be discussed. No doubt it would be the job offer Tim had mentioned.

"Yeah. You can't pass up a free meal, right?" His light tone changed to concern. "How are you sleeping?"

"Not so good. The nightmares are making it impossible."

"Maybe you should talk to someone, a professional."

"I'll be okay," Beth reassured him.

"I know you will, but you've been through a lot. Any more panic attacks?"

"Nope, but I haven't ventured outside, yet. I thought I would wait till you got back."

"Sounds good." He paused, "I have to go. I need to touch base with a friend of mine before I head back."

"You don't have to come back today if you're needed there," she told him.

"I will be in late tonight. I can get everything I need to get done today. So, I will see you in the morning."

"Okay. I can't wait." After she hung up the phone, her pulse quickened at the thought of him coming home. Would it be his home for long? She couldn't ask him to stay. She wouldn't. Beth climbed out of bed and slowly walked to the window. Her hands shook as she grabbed the curtains. Slowly, she opened them only a sliver, peeking out at the river in front of her. What was she afraid of? The water? She pulled the curtain open a little more, watching the four little boys with their fishing poles casting into the water. Their giggles and screams floated through the air into her window. This was supposed to be a happy place, not one of dread. She reached deep within her and opened the curtain wide. She could do this. She was not a victim. This was her home, and she was safe. She chanted to herself, "I am strong, I can survive this. He will not win."

Out of the corner of her eye, she saw Selah with a smile on her face. The young woman only nodded, her hand holding a small piece of patchwork. "You are safe," she said, "but he is still watching. Be careful." Beth continued to chant her new mantra and opened the window to let the breeze blow through the house. The fresh air renewed her spirits as it filled the room. The boys turned around and waved at her from the pier. She waved back and then walked to her dresser to decide what to wear for the day.

She slowly walked down the stairs to the gallery space to see beautiful pieces hanging on every wall. There was some pottery on the relocated cellar shelves. Classic and modern pieces all picturing seascapes. The color of water surrounded her, and she was in her own personal hell. She found a chair in a corner and took in all the work Martin had accomplished during her recovery time. He did an excellent job. Beth could hear someone talking in the kitchen. She strolled down the hall toward the conversation. She recognized Hellen's voice, and there was a male's voice.

As Beth rounded the corner to peer through the doorway, she spotted Deputy Felton with a sandwich in his hand. Hellen was stirring something on the stove. The kitchen was simple and elegant; exactly what she needed for the gallery.

"Well, look who decided to join us for lunch." Deputy Felton rose from his seat and offered it to Beth. "Here, have a seat. I'll get another from the other room."

"Thanks," Beth said quickly, looking at Hellen for an explanation. She was suddenly uncomfortable with her appearance. Her hair was wet from her shower, and she had dressed for comfort, not visitors.

Hellen shrugged. "Do you want some soup? I'm getting ready to call the boys in for lunch."

"Sure, I'll have some," and then whispered, "What is he doing here?"

"He dropped by to check on you. I think it's kind of sweet." She whispered back. Then Bill returned to the room with another chair, "Bill, did you get enough to eat?"

"Yes, thank you." Turning to Beth, "How are you feeling? I was worried when they said you weren't allowed any visitors."

"Nothing to worry about, I'm doing a lot better. I've been resting a lot."

"Well, you look great." He looked her up and down as if he was taking inventory.

Beth glanced down at the scabbed over rope burns on her visible wrists, wishing she had chosen a long sleeve shirt, her bruises now yellowing with age. "Deputy Felton, you shouldn't say things that are untrue."

"Please call me Bill," he corrected her. "I would never do that. You are just as beautiful as ever."

"Thank you." Hellen put a bowl of soup in front of her on the counter with a smile, ignoring her discomfort growing. "Thanks, Hellen."

"I'll be right back." Hellen quickly said over her shoulder and headed out the front door to get the boys.

Beth's skin grew goose bumps and her hair prickled. Bill leaned closer to her, "You really should learn to take a compliment. You don't want to seem ungrateful." His mustache tickled her ear. Déjà vu kicked her body with a jolt of adrenaline.

She started to shake, but she willed her body to remain calm. *What should she do?* "If you will excuse me, I should go back upstairs. I'm feeling very tired. Thank you for dropping by." Beth slid off the chair and backed out of the room, her face like stone. She wouldn't let him see what she now knew. Bill was her kidnapper.

When she was out of his vision, she ran to the front yard scanning to see where Hellen was. She spotted her at the large tree. Her breath wasn't cooperating with her will to run across the yard. "Hellen, call the police, call Deputy Whitaker."

Hellen gave her a confused look. "What? Why?" Beth's voice tried to compete with the boys pushing dump trucks through the mud at Hellen's feet.

Beth couldn't catch her breath. "Call..." it was hard to form a sentence... "Tim." And everything faded.

* * *

BETH SHOT STRAIGHT UP when she woke. Panic still raced through her bloodstream from her discovery. She realized she was back in her bedroom. The drapes were pulled tight, and it was dark. A shadow in the corner shifted in their seat at her movement. She couldn't tell who it was.

"Hello?" Her voice wavered with fear.

"Beth..." it was a female voice. "You scared us to death."

"Hellen?"

"Yes, honey?" She asked. "Tell me what you need."

"Did you call the deputy?"

"What? Why?" her voice was confused.

"I need to talk to Tim. Can you please call him for me or get me my phone and his card? I will call him. I remembered something important." Beth started to feel anxious. "Has Bill gone?"

"Yes, he helped me get you into bed," Hellen said as Beth felt the sheets against her skin noticing her clothing was missing. "Then he said he had to get to work."

"Did he help," Beth hesitated, her voice shaking "...help you take off my clothes?"

"Of course, not. He just helped me get you to the bed. What is this all about?"

"Just bring me my phone and Tim's number please."

"Okay." She crossed the room to the dresser and returned with both items, handing them to Beth.

"Thank you. Give me a minute, will you?" She glanced at the door.

Beth watched Hellen close the door and dialed Deputy Whitaker's number. He picked up almost instantly.

"Deputy Whitaker speaking. How can I help you?"

"Deputy Whitaker, this is Beth Pearse. I know who it was. Can you come over to the house please?"

"I'll be right over. Do you have someone with you? Is Sam back?"

"No, he isn't back yet. Hellen is here with me."

"Okay, stay at the house. Give me ten minutes." She heard his car ignition, and he disconnected.

Beth pushed the button for the intercom, "Hellen can you bring me some water, please?" Her nerves left her mouth parched. He wouldn't be long, she told herself.

"Of course. Do you need anything else from the kitchen?"

"No, thank you."

Soon there was a knock at the door, and Hellen popped in with a glass of water. "Everything okay?" she asked.

"Yes, Tim is on his way over. Can you make sure that no one else comes in the house? I don't want any more visitors today."

"Of course," she smiled. "It was good to see you outside, but maybe you pushed yourself too much today. Let's take things slower."

"I know who it was." Beth blurted out before she lost her nerve to say it out loud.

"What?" Hellen appeared shocked.

"I know who took me that night. It will be over soon."

"Is it that man the guys have been looking for?" Hellen volunteered.

"Who is that?" Beth asked.

"Some guy that was working at the hardware store. No one has seen him since the night you disappeared. I can't remember his name. Jose told me that Martin thought he recognized him, but then changed his mind."

"No, it wasn't him. I've never met him."

"So, it's someone you know?" Hellen looked astonished.

"Yes. Please send Tim up when he gets here."

"No problem." Hellen left the room and returned with Tim five minutes later.

The deputy crossed the room and took a seat next to her bed. "Okay, I'm ready. What do you remember?"

"Hellen, can you excuse us, please. I want to talk to Deputy Whitaker alone." She saw Hellen hesitate, so added, "really I'm okay now." Beth glanced around the room and saw her ally, Selah, rocking in the corner. Sam even remembered her rocking chair from the flat, he thought of everything. After Hellen had closed the door behind her, Beth started.

"It was Bill Felton." Tim tensed, and Beth knew what he was thinking, "I know that you are friends, just listen to me, please. It was him. He keeps showing up at weird times. I never noticed it before, but today he used the same phrase my kidnapper did when he took me."

"You're sure?" Tim countered.

"That night the man told me to 'shut up, ungrateful bitch.'" A shudder ran through Beth remembering that night. "Then this afternoon he told me, 'You don't want to seem ungrateful.' It was the same voice, I swear."

"Okay, then what happened?"

"I must have been drugged because I passed out when I screamed."

"Do you remember anything else that would identify him?"

"No, um, wait, the feel of his mustache on my ear when he was talking to me. That was the same this afternoon."

"You say this happened this afternoon?"

"Yes, he had lunch here at the house. After Hellen left the room, he leaned very close to me and whispered in my ear." Beth started to shake uncontrollably. "I know he's a cop and your friend..."

"First, I need you to relax. I will take care of this. My priority is to keep you safe. We will bring him in for questioning." He put his hand on Beth's trembling one. "Calm down and breathe for me." Beth released the breath she realized she was holding when he spoke. "Okay, that's better. Stay at the house. I will have a deputy posted before I leave."

Beth could only nod. She tried to tell herself things would be okay, but now one of Sam's friends was going to be arrested because of her. Tim caught her gaze and gave her a strong smile. "It's good that you remembered. Now we can finish this." He left her alone in the dim room.

Selah stepped out of the darkness. "He's a good man. You can trust him."

"But I don't think he believes me," Beth said.

"It's hard to think that a friend can do evil things, but he is good at his job. He will make sure that you are safe. I heard it in his voice."

Beth heard the same assurance that Selah had in his voice. He wouldn't stop until she was completely safe, she knew it. Beth got dressed and headed downstairs. Hellen was playing outside with the boys, and she saw Sophie under the large tree as well. True to Tim's word, there was a deputy posted on the porch. She opened the door, took a deep breath and stepped out of the house. Giving the deputy a nod, she walked over to the group of young boys doing demolition under the tree.

"Hi guys, how's the road building?" All four faces turned toward Beth and beamed.

"Beth," they all screamed, jumped up, and ran to wrap their arms around her.

Beth's eyes turned glassy. "Oh, my goodness, what a hug! Thank you."

"You're welcome," they squealed and pulled her down to the ground to their dirt project.

"Ça va?" Sophie asked, knowing that the answer may not be entirely truthful.

"Bien." Beth met the knowing look head-on. "Soon we will be all better."

"Oui, very soon." She brushed Beth's shoulder lovingly.

"Mama says the policeman is here to keep you safe," Phillipe said.

"That's right. He is here to keep us all safe." Beth agreed. "We should have a picnic and talk about the festival next week."

"Oh yes, a picnic for dinner," Hellen agreed.

"Are you going to be able to stay for the festival?"

"Oui, we planned to stay through your opening. Are you still going to open for the weekend?" Sophie asked.

"Thanks to Martin, it looks like we are all ready. We will still have to plan for the reception." Beth mentioned.

"Already done," Hellen piped up.

"Wow, you guys have done so much. How am I ever going to thank you?"

Hellen leaned over and gave her a hug. "What are friends for? Besides, I have to keep you happy so you will stay. It's been nice having a girl around to talk to."

"I have such good friends. Now if the drama will just die so I can get on with life…" Beth said with a shrug.

Sophie laughed. "You are already used to the small-town life. Brad would never believe how you've changed."

Beth gave her a smile. "No, he wouldn't, would he? The new and improved Beth."

They all three leaned in together for a hug. "Now who is going to get fried chicken?" Beth asked.

"I'll go," Hellen volunteered, shifting off her knees to get up from the ground.

"Okay, we will get everything ready, and the boys can stay out here and play," Sophie said.

"Sounds like a plan. Don't forget to pick up a nice bottle of wine." Beth added.

"And what type of wine goes with Fried chicken?" Hellen and Beth looked at Sophie for the answer.

"What? Just because I'm French, I know the answer to the wine question?" She stood up and put her hands on her hips. All three women burst out laughing. This afternoon would be a good one,

Beth thought, in more than one way if Tim kept all his promises. She and Sophie waved at Hellen as she pulled out of the driveway.

"Boys, we are going inside to get everything ready for the picnic. You stay here. Do not move from this spot. Do you hear me?" All four heads nodded in agreement with Beth and continued to push the trucks through the mud.

EXISTING ELEMENTS

The precious cargo in his satchel was driving Sam crazy. He didn't know what he would do if something happened to the diary that he and Beth found. He needed it though for the next meeting he had today. The young lawyer he spoke to on the phone the day before had been more than a little suspicious of his inquiry. Fredrick Brown was a young, up and coming defense attorney in the Raleigh area. His face was in every regional magazine over the last year since his big win at the state supreme court. Sam didn't blame him a bit.

The coffee shop was a small one close to the University. Sam would find an out of the way booth so the two men could talk. It had taken more than a few pulled strings to track down the correct Brown family, but Sam was sure that he had the right branch. His friends in the history department at East Carolina helped tremendously with the research. Boy, did he owe them big time. Now if only Mr. Brown would listen to what he had to say.

Sam stepped up to the counter and ordered a black coffee with the barista giving him an odd look. She poured the cup of liquid and slid to over the counter.

"Let me know if you need anything else." She smiled sweetly at him.

"Will do," he responded dismissively, disappointing her.

Sam took a seat out of the way and waited for the lawyer to arrive. He didn't have to wait long. The gentleman was very prompt, and Sam felt underdressed as his appointment approached the table in a designer suit.

Holding out his hand, "Fredrick Brown."

"Samuel Howards." Sam shook his hand.

"I don't have much time," Mr. Brown said matter-of-factly.

"Okay, no problem. I wanted to touch base with you on an artifact from your family's history."

"And how did you receive this item?" he asked.

"It was found in a house that I am working on, as I said on the phone. I am a historical preservationist."

"Yes, I checked on you after our conversation."

"Really?" Sam's eyebrows went up in surprise. This guy was suspicious. "Anyway, it is a diary. I have reason to believe that this was your great, great, great grandmother's diary."

"That is impossible. You see I have the information from my lineage and there is a dead end in 1862 when my second great grandfather was found on the river bank and raised in Bath."

"I think if you read the diary, you would find that the information is quite a good match. Of course, it is not concrete. There are no paper records of his birth because of being a foundling, but the diary does coincide with the timeline."

"I disagree. There has to be paperwork of his birth somewhere."

"Would you like to hear about the author of the diary?"

"I will listen, but I only have a little while longer."

"Okay, I will get started then," Sam said, frustrated. "The woman's name was Selah Brown. She was a Freeman originally from a plantation west of Wilmington, North Carolina. According to her diary and the papers that were inserted into the book, she bought her freedom herself by selling quilts and working as a seamstress. She worked in Washington and was raising money for a trip North for her child and his father, a boat captain. The night that she was supposed to leave there was a bad storm. She was killed, and her child went missing. The diary ends suddenly that day."

"And how do you know she was killed?"

"I'm not at liberty to say," Sam said.

"So, you aren't sure." The man commented.

"I will not say," Sam said back.

"And are you sure the child survived?" the man said.

"According to the newspaper, there was a foundling child after the storm," Sam said as he leaned down and pulled the diary out of his satchel. He read the article himself at the library, claiming the child's survival was a miracle.

"What do you want from me?"

"I would like you to come and meet the woman who found the diary. She had a traumatic month, and it would mean a lot to her. That's all that I'm asking." Sam stated.

"That's all?"

"That's all," Sam reinforced and placed his hand on the small book laying on the table.

"When would you like me to come and meet her?" He asked, his eyes drifting to Sam's hands.

"Do you have time in the next few weeks?"

"I think I could arrange one afternoon to drive to Washington. I will let you know when my schedule will permit."

"Thank you, sir. Would you like to take the diary with you?" Sam offered him his hand, and Mr. Brown shook it firmly "Thank you for your time."

"You're welcome, and no, I'll leave the book with you. Thank you for contacting me although I am still not sure your story is accurate."

"Thank you for listening." Sam was overly gracious. He knew that it would mean a lot to Beth to meet him even if the story was based on coincidence. Mr. Brown said goodbye and left the shop, while Sam stayed and finished his coffee. He hoped this would work out. He would cross his fingers.

Sam checked his phone. There were a few missed calls, mostly colleagues from the symposium congratulating him on his presentation and a text from Tim.

Tim: Call me when you have time.

Sam hit the call button and waited for his friend to pick up.

Tim picked up on the second ring, "Hey man, how's your day going?"

"It's been busy here. What do you need?" Sam asked.

"Just wanted to let you know we caught the guy. He's in custody and won't shut up," Tim bragged.

"What?" Sam exclaimed.

"Yep, he's in lockup." Tim's grin could be heard through the phone.

"But how?"

"Beth was able to remember some stuff this afternoon, and we were able to pick him right up."

"Thank goodness. Does Beth know?"

"Not yet. I was getting ready to ride over there. When are you coming home? She's pretty fragile, you know."

"She's stronger than you think, man. I'll be home late tonight." Sam said.

"Okay, come by and see me tomorrow sometime."

"Will do. When you go over there and give her the good news, ask her to call me after you finish."

"No problem. It will probably be about an hour."

"Sounds good." Sam hung up. He strolled through the streets on the way back to the hotel, the students passing by him with their whole lives in front of them. The hard decisions are not made when you're eighteen or even twenty-one. They are made when you have a career, and you chose to be happy instead of prestigious or rich. They are when you have it all offered to you on a platter, but you turn it down because you value love more. He was about to make a decision like that. He stopped to people watch in the park across from his hotel, and his phone rang.

"Hi, sweetheart. How are you doing?"

"It's been a hard day, but a good one," Beth answered.

"I heard. Tim called me earlier. Are you okay?" Sam asked.

"Yeah I know he told me you want me to call. I'm doing okay.

Hellen and Sophie spent the day with me. The boys have kept it interesting."

Sam laughed. "I can imagine. How much mud are we going to have to clean out of the gallery before the opening?"

Sam's laugh was contagious, and Beth joined in. "It's not too bad."

"I'll see for myself tomorrow." It was good to hear her laughing. He missed the sound.

"Are you still coming home tonight?" She sounded anxious, and he thought he could hear some longing there as well.

"I will be coming in late. I'll bring you breakfast and then we can have a look at your special room," Sam teased.

"I forgot about that." She laughed again.

"You mean you have been good, and you haven't even peeked?" Sam asked.

"I've been too busy to peek," she said.

"Okay, I trust you. I'll see you tomorrow," he said.

"Don't be late. I don't know how long I can be good," she teased.

He laughed and disconnected. The thought of the drive home made him wince. *Oh, this is going to be painful.* He walked back to the hotel and packed his bag. The valet brought his truck around to the front of the building, and Sam threw his bags in the back. His satchel went in the cab with him, and he set off into the six o'clock rush hour traffic.

BACK NAILING

*W*ednesday, October 1, 2014

Sam barreled through the swinging glass doors at the front of the Sherriff's department demanding to see Tim. Chair legs scraped across the floor as the other deputies stood at their desk with their hands on their weapons in case there was an escalation.

"Tim, where is he?" Sam headed straight to the deputy's desk.

"Hold on there, man." Tim put his hand out to keep Sam in place. "He's in custody, and we will take care of everything. You need to calm down."

"Does she know he's here?"

"Yes, she does."

"I want to see him. I want to see Robert and ask him how he could do it."

"Wait. What?" Tim looked confused.

"Robert took her; where is he?"

"Sam, it wasn't Robert. It was Bill." Tim raised his voice to penetrate Sam's thoughts.

Sam shook his head and looked Tim in the eyes. "What are you talking about? It was Robert." The information wasn't making sense. *Bill wouldn't do something like that.*

"No Sam. It was Bill that took her to the island. He has admitted it."

Sam froze, his mind replaying all the events of the last week. "It was Bill?"

"Yes, it was Bill." Tim grabbed his arm and lead him to the chair by his desk. "Apparently, it is an obsession thing. He took her and then he was going to save her so she would think he was a hero. The plan was disrupted when Robert tied him up in his shed."

"So, Robert did tie him up in the shed?" Sam sat in the chair with a thud. All the officers sat back down at their desks.

"Yes, and we are still looking for him because of that." Tim took a seat next to him. "You need to talk to her about the second guy. We're going to release his picture to the news. If she sees it..."

Sam shook his head. "I don't know how to. She just found closure, and now we're going snatch it away. I'm not sure if she could handle it. She wouldn't even leave her room when she was afraid. I need to help her feel safe. If she knows, there is still someone out there..." The anger he felt just moments earlier turned to pity. *Why? Why would Bill do something like that?*

"She is strong enough to handle it. You told me yesterday how strong she is."

"But how can I help her feel safe if we don't know where he is?"

"She loves you. Everyone can see that. I can't tell you how she will react, but you've kept it from her long enough."

"Okay." He wasn't ready to watch her fall apart.

"I'm just telling you the news will release it tonight. You need to talk to her."

Sam rose from the chair and held out his hand. "Thanks. I'll see you later, man. Thank you for taking care of her." He waved at his friend and walked toward the front door.

"Sure. Now go see your girl and show her that room, before you drive her crazy." Tim laughed.

Sam clapped his hands and rubbed them together. Time for some breakfast.

* * *

THE DOORBELL RANG AGAIN and then it rang a third time. Beth shook her head to clear the grogginess from her head. Who would be coming at this hour? Then she remembered, Sam was supposed to come for breakfast. Her heart started to pound, and excitement filled her. She grabbed her robe and wrapped it around her as she walked to the stairs. Taking her time on the stairs, she made it to the front door before he rang it a fourth time. She swung the door open wide. He stood there grinning like a cat.

"You took your sweet time…"

She interrupted him wrapping her arms around him and giving him a long deep kiss.

"Well, good morning to you too." He slid her close and smiled before placing a tender kiss on her forehead.

She smiled wide and pulled him through the doorway after glancing outside for invisible onlookers. "Good morning. How was your drive?" She saw the tiredness around his eyes, or maybe it was something else. "How late did you get in?"

"That's not important. Let's have some breakfast. Ms. Martha picked out the fluffiest biscuit for you." He walked toward the kitchen and placed a brown paper bag on the counter.

"Ms. Martha?" Beth wondered, following him.

"Yes, she's like a mom to me. I'll introduce you one day. She makes the best cheese biscuits. Here. Do you have any orange juice?"

"I honestly don't know. I haven't been in the fridge lately." She sat down at the table.

Sam walked over and opened the refrigerator. "Looks like we have cranberry and pineapple juice. Which would you prefer?"

"I'll have cranberry, please."

"Yes, ma'am." He grabbed the bottle and filled a glass for her. Then he unpacked the bag, setting a large roll oozing with cheese in front of her. "You should eat it while it's hot. That's when they are best."

Beth took a big bite and the warm cheese melted in her mouth. It tasted heavenly. She was enjoying the biscuit when Sam came up behind her. He kissed the top of her head and trailed down kissing her ear whispering, "Are you ready to see your room now?"

She jumped up, bumping into him. "Yes, let's go."

"You aren't going to finish your breakfast?"

"I can do that later." Beth couldn't wait to see it, her own special place, just for her. She grabbed Sam's hand and pulled him up the stairs. She stood in front of the double doors, waiting, for what she didn't know. Sam opened the doors for her to see the room. Beth slowly went in, taking in every detail. It was an office and library with built-in bookcases along the right side of the room, and as she walked further into the room, she saw it. The desk at the window had intricate trim that she knew he had done himself and the wall was covered in different colors. It drew her in closer. She touched the wall and realized that it was clear plexiglass and underneath was folded fabric. In between the studs in the walls, there were hundreds of pieces of fabric making an elaborate collage of color.

"Where did the fabric come from?" she stepped back looking at walls and then turned to Sam.

"It was here in the walls. I think it was probably Selah's. You know, for her quilts." He smiled at her and warmth filled her body.

Beth ran and gave him a hug, whispering in his ear, "Thank you. It's so beautiful. This is amazing. You have captured the soul of the house." Giving him another hug, she noticed it for the first time. In the corner of the room on an easel was the Miró. The painting from his house that she loved so much and now she knew why. She looked up at him and smiled. "It's me standing on the beach, waiting for my next journey to start."

"Of course, it is. That's why it belongs here." Sam said.

"Come with me, Sam," she said so quietly she was afraid he didn't hear her.

"What?"

"Help me start a new life," she said louder to make sure he heard her this time.

"Of course, I will," he answered.

"I know you have that great new job in Raleigh and the commute sucks, but maybe you could come and see me on the weekend. I don't need a lot."

"Wait a minute. There is no job in Raleigh." Sam put his hands on each of her cheeks looking directly into her eyes. "Do you remember that night on the beach? The night when we talked about all the reasons why we loved it here? Do you remember?"

She saw the desperation in his eyes. "Yes, I remember, but that was before the conference; the job offer. You have so much going for you in Raleigh. I can't ask you to give that up." She wanted to be supportive, but in her heart, she knew she really wanted him here in Washington.

"Beth, you aren't listening. I received that job offer months ago, just after I started on your house. I knew then I couldn't accept it. Raleigh is not where my heart is. My heart is here with you." He pulled her into his arms and her body folded into his. She looked up at him and leaned toward him as his lips took hers. She knew that he would stay here with her forever.

"I love you, Beth Pearse. So, let's get this adventure started." He held her tight against him and spun her around until she couldn't see anything but him.

EPILOGUE

*F*riday, October 17, 2014

Beth woke to the laughter of children and music floating through her open windows. "This street is amazing," she whispered out loud as she slipped out of bed and walked to the window to slide it closed. It had been a couple of weeks since she came home to her safe haven. With some help, she finally conquered her fear and could enjoy the water view Sam had given her. She stood there watching the school buses unload into the waterside park. It was going to be a beautiful day.

"Where'd you go? Come back to bed," Sam groaned.

"We need to get up," Beth said over her shoulder, "The school groups will be here soon. The Estuarium is already letting them in."

"Let them. Come back to bed. I want you to myself for a little while longer." He lifted his arm and motioned her to come closer. Beth slowly closed the space between them and he snatched her, pulling her under the sheets. She squealed as he tickled her ribs.

"Stop it. I thought you wanted to go back to bed."

"I didn't say to sleep," Sam said, his tickles turned into caresses, and she gasped as he kissed her neck.

"Sam, we really need to get going. Didn't you get enough last night?"

"I can never get enough of you, Beth." He kissed her again, his lips traveling down to her shoulder.

Beth laughed in between moans, "That's what I love about you."

Sam groaned when the doorbell rang. "Just ignore it. The 'closed' sign is out. You don't have to answer it."

"You go get the door. I'll get dressed." Beth jumped out of bed and went across the hall to the bathroom. She heard him fussing as he put on his pants and pulled a t-shirt over his head. His footsteps disappeared as he headed downstairs. After a few minutes, he yelled up the staircase.

"Beth, it's a surprise for you."

She rushed as she finished brushing her teeth and ran a brush through her hair. She knew he had bought her something. He spoiled her all the time, blaming it on being Southern, but she knew better. She went down the stairs and rounded the corner to see Sam talking with a nicely dressed African-American gentleman.

Sam motioned to the man. "Beth, I would like you to meet Fredrick Brown. Mr. Brown, I would like you to meet Beth Pearse." The young man held out his hand, and Beth took it.

"It's nice to meet you. Are you here to see a painting? Perhaps I could interest you in a Seago beach piece." Beth smiled.

"Nice to meet you as well. Actually, I was here because Professor

Howards told me that you might have a piece of my family's history." Mr. Brown stated.

Beth looked at Sam with questions in her eyes. Sam explained, "After doing some research, I believe that Mr. Brown is a direct decedent from Selah."

"That means…" She stopped short of finishing her thought.

"That's right. The infant Brown survived the storm. He didn't die with his mother."

Beth closed her eyes which had started to brim.

"Ms. Pearse are you okay?" the man asked.

"Yes, I'll be fine. Oh, look we have forgotten our manners. Won't you come in and have a cup of coffee? The children will be here soon." Beth took the man by the arm and invited him into the house.

"The children?" he asked.

"Yes, the school children visit the gallery after they go to the State Estuarium. Beth's gallery has turned into quite the tourist spot," Sam explained.

"I don't know about that. The art doesn't stand a chance after they watch the guides feed the alligators, but hopefully, it sparks interest with some of them." Beth brushed off the compliment as the trio sat down at the kitchen table.

"You do have some beautiful pieces," Mr. Brown agreed.

"Thank you. Do you take cream in your coffee?"

"Yes, thank you."

"You enjoy your coffee, and I will go and get the diary." Beth left the two men sitting in the kitchen and went upstairs to her office.

The rocker in the corner was rocking away, and she knew that Selah was there.

"Selah," she called. "Your grandson is here. I'm going to give him your diary." The rocker continued. "I know you are listening. He will know where he comes from."

She left the door open and rejoined the men downstairs. Gently, she laid the diary in front of Mr. Brown.

"Here it is. There are a few things with the book, a picture of Selah and her Freeman papers. I appreciate the opportunity to read the diary, but it belongs to you." Beth smiled at him.

"Thank you for taking such good care of it. I'm still not convinced of the connection. But I will read the diary. If it is not my family, I will return it to you. Professor Howards tells me that you have a very nice Underground Railroad Museum in Washington."

"That's right. Most of the artifacts we found in the cellar went to them." Beth was so proud of her donation. "You should go visit, especially if your family was from this area."

"I might just do that. Well, I better get going. I have appointments this afternoon. Thank you again." He held out his hand to Beth.

She shook his hand and followed him to the door closing it behind him. She let out a huge sigh. Sam was standing behind her.

"What do you think?"

"It's him. He has the same mannerisms. I'm certain."

Sam's eyebrows went up with surprise, curiosity showing on his face.

"Don't ask me how I know, please." Her lips turned up into a smile.

"I know better." Sam wrapped his arms around her. "We better get ready for the kids."

"I'm going to run to Rachel's for breakfast really quick before we open. Do you want anything specific?" Beth kissed Sam, and he released her.

"No, I'm good. Ms. Martha made me promise I would come by for biscuits. You go ahead. I'll see you this afternoon after I finish at the office." Sam kissed her again.

She slipped out the door and headed down to the waterfront to the bakery. The beautiful weather had the town full of people this morning. As soon as she stepped into the restaurant, everyone yelled good morning to her. "Good morning, guys."

Rick asked giving her his brilliant smile, "What can I get you on this perfect day? You want your regular?"

"Yes, thank you," Beth answered, winked at him, and stepped out of the way of the next guest in line. The young man blushed and then turned his attention to taking the next order. WITN was on the TV in the corner, and they were appealing to the public to help find someone. It caught her attention. She moved closer to the set.

"The Beaufort County Sherriff's Department is asking for help from the public. Please take a look at this photo and call if you have any information about the man pictured. He is a person of interest in an active case. The sheriff advises not to approach him, call 911 immediately."

The photo flashed on the screen, and Beth let out a gasp. She knew that sweatshirt. She stared even closer at the man's image. The blood drained from her face. There was a movement to her right as she felt Rick jump the counter and hold her up as her knees went weak.

"Beth, what's wrong?" Rick asked, "Honey, what happened?" She couldn't make her mouth move. "Is there someone I can call for you?" His voice turned desperate.

Beth held out her phone and unlocked it. Her hands were shaking, and her brain couldn't make sense of anything. Her reality was collapsing with every flash of the photo on the screen. "Call Sam," was all she could manage.

Rick held the button down and told Siri to call Sam. The phone took over, and Sam answered right away. Holding the phone to her ear, Rick supported Beth's head in his lap.

"Hey, sweetheart. How's Rachel's?" Sam asked.

She tried to respond, but nothing would come out. She pushed the phone to Rick's face.

"Mr. Sam, this is Rick at the bakery. Something is wrong. Can you come over?"

Beth couldn't hear his response.

"She was watching the television, and now she's white as a sheet and not speaking. Can you come now?"

Rick put the phone back to Beth's ear and said "Okay" loud enough for Sam to hear.

"Sweetheart, what is wrong?" his words were short and breathy. He must be on his way.

She struggled to push the words out. They barely escaped as a whisper, "Brad is alive."

The End

SNEAK PEEK

SLEEPING MALLOWS
THE WATER STREET CHRONICLES BOOK 2
COMING SPRING 2019

August 12, 2013, Pamlico Sound NC

The sailboat drifted silently in the sound. The wake of his rubber boat rocked it ever so slightly as it disappeared from view. He would report it when he got back in town and let the local authorities take care of it. He needed to finish this run to the gallery on the island.

What a shame. They were such nice people. The ride to the rendezvous point was just what he needed to keep him on schedule today. The short chat on the dock in Washington was the only expense to secure the ride.

"Hi, I'm Robert. Have you seen a blue and green twenty-footer around? I was meeting my ride this morning, but that was an hour ago."

"Nope haven't seen them," the husband said.

"I guess that ruins my day."

The wife looked at him with a nod and a smile. "That's a shame."

"Where are you headed, Robert?"

"I was headed to Ocracoke for a delivery." He plastered a half-smile on his face and added a shrug to help sell his story.

"Alfred, we could give him a ride. It's not *that* far out of the way."

"Oh no. I couldn't take you out of your way, ma'am. But it's kind of you to offer."

Alfred clapped him on the shoulder. "It's no trouble. Come aboard. You can keep her company while I steer."

Robert grabbed his backpack and the shipping tube from the bench. Stepping aboard the sailboat, he offered his hand to the wife first and then the husband.

"Thank you so much I really appreciate this. Where are y'all headed?"

"A weekend trip to Oriental. One last trip away before our boy heads back to school."

"Sounds great."

"Come on down and have some coffee. I'm Lilly by the way." She disappeared down the hatch, and Robert followed.

Down in the galley, she was gracious, filling his coffee over and over as his eyes studied the painting on the wall.

"You know, Robert. I think I have a daughter your age. Are you single?"

"No, ma'am. Married." He held up his left hand and showed her his ring.

She blushed and turned her head back to the small counter, busying herself. "Oh, okay."

Perhaps they wouldn't notice if he took the painting before they made landfall. It would make a nice addition to the shipment. The wife kept talking about this or that. He didn't bother to remember the rambling chitchat. The debate about the painting repeated in his head until the horn sounded. Her husband was an excellent sailor and made good time to Ocracoke. Now it was time to get rid of the witnesses. His boss would insist.

A small boat pulled alongside, and a man boarded the sailboat, pistol drawn. Her husband tried to fight the gunman off, but there was no competing with a professional. Robert just stood back and watched. She screamed "Help him," but there was no one willing. He didn't even avert his eyes as the old sailor's body fell to the deck and his partner trained the gun on the woman.

Robert went down into the galley and grabbed the painting off the wall. He looked around. There was nothing else of value to him. Everything was as the couple unpacked it this morning, including the cell phone sitting on the table in the small galley. This was getting messy. He returned topside to see one last flip of a body shaped form wrapped in canvas slide in the boat next to another roll of canvas.

"Was this necessary?" Robert pointed at the wrapped bodies in the bottom of the smaller boat.

"Oui, C'est nécessaire."

"Okay, let's make this quick. I need to get back to the mainland." Robert jumped down in the boat and secured his cargo.

The other man nodded and revved the motor and turned the boat towards the island.

As the sailboat disappeared from view, Robert twisted his ring in thought. Would he ever be able to return to her? After today, he doubted the day would ever come.

~~~

October 20, 1861, Pamlico Sound NC

Abram learned a long time ago silence serves a man well. *It keeps you out of trouble, and if you listen in the silence, you learn an infinite amount.* He steered the workboat against the tide, listening silently. The tide was descending quickly signaling the storm over his shoulder was building strength and would soon arrive.

As Abram stood quietly, he listened for changes in the sounds of the waves, changing the boat's course when necessary. He was an expert navigator and knew the shoals like the back of his hand, but they were dangerous and changed almost monthly. A storm like this could place debris in his path where there had not been any for centuries. He rescued many ship captains boasting about their experience too loudly to hear the sea. *Tonight's pickup is too important not to arrive.* His precious cargo had monetary value, but not to him. This voyage was one of the heart, and he never felt emotion like this for anyone. Selah was waiting for him, and the year it took to get back to her felt like an eternity.

He turned his eyes to the heavens, praying that God would see them through this. They picked this date a year ago. There was no way of knowing a hurricane would be blowing in on the Outer Banks. The wind was picking up. He didn't feel like an expert at the moment. Every bone in his body told him to seek shelter, but that would not get him closer to the port of Washington, where she was waiting. He had to press on.

The boat gave a sudden jolt and dragged along the bottom. Abram jumped into the shin-deep water and checked the hull.

No holes, so that meant nothing solid. Without his weight, the boat traveled easily across the sandbar. He pulled out his spyglass and peered into the distance. He was almost to the turn. The river water would be easier to navigate, but the tide would be working against him. It was not stronger than his determination though.

The sun was setting in the west. *I better make good time across the sound if I am going to meet her on time.* Seafoam was building on the sandbars making it easier for him to move past them. Seaspray soaked his shirt through making it cling to his chest. Droplets of salty water glistened on his dark skin and his muscles throbbed from the exertion of the day. Thoughts of her pushed him harder across the water, and soon he was fighting the current to enter the river. The trees on the bank bent to the ground as the wind tore them from the rain-saturated soil. This storm was going to bad. It already showed its strength, and he could see the worst was still to come.

He was alone out on the river. Normally, it would be filled with schooners and other freight ships on their way to the next big port from Washington. But the storm was growing worse, and the smart captains were in port waiting out the storm. *I will make it in time, but we will not be able to leave until after the storm is gone.* He knew the backside of the storm would be worse and the tidal surge could be deadly. The small boat skimmed the waves and hours later as darkness fell he tied the boat to a slip on the pier. Soaking wet and exhausted, he slipped through the streets, cutting between the warehouses lining the bulkhead and turned down Water Street. Staying in the shadows, he headed towards the grand house at the end of the street. His pace quickened when he saw the waves licking the edge of the front porch. He fought against the waist deep water and rounded the house to see the small shed where he was to meet Selah was gone and she was nowhere to be found. *Maybe she's hiding in the garden.* He jumped over the garden gate. Leaning against the big oak, he gave up his silence and yelled her name.

"Selah. I'm here. Selah." But there was no answer. Anger filled him. *Where was she? Did she change her mind? No, she wouldn't. Not after she had written. She was ready for him to come.* His anger turned to anguish. What happened to her?

He ran to the front door of the house. Not caring what they thought of him, he beat on the door. "Open the door." He yelled. "Ya know where she is. Open up. Selah."

A branch of the large oak fell in the side yard only to fall on a pile of debris. The wake it caused sent the river water onto the porch. He beat on the door again. He saw a lantern through the window come closer to the entrance. Slowly the door opened.

"What do ya want? You know better than ta come ta the front door. You should've come to the slave entrance round back." An older black man dressed in a suit stared back at Abram with disdain. "You shouldn't be out in this storm. Go away."

Regaining his composure, Abram calmed himself then yelled only loud enough to be heard above the wind. "I am looking for a young woman who stays here. Selah's her name. I'm worried about her and want to make sure she's safe."

"There is no woman here, slave or free, by that name. I said go away." He closed the door.

Abram stood on the porch stunned. He knew she stayed here. *Why would he lie?* The saltiness of his tears diluted the rain on his face. *Where was his precious Selah?*

With a crack of thunder and a flash of lightning, his heart broke into a million pieces.

To Be Continued…

ABOUT THE AUTHOR

Tammera Cooper grew up on the Rappahannock River in Virginia watching the riverside community change with the times but remaining the same in spirit. The waterside lifestyle is in her blood and influences her writing every day.

Currently, she lives in Washington, North Carolina writing and sharing the small town's history with her readers. She is a member of the Pamlico Writers Group, Women's Fiction Writers Association, and Romance Writers of America.

You are welcome to touch base with her on her website: https://www.southernromanceonthepamlico.com/

Twitter: tlc_writer

Instagram: tlc_writer

Facebook: Tammera Cooper

CPSIA information can be obtained
at www.ICGtesting.com
Printed in the USA
LVHW091721220519
618749LV00005B/680/P